EMMA AND THE BANDERWIGH

TALES OF WIDOWSWOOD
BOOK ONE

MATTHEW S. COX

DIVISION ZERO PRESS

Emma and the Banderwigh
© 2015 by Matthew S. Cox
Second Edition © 2018
All Rights Reserved

ISBN (ebook): 978-1-949174-50-2

ISBN (print): 978-1-949174-51-9

CONTENTS

OUT OF THE WOODS

Tough bristles raked at the wood while Emma worked the large broom back and forth across her front porch, careful to keep her toes out of the way. The end of the handle reached up past her head. Uneven boards shifted with her weight as she inched across the porch of her family's modest house, accompanied by a steady rhythm of scratching. She kept her gaze down, avoiding looking into the dark pines of Widowswood so close to her home. The murk among the trees felt alive—as if it stared at her—even though such things only happened in Nan's nonsense tales. Yet, as much as she couldn't believe them, she still refused to look up.

Her grandmother's stories of monsters scared *small* children, not a girl of ten years.

The wind whispered at the trees, but no breeze reached the village. She leaned on the broom while wiping sandy grit off the bottom of her foot against her shin. An eerie roar, deep, pained, and not quite human, rang out in the distance, startling birds from the treetops.

Emma jumped and clutched the broom handle to her chest, not breathing. She stared into the woods. Darkness lurked in the gaps of the forest, but nothing moved. The stillness broke a moment later with a shout like the first, only the noise seemed less monstrous, merely an unseen huntsman's bellow echoing among the boughs. She relaxed, and resumed sweeping. Da would be home soon. As usual, he'd been out all day with the village watch. His patrol would end when the sun set.

She made it three quarters of the way across the porch when a sudden breeze carried spinning whorls of dirt from the road back over where she had swept, ruining her work. Emma grumbled, trudging to the right to start again from the beginning. Da had chosen to build their house at the village edge, where the street was little more than a wide footpath worn in the grass. Emma scowled at the drifts of grit and rushed to clear the re-dirtied porch with a series of haphazard swipes.

Why do I do this at all? It'll only become dirty again in an hour.

Satisfied with her slapdash effort, she stepped with care around the already-swept patches and worked the broom back and forth at the point she left off. Her knees peeked out from under grey flax. She'd soon need a new dress, having grown too big to wear this one much longer. Emma had already worn it well past the point of Da's approval. Mama seemed at ease with it, even if it did leave her looking like an urchin. The threadbare garment had a torn seam, frayed threads, several holes, and kept sagging down off her left shoulder. Emma adored it because Nan had made it for her. She would much rather wear it than something from the town tailor, crafted for no one specific. This dress was *hers*, and it made her feel safe.

She stalled, leaning on the broom again with a somber stare at the distant buildings. The Watch paid well, and his distant family had money, not that she had ever met them. Da could afford to buy clothes —nice clothes—and did not care for her traipsing about in 'a rag.' Emma wanted to wear this dress until it didn't fit anymore or fell to pieces. Nan was old, her fingers not as nimble as they used to be, and she feared her grandmother wouldn't be able to make another one.

A lump formed in Emma's throat. The wind picked up again, rustling the forest and tousling her hair. Nan wouldn't be with them for much longer. Two of Nan's friends had passed recently. It had been two years since Da's old dog, Wooly, had refused to wake up. She had been eight then, and still cried a little whenever she thought about the mutt. That dog had been old for as long as she could remember, and from the way Da spoke of him, he'd lived surprisingly long for a dog. Emma stared at her toes, wondering how much worse it would feel to lose Nan than a dog. She knew the day would come, but that didn't make the idea hurt any less. She wanted to spend more time with her grandmother, but most of her day went toward taking care of her little brother Tam while Mama went into town and Da kept everyone safe.

It made her feel important, helping ease the burden on Mama and allowing her daily visits to the villagers to resume. Everyone loved her mother, and people had always come by the house to visit while she'd been stuck at home with Tam.

The *snap* of a twig nearby made her glance into the murk of Widowswood with a twinge of unease.

Nothing is watching me. Stop being childish.

Emma turned the broom, spinning it on a long clump of bristles. It felt like forever ago since she'd been Tam's age and her only worry had been how she would play. She set her jaw in determination and resumed sweeping. *It's okay. Mama needs my help.* Soon after Emma made it to the far end of the porch, Mama appeared on the road in the distance, walking out from where the village buildings grew too thick to see past. She waved, and Emma stood as tall as she could to return it. Her mother chatted with a few wandering people on her way up the long, curved trail leading from the town proper to their home. Feeling guilty, Emma hurried back to the poorly swept areas.

Mama walked up onto the porch, pausing for a warm hug. "How is the house?"

"Good, Mama. Tam's inside, Nan's having a nap."

"No faeries steal anything?" She winked.

"Mama," said Emma with a bit of groan in her voice. "I'm too old to believe in faeries. Bad luck and carelessness aren't the work of little magical people no one can see."

"So smart, Emma." Mama gave her a light pat on the cheek. "Come help me with dinner when you're done here?"

"Yes, Mama."

Emma wiped the grit from her feet again and spent a few minutes chasing sand off the porch.

"Apple for a bit?" chirped a tiny voice.

The sickly sweet scent of fermenting fruit lofted on the wind. Emma pulled her hair out of her eyes and glanced down the three steps to the road. A grimy redheaded girl a year or two younger than her shied away from Emma's stare, digging her toes into the road and forcing a smile. Her once-white dress was ripped and stained, in worse shape than Emma's. She held out a wide, flat basket with a number of sorry-looking apples, most of which seemed to have been plucked from the ground. Small cuts and scrapes marked her legs, evidence of hours spent roaming the forest underbrush. Faint dark discoloration painted the child's cheek below her right eye. Even at ten, the sight of the other girl filled her with a motherly urge.

"Minnit," said Emma, spinning on her heel and leaning the broom against the wall. She darted inside and found Mama cutting vegetables by the large iron cauldron.

A plump robin perched on the tiny window above the cooking area chirped, tilted its head at Emma, and chirped again. Mama whistled on and off at it, as if mimicking bird noises.

Emma rolled her eyes, thinking back to her mother claiming she spoke to the birds. "Mama, can I have a copper bit?"

"For what, Em?" Mama stilled her knife and smiled. Her long raven tresses had a faint curl, and her eyes held the deep blue color of sapphires. Everyone called Emma a smaller version of her, and would look the same when she grew up—a fate Emma proudly accepted. She wondered if Nan had been pretty too.

Emma pointed at the door. "Kimber is selling apples again. She looks hungry."

A look of worry flashed in Mama's eyes. She set the knife down and crossed the kitchen in two steps to peer out the curtained window. With a sigh, she moved to a drawer and rummaged out a brown cloth pouch. Emma folded her hands in front of herself, waiting, eyeing a round wheat bread as big as a cat's head among the vegetables.

"Go ahead, Em." Mama handed her two copper coins, and the bread. "Awful the way that man treats the poor girl. I've half a mind to have your father pay that drunken lout a visit."

Emma smiled, hugged her mother, and scurried for the door. Kimber waited a short distance from the porch, swaying back and forth with an eager expression. When Emma held out the two copper bits, the girl's eyes watered up. She hefted the basket.

"Thank you, miss Emma. Take any two you please."

She sifted among the apples, searching for ones without obvious worms. Many still had bits of branch clinging to them. She chose two that didn't look rotten, and left the large roll in their place. Kimber's deep green eyes widened in astonishment. She studied it for a moment, almost afraid, then bit her lip and glanced over her shoulder at town, turning her body as if to hide the bread from anyone in that direction.

"Kinnae sit 'ere an' eat it?" Kimber shot a frightened, sad stare into the dirt path.

"Kay." Emma gestured at the porch, and joined her on the step.

The younger girl held the round loaf to her face like a squirrel with an acorn and gnawed on it as though it would be ripped from her hands at any moment. She peered up every few bites with smiling eyes. Emma's happiness dimmed at the realization some of the dark spots on the girl's face didn't come from dirt, but bruises.

"Come back if you're hungry again." Emma traced lines on the ground with her toe.

Crumbs fell out of Kimber's grin. She mumbled something like "thank you" past a full mouth.

"Sorry you get hit." Emma scowled in the direction of town. "I should tell my Da."

The red-haired girl stopped eating, a mournful stare at the half-loaf in her hand. "Is okay. Papa's not bad alla time. Only when he's got his pay and 'as faeberry wine." Kimber jammed the bread into her mouth again.

Emma smirked and leaned back on her hands, gazing into the waning daylight. Nan would say she should ask the spirits to aid the other girl. Da thought people should pray to the gods for help with events outside their control. She picked at a frayed thread by her hip. Spirits and gods weren't real, and even if they were, they wouldn't care about one tiny waif among all the people of the world.

Kimber spent a minute picking crumbs out of her dress and eating them before she jumped up and curtsied. "Thank ya for the bread, Miss Emma."

"I'm not old enough to be a 'miss' yet." Emma frowned. "Thank my mum for lettin' me."

Mama's laughter leaked onto the porch.

The girl stood, faced the house, and raised her voice. "Thank ya, Miss Emma's Mum."

Kimber carried her basket of pathetic apples off down the street to the next house. With a sad sigh, Emma resumed her sweeping. Tam hated chores. Emma didn't mind them, or that he didn't do any. The more she did, the less her mother had to do. The boy was only six, too young to understand much beyond the faerie tales of dragons and knights that Nan read to him. In many ways, Da was a bigger version of Tam. Both demanded Mama's constant attention to keep their clothes in order. Neither could cook, and more often than not, it seemed neither could dress themselves.

Emma giggled.

It took her another fifteen minutes to sweep to the edge of the porch. Nan's face appeared in the window, smiling. Emma grinned in response, still working the broom. A moment later, a chance shift in the wind blew into town from the woods. It gathered strength, as well as the dirt from the porch, and carried it in a tiny whirlwind down the street. Emma cringed at the gust that almost knocked her over. When it died down, she held the broom up and blinked at the porch, ready to sweep again, but the wind had left it spotless. With a satisfied grunt, she turned to go inside, but startled at a sudden motion on the road.

An older girl, perhaps sixteen, stumbled down the path leading from the village into Widowswood. She emerged from the gloomy tunnel of twisted, leaning trees, wan and dazed, in a garment made of leaves and twigs that barely covered her. Emma stared, transfixed. The young woman moved only her legs, arms dead at her sides. Sickly and thin, every rib showed clear under her skin. Her mouth agape, she staggered forward in a rickety gait, almost as though she had forgotten how to walk. She paid no attention to Emma. Her grey eyes held no spark of life. Unkempt brown hair hung down to her ankles, loaded with twigs and scraps from the forest floor. The barely-alive girl halted twenty paces distant and swayed in place. She raised one hand to cover her mouth, gawking at the village as though she couldn't believe it real.

Emma, stunned at the sight, lost her hold on the broom.

The *clack* of the wooden handle striking the porch made the strange girl yelp and startle. She looked up, staring at Emma as if she had no idea what another human being even was.

"Mama!" Emma wanted to shout, but whimpered. She swallowed, backing into the wall. "Mama!" she yelled, then sidestepped closer to the door. "Mama, come here."

Her mother appeared at the door. "What's the matter, Em?"

Emma pointed. Mama's eager smile fell away to a look of worry. She gathered Emma into the house with a hand on her shoulder.

"Go inside, Em. Help Nan."

2

WHAT STRANGE THINGS IN DARKNESS DWELL

*E*mma walked backward into the house, unable to pull her gaze away from the wasted figure standing motionless in the road until Mama, still outside, closed the door. Warm air with the scent of garlic and baking potatoes did little to ease her nerves. Emma kept going until the edge of the table hit her back, bumping it hard enough to knock over an unlit candlestick. She whirled toward the clatter, but gasped at finding her grandmother close behind her.

Nan stroked her gnarled fingers over Emma's hair. "What's got your blood hiding? You're pale like a banshee."

"There's a sick lady outside. Mama told me to help you."

"Well, now. Sick people don't often scare you."

"Uhh." Emma gave her grandmother a helpless look. "Something's wrong. She felt strange."

Wisps of Nan's white hair drifted to the side, draped over her black shawl. The wailing wind seemed impart a chill to the house despite the glowing orange fire. Emma shivered. Nan leaned her head as if to peer out the wall like a window, milky eyes widening.

"She's alive," said Nan. "Go wash your hands."

Emma ran out the back door and over to the pump ten paces away. She worked the lever until a spurt of water came out and rubbed it over her hands and arms. A sprawling meadow filled the land between the rear of their house and the tree line where Widowswood curved around the village. Bugs of all sizes zoomed and fluttered above the grass. A large, white butterfly meandering in a drunken spiral caught her attention, stark against the distant forest. She froze, water dripping from her fingers. The puddle around her feet turned cold in an instant. For no reason she could explain, she found herself staring at the forest again.

Something unseen among the trees watched her.

She darted back into the house, slamming the door hard enough to knock Da's spare riding tack from a peg on the wall and leaning all her weight into it as if her little body might make the difference between the monster getting in or not.

"Emma!" shouted Nan, clutching her chest. "What's gotten into you?"

Her heart raced. Emma looked at the door, at Nan, back at the door, and then at the bit, bridle and gloves at her feet. She felt silly for being afraid of the dark. "Nothing. I'm sorry for making you jump."

The eeriness faded. *Why am I acting like a little kid? Grr. I'm not six anymore.* Angry at herself for being scared, she hung Da's things up. Then, Nan guided her to the table, slid a bowl of dough in front of her, and dropped a cloth next to it.

Emma dried her hands and set to task without protest, kneading. Tam sprawled on the floor closer to the bed, his stick-knight battling a shrub-dragon. She smiled, watching him play while she worked for a few minutes in silence. Nan portioned out various spices and herbs for the rest of the baking.

Minutes later, soft thumps on the porch approached the door. Emma looked up, hoping to see Da. Whatever lurked in the woods wouldn't dare try anything with him home.

I'm being childish again. Emma sighed at herself.

Mama rushed in. She didn't look at anyone, hurrying to gather a few items from Nan's cabinet, the one they forbade her from going near. Emma froze, forearm deep in dough, watching her mother collect a few pouches. Without a word, Mama ran back outside.

"Nan? Who do you think that lady is?"

One of grandmother's few remaining teeth peeked out of a grin. "Oh, nothing you'd believe. I shan't waste my breath on it."

Emma continued kneading gooey dough between her fingers while Nan poured herbs into the mass. She gave it two squeezes before puffing a strand of hair out of her face and staring. "Nan."

"Fine, fine." The old one settled into a chair. "Her name is Hannah. Before today, the last anyone saw of her was ten years ago." Nan rocked back, tapping a finger to her chin. "I believe she vanished only two weeks after you were born. She was about Tam's age then."

At the sound of his name, the boy perked up. Sensing an imminent story, he scampered over and scrambled up to lean his elbows on the table, knees on a chair. Emma took more pinches of herbal seasonings, adding them to the dough between folds.

Shouts rose up outside, growing into cheers and praise to various gods, mostly Rhiannon the Matron or Baragen the Harvest Lord.

Emma rushed to the window, holding her hands up to keep from smearing dough all over. Smooth glass chilled her forehead as she strained to peer toward town where a crowd had formed. Hannah shivered at the center, wrapped in a bright blue cloak of the kind worn by the town watch. It seemed as if everyone had come out to welcome the lost daughter of Widowswood home. A wobbly, heavyset woman with a shock of white in her chestnut hair required the aid of two men to avoid collapsing.

"Em, you're making Nan not tell the story!" yelled Tam. "Come back."

"Hannah! My daughter!" shouted the large woman before breaking down in sobs. "Are you really here?"

"We thought you dead," cried an elderly man.

Numerous people burst out in cries of joy or wails of sorrow.

"Why isn't she speaking?" yelled a youngish male voice.

"What's happened to her? Oh, my Hannah!" A man older than Da, but younger than Nan, lifted the girl off her feet into a desperate hug.

Hannah's mother grabbed and pawed at her, as if searching for injuries.

After a moment of hanging limp, Hannah raised her arms and held on to him. Seconds later, she lifted her head and looked at everyone.

At that, the crowd erupted in cheers.

Mama made her way into the group of villagers, took Hannah's hand, and coaxed her to drink from a small bowl.

"Em! Em! Em! Em!" Tam chanted her name while slapping his hands on the table.

"Alright." Emma sighed and trudged over.

She took her place by the bowl, jamming her hands into the dough while trying to peer out the window.

"Well, most everyone thought she wandered off into the woods. But nobody could find her." Nan finished the chopping Mama had started, and shoved everything into the cauldron. "I can see that distrustful look in your eyes. Just like your mother was at your age." She winked.

Emma folded and mushed the soon-to-be bread. "A child wouldn't come back from being alone in the woods. That's why you don't let me an' Tam go there."

Wrinkles accented Nan's grin. "Do you think someone took her?"

"Goblins!" blurted Tam. "Goblins got her."

Nan chuckled. Emma rolled her eyes.

"Not goblins, I'm afraid, Tam. Goblins would have put her in the stew." She pointed a curved finger at him, wagging it. He laughed. "This… No, this was something worse."

"Worse?" Emma made a face. "She's still alive. That's not worse than being goblin stew."

"Emma, you don't believe in this sort of thing, so I won't waste what few breaths I have left on it." Nan dropped the metal lid over the cauldron to end her sentence.

"Nan, you're not gonna die," muttered Emma. "And there's no goblins and no monsters. Just bad people. I bet bandits had her, and made her cook and wash for them. When she got sick, they let her go home."

"Sounds like you've already got the world figured out." Nan picked out seasonings for the soup, dropping them in pinch by pinch. "Don't need me ruining it for you."

"Story!" yelled Tam, before he gave Emma a raspberry.

"No!" Emma leaned over the bowl to shield it. "Don't do that near food."

Tam laughed.

"Please tell me, Nan." Emma grunted at the dough, her arms already tired.

"Do you believe in goblins?" asked Nan.

The boy nodded.

Emma shook her head. "Of course not."

"Faeries?"

"Uh-uh." Emma glared at nothing in particular. "That's all stuff to scare little kids with."

Nan leaned back, drawing a soft creak from her chair. "Dragons, elves, wizards?"

"Dragons can fly!" added Tam.

"No, no, and no." Emma tried to blow a stray bit of hair off her face. "You're being silly."

Halfway between anger and laughter, Emma's expression made Nan chuckle.

"What about magic?"

Emma sighed. "There's no such thing."

"What of the wizard in Calebrin? Your father met him when he was a boy."

Tam waved his hands at her, making plosive noises as if he were some great wizard throwing fireballs.

Emma shrugged one shoulder out of her dress. "Probably an alchemist with some trick fire to scare people. Stop it, Tam. Don't spit in our food."

He stuck his tongue out at her. She sighed, unable to stay angry at that face.

Emma waited for a moment, but when Nan didn't say anything more, she looked up. The old one seemed to have gone still in her chair, with no trace of her usual wheezy snoring.

"Nan?" asked Emma.

The elder didn't react.

Emma crept closer. "Nan?"

Nothing.

"Nan!" shouted Emma.

Her grandmother didn't move.

Emma grasped her by the shoulders. "Nan?" Emma shook her. "Nan!"

"Calm down, girl." Nan's eyes popped open. "I'm not dead. You're not trying to rush me into the ground, are you?"

"No!" She sniffled. "You scared me. Why did you fall asleep like that?" Emma pouted and took two steps backward.

"I wasn't asleep, dear." Nan winked. "Hannah was taken by a Banderwigh."

Tam's eyes widened, his little hand slipped from his chin as his mouth gaped. "Bander wee?" He clearly had no idea what sort of creature that was, but appeared frightened.

Emma trudged back to the bowl, more than a little annoyed at Nan for teasing her. She picked up the glop of dough, spun it over and flung it back down. "Banderwigh? Is that another one of your faerie monsters?"

Nan's dry chuckle turned into a cough. "Indeed. I've only known of one person who's ever claimed to see him. Though, I think it is more of a *they* than a him. They're fairly rare, never more than one around a place, you see."

"I still think it was bandits," said Emma, patting the dough into shape.

"Bandy-wee!" belted Tam, cheering.

"They are solitary things. The Banderwigh lives in the darkest parts of the forest and feasts upon sadness." Nan leaned forward, raising her claw-like hands over the table. "It walks the land under cover of night, taking children away from hearth and home to lock them in a little place where no one can find them." Her stare grew eerie. "There, in the dark, it makes them sad and drinks their tears to feed itself."

The boy shivered, and scooted under the table to cling to Emma. She frowned.

"Don't listen to her, Tam. It's just a story to scare little boys inside at night." She sprinkled some flour on a pan and dumped the unbaked bread out of the bowl. "If this monster takes people, why is Hannah back? Doesn't it eat them or something?"

Nan clucked her tongue as she stood to grab the pan. "The Banderwigh eats sorrow, child. It drained poor Hannah of all her tears. The girl must be dead inside now, a mere shadow of a person."

"That's silly," said Emma. "Monsters don't make people go nutters. Livin' by herself in the woods made her go nutters. She's so skinny 'cause all she had to eat was nuts and berries. What does this *monster* look like?" She kissed her brother atop the head. "It's just a scary story, Tam. No one's ever seen one."

"Are you so sure?" asked Nan, with a scary gleam in her eye. "A man, older than your father, covered in shaggy black bear-fur and unshaven"—she waved her open hand around her face—"with wild hair and a giant woodsman's axe. His eyes burn with the yellow light of the Netherworld. He's neither dead nor alive. Some say cursed."

Emma frowned at the dough, prodding it with her fingers. Nan's words were scary, but she couldn't bring herself to believe such fancy. The old woman being so serious about it only convinced her Nan tried to give her a fright. Despite thinking it a silly story, she found herself holding on to the table to keep from shaking.

"Probably just some poor old man who lives alone in the woods that people are afraid of for no reason." Emma made a face at her flour-coated hands. "People always make up stories when they're scared, or they don't wanna do something."

Nan smiled, stood with a grunt, and ambled to the stove on three legs, two living and one wooden. She hooked her cane in the crook of her arm and opened the metal oven. After putting the bread inside, she closed the door and added another two hunks of wood to the fire. Emma wiped her hands on a rag. Nan wobbled closer, leaning two shaking arms on the stick to prop herself up as she fixed Emma with a stare.

"How likely is it that a girl of six survived on her own in Widowswood? Do you think bandits would keep a pauper's daughter for ransom? What of the wolves, or the goblins, or the emerald creepers?"

Those, Emma believed in—spiders half the size of a horse, with bright green hair. She believed in them because she'd seen one once. Dead, on the back of a merchant's wagon, but real. Two weeks' worth of nightmares came from that, but she'd been only five then. Nan mentioning them made Emma imagine being six and running into one alone in the woods—one that wasn't dead. She crossed her arms over her chest, shivering, giving Nan an accusing look for making her think such thoughts. Tonight, her dreams would be wrapped in spidersilk.

Nan chuckled. "Emma, come help me—"

The door flew open and smacked into the wall.

Emma gasped, grabbing the edge of the table with both hands. Da walked in amid the clatter of light brigandine armor and a broadsword tapping his leg. All thoughts of giant spiders and child-stealing monsters with axes fled her mind.

Da started to smile at her, but sighed. "Em, it's high time we got you some proper clothing. You look like a beggar girl."

She pulled the dress out to the sides, appraising it. "But Da, Nan made this…"

"Yes, she did. Two years ago, and you've worn it to death. It's falling apart." His steps thudded over the floor as he crossed the room to hang his cloak on a peg and lean his weapon against the wall. "Tomorrow, we're going into town."

"Yes, Da," she said, staring down at her dirty feet.

He rounded the table and put hand atop her head, drawing her into a gentle, but brief hug. He picked Tam up, spun the giggling boy around twice, and set him back in the chair. Emma smiled as he moved into the back room remove his armor.

Nan tapped her cane on the table. "Come, Emma, help your old grandmother finish supper."

3

A STORY UNSEEN

*A*fter dinner, Da worked out guard salaries and schedules in his logbook. Emma had perched in his lap with her cheek on his shoulder, something she hadn't done for at least two years. Even without such things as monsters being real, the dark forest *was* scary. He took it as an attempt to beg him off replacing her beloved dress. Emma didn't care to correct him.

About an hour later, he closed his book and sat with her a while longer before carrying her to the great family bed. Tam had fallen asleep on the rug by the smoldering fireplace. Emma changed into her nightdress while Da retrieved Tam, set him on the bed, and peeled the boy's tunic off, leaving him in his skivvies.

Emma scampered to her spot by the wall beneath the windowsill and curled up beneath the heavy blankets, staring up at the dusty boards of the ceiling. The quiet time between dinner and bed had ended too soon for her liking. Every creak the wind drew from the house made her think about the creepiness in the woods that morning. Nan's story hadn't helped. Surely, the sense of being watched couldn't have been anything like a Banderwigh.

Tam snuggled against her. The warmth of his bare back against her cotton nightdress lulled her closer to sleep. Da went outside, standing with Mama on the front porch, the low murmur of their voices audible outside the wall. Tam decided to take advantage of their parents' part of the bed being open, and flopped away from her, arms and legs held out to take up as much room as he could.

Nan grunted, easing her weight into a stool by the side of the bed. She clutched a leather-bound book, winked at Tam, and opened it. She licked a finger, twirled it in the air, and turned the first page.

After clearing her throat, Nan spoke in a grand whisper.

"Many years ago, there lived a young knight by the name of Aemon Steelsong. He was the most trusted of the King's soldiers."

Emma stifled a yawn. *Knights again. Is he killing a dragon or saving another princess?*

"One day," said Nan, "minutes before sunrise, a creeping shadow slipped through a window into the castle. It had the shape of a man but no legs, and floated down the hallways unseen and unheard. When it reached the master bedroom, it breathed an icy pall upon the King."

"A pall is bad, right?" asked Emma, grinding the back of her hand into her eye.

"Shh!" yell-whispered Tam.

Nan held the book to her breast, peering over it. "Yes, Em. It was a powerful curse of dark magic." She lowered the book and turned a page. "King Ralas fell into a deep and terrible sleep. His skin turned blue and flaked with ice, and shadows hovered on his breath."

Tam pulled Emma's arm over his chest and held on.

"With the king near death, the weight of leadership fell upon the shoulders of his daughter, Princess Isabelle, a girl of only fifteen."

"That's old," whispered Tam.

Emma faded in and out of sleep as Nan went on, telling of a wizard, loyal only to money, who wanted to wrest the crown away from the young princess upon her father's untimely death.

It had been some time now since Emma had lost interest in princess tales. Even the old faerie stories seemed childish and boring. Tam loved anything involving dragons, knights, or wizards. Da claimed to have seen a real wizard in the north, in the large city of

Calebrin, before he met Mama. Half awake, Emma mumbled at the thought of it.

Wizards, bah. Someone made up banderwighs to scare kids in at night. Wizards are stories to scare grown-ups with.

"People thought the princess part elf for her beauty, and for her kindness. One glance from her bright blue eyes could leave a boy dazed."

"Eww," said Tam. "Who's Aemon gonna fight?"

Nan held back a chuckle. "No one really knows if the princess got her looks from the Astari, but she was pure as the stories claim the elves had been. The wizard took advantage of her trusting nature and tricked Isabelle right out from under Aemon's nose. He convinced her the only way she could cure her father was to go into the dark and forsaken woods"—Nan leaned over Tam, making him shiver—"and retrieve a sprig of Nymph's Breath from where the Astari Elves once dwelled, long before humans came to the land. He lied, and told her the rare plant would die if any but an innocent girl touched it."

Emma rolled her closed eyes.

"Was Isbel imacent?" asked Tam.

"Oh, yes." Nan winked. "So innocent, in fact, she believed the wizard's lie and ran off into Mur'Elonnae, the Forest of Ancestors, to fetch the herb."

"Elf words?" asked Tam.

"Yes," said Nan.

Emma's head felt like stone. After a short sense of falling, she found herself running into an unfamiliar forest, rustling in a puffy pink dress. *Stupid princesses.* She scowled at thin, silver slippers tight and uncomfortable. Her ungainly outfit snagged and pulled on the underbrush. She felt ridiculous, and wondered why any girl would wear such a thing—especially while running into the woods in the middle of the night.

"Isabelle left her horse at the forest's edge," said Nan. "She tucked her long, golden hair into a thick hood, and tightened a belt around her riding leathers. In her haste to save her father, all she had brought with her was a single torch."

Emma's pink princess disintegrated. Her eyes fluttered open. Nan waved her hands about while describing great birds swooping down at Isabelle, chasing her deeper and deeper into the forest.

"These were not normal birds, not buzzards nor eagles." Nan added a twang of avian caw to her voice. "They had the faces of ill-tempered old men, and wailed and screamed at her for disturbing their sleep. Whenever she swung her torch at one, it cried out with an awful screech."

The scarier the story became, the closer to Emma Tam moved, until he curled against her in their usual cramped sleeping position.

Nan settled back in her seat. "Isabelle wandered lost in the woods, and couldn't find her way out."

In her waking dream, Emma raced about in a hapless circle, with a torch in one hand and a star-capped princess wand in the other. The morning's eerie wind took her dream out of her control, filling the murky spaces between trees with real dread.

"She sensed it would be dark soon," said Nan, "and so she made herself a place to sleep, knowing it dangerous to wander alone at night."

Emma whined in her sleep. Every turn her dream-self took left her more and more confused. She startled awake and jumped again at the sight of the wrinkles on Nan's face changing with every spooky expression she made.

"It was not until the next morning that Sir Aemon found her missing, and set off at once to find and rescue the princess. Of course, the wizard expected this." Nan held up a finger. "He desired to lure Aemon away from the castle."

Emma struggled to stay awake, even for another boring 'knight-saves-the-princess' tale. She wanted to be with Nan while she still could. The old woman only tried to amuse Tam. Acting bored and disinterested felt mean. She also feared giant green spiders waited for her if she closed her eyes. A little anger curled her lip into a snarl. She'd never been afraid of the dark before, even at Tam's age.

Her grandmother noticed her paying more attention than usual, and it brought a gleam to her eye. Despite her effort to listen, Emma's eyelids grew heavy and she caught herself nodding off. Nan's voice sounded different, dream-like, as though she had become another woman, a character from the story.

"Aemon ventured into the woods in search of the princess, but the wizard had summoned a demon who took the form of a beautiful woman. She charmed him with a stare, and fed him a brew that transformed him into a statue of living ice. As it turned out, Princess Isabelle found Aemon, and needed to rescue *him*," said Nan.

Tam grumbled.

The old one's voice blurred as Emma drifted in and out of sleep. She caught bits and pieces of the story: a fairy queen with a promise of a potion that could help Aemon, running around the forest, and something about Isabelle being captured and locked in a dungeon.

Nan's retelling swelled into a new life within her half-dream—one that made her think she smelled the must and leather as Princess Isabelle decided not to wait around to be saved. Emma's head dipped forward onto Tam's shoulder.

She floated from her safe, warm bed into a musky underground hallway of wet grey stones, where a fifteen-year-old girl with perfect blonde hair struggled against the barred door of a tiny cell. Creatures under the control of the wizard had captured her in the night, stuffing her into a bag and dragging her deep within the forest. Her clothes looked expensive, but made for travel or fighting: leather armor, pants, and heavy boots. Much to Emma's surprise, Isabelle looked angry rather than terrified.

"Aemon was a dutiful protector." Nan's voice floated out of nowhere. "He'd made her promise never to leave herself defenseless."

Princess Isabelle took a dagger from a sheath at the back of her belt, and wedged it into a gap by the lock. She grimaced when it slipped out, and almost stabbed herself trying to catch it before it could bounce out of the cell. The princess's blue eyes burned with determination, and she continued working the blade back and forth until the door gave way.

"And so, Princess Isabelle crept through the dungeon until she found a guard asleep at his post. No man, but not too far from one," said Nan's disembodied voice. "A head shorter, pudgier, and much, much, smellier."

Tam's giggle echoed from the shadows.

"His dark green skin as tough as armor, arms thicker than her legs… but, he slept."

Emma's dream self followed behind Isabelle while the older girl tiptoed up to the snoring creature and helped herself to a plain sword on the table. With a grin of victory, Isabelle darted up a flight of stairs toward daylight.

The crinkle of paper moving came from everywhere as Nan turned a page.

"Pale fog rolled among the trees outside. The dawn brought a damp chill. Princess Isabelle didn't know where she'd been taken. Two more man-creatures like the sleeping guard, no taller than her but much thicker and stronger, walked out of the mist. Isabelle pulled back her hood, letting her hair fall to her waist and flashing her wide blue eyes. She hoped her sweet smile would make them not want to hurt her."

"Wrong!" cheered Tam's disembodied voice. "Hobgoblins don't like pretty princesses."

Princess? The thought nudged Emma back from the edge of sleep. *A princess with a sword?* She propped herself up on one arm, squinting at Nan who waved her hands around to illustrate the ensuing sword fight. Emma shifted, pulling her heels under her.

"The wretched creatures hissed and spat, and attacked Isabelle with knobby claws." Nan mimicked a clawing gesture, which made Tam squeal. "Their eyes burned with hate for anything pure. When they failed to grab her, they drew crude clubs from their belts. If she got away, the wizard's plan would fail, so for him, they would kill her."

Nan flipped pages as she half-described-half-demonstrated a girl holding off two hobgoblins with her blade and agility.

As the princess fought, the burden of responsibility slipped from Emma's shoulders. She stared with rapt attention, gripping her knees, her mouth hung open. When Isabelle cut one of the monster's hands, forcing it to drop its weapon, Emma grinned.

"Enraged, it grabbed her arm and tried to bite her throat." Nan grabbed at Tam, who screamed. "Isabelle jumped away, but its claws raked over her hand, taking her sword."

Emma bit her lip when the princess stumbled, clutching the sheets to her chest with wide eyes.

Nan grinned. "Or so they thought. Isabelle's fall was a trick, and when the monsters tried to jump on her, she rolled out of the way and got to her blade. They'd piled on each other, and before they could get up, she stabbed them through to the ground."

Tam made a sputtering noise.

Nan glanced at him. Emma shoved at his back.

"Something the matter, Tam?" asked Nan.

"That's silly. Princess can't beat up hobgoblins wif a sword. The knight's gotta save her."

"Sir Aemon's frozen!" Emma blurted, not even realizing she had been so into the story. "She's gotta find the Hearthfire potion the faerie queen told her about to thaw him or he'll stay trapped in ice forever."

Nan smiled at Emma, making her feel childish.

"Knights saves princesses," said Tam.

"Not all the time," whispered Nan.

"Nan, does Isabelle find the potion?" Emma pulled Tam into her, wrapping her arms around him as if clutching a living doll. He squirmed. "Does she break the spell? Do they get married?"

"Eww!" wailed Tam.

The door creaked open, admitting a pair of yawning parents.

Nan snapped the book closed. "Well, Emma. I suppose you'll find that out tomorrow night."

Emma whined, drawing in a breath to protest, but gasped when she saw the cover of the book: plain brown leather with the seal of the town guard. Sleep left her mind at the sight. *Nan's got Da's logbook. That's not a storybook.* She swallowed the urge to cry. Nan couldn't see what she held. The story came out of her head, not the book. *Nan's going blind.*

She crawled over Tam to get to Nan's lap, crying.

"What in the name of Belephir did you tell them?" asked Da.

"Just a story," said Nan. "Just a story about things your daughter is too old to believe in. It certainly wasn't a sad one." The old one gave her a pat on the back. "Come now, Em. There's nothing to cry about. It's time for bed."

Emma didn't move until Da plucked her from Nan's lap and deposited her on the bed. She crawled between Tam and the windowsill, watching old woman amble off down a short hallway to her separate bedroom.

4

THE TRADER

*E*mma sat at the table, swinging her feet back and forth, staring down at her toes scuffing the floor. Da hadn't said a word when she had changed out of her nightdress into her favorite article of clothing, but she dreaded the day would end with her having to give it up. She couldn't deny that it didn't really fit well anymore, tight around the chest and a little too short. But wearing it felt like a constant hug from Nan.

Two small rolls and some fruit sat untouched on the wooden plate in front of her. Tam had already gone outside to play in the meadow behind the house. Da took his time eating, splitting his bread and adding a hunk or two of cheese.

"Y'avent touched your food, girl," said Da. "We're going into town when I'm done. I'll not wait for you to finish if you aren't even trying."

Tears ran down her cheeks. "But, Da, I have a dress. I like this one. Nan made it."

"We've been 'round this before." He took a bite, pointing at her while murmuring, then swallowed. "I'll not have my daughter being thought of as some beggar orphan. You look like that Drinn girl. Fauen thinks we're not takin' proper care of you."

"Oh, is that what this is about?" asked Mama. "Your reputation?"

He put his roll down. "Half the town thinks we refuse to feed and clothe her."

"I talk to them, too, and they most certainly do not." Mama winked at her. "She'll grow out of it."

"She already has grown out of it." He gestured at her.

Emma picked up her bread, nibbling at it with disinterest. "Nan can't make another. She can't see the needle anymore and she's not got much time left, like Wooly." She rubbed the coarse cloth over her leg. "It's like she's wif me."

Both of her parents stalled at the unusual childishness in her voice, staring. Mama frowned and came over to rub her shoulder.

"That ol' bat will outlive me," muttered Da.

Mama squeezed Emma's shoulder. "It is the way of all things, child. You shouldn't be sad. She will rejoin the woods and the animals." She kissed Emma atop the head. "Death is only the start of a magical journey."

"You know she doesn't believe in all that"—Da waved his hand over the table—"that faerie story stuff. What's this about Nan not seeing?"

"And you do?" Mama smiled at him, patted Emma on the back, and set about collecting empty plates.

Emma pointed at the shelf. "Nan was pretending to read from—"

Armored boots tromped to the door, followed by the expected loud banging—no one jumped.

"Captain Dalen?" shouted a man outside.

Da moved to answer, adjusting a burgundy tunic on the way. Emma shifted in her chair, sitting sideways to watch. Six members of the Widowswood Town Watch waited outside, five in the street.

"What is it, Haim?"

"Captain, there's been a break in at Carrow's Field. Someone got into the house last night. Lucky thing the boy woke up. Screamed himself hoarse, he did. Woke the whole family s'well as the neighbors. The mum got a glimpse of a burglar runnin' off into the night. Big, hairy fellow."

"Damn bandits." Da left the door open and went for his armor.

Emma's head turned to follow him across the room. "Em, I need to go." He heaved his breastplate on and buckled it under his arms. "We'll go to the tailor tomorrow."

She gnawed on the hard roll. "Okay. Don't get hurt."

Once he'd gotten his armor and sword in order, he tromped over and ruffled her hair. "I won't. It's just a burglar. They'd rather run than fight."

Mama handed him a leather-wrapped bundle and kissed him. He tied it to his belt, kissed her again, and rushed out to meet the guardsmen.

Emma grasped the seatback, peering over it at as Da left. The scent of weapon oil still hung in the air. After the door closed, she continued staring until Mama ran a hand over her head. She looked up, unable to hide her worry.

"Em, what's got you worked up so? It's not the dress business, is it? You should be happy you can wear that rag another day."

She swung her legs around, sitting proper. "I don't know why I'm scared."

"He'll be alright. He's got the whole town guard with him."

Having a delay in the inevitable trip to the tailor did give Emma back some appetite. The berries went down faster than the bread. Mama puttered around at the cabinets while Emma ate. By the time she finished her breakfast, her mother had set a small pouch at the corner of the table.

Emma picked it up and shook it. Coins.

"Be a sweetheart and run to Marsten's shop. There's a list in there."

She let the pouch dangle from two fingers. "You've not taught me to read."

Mama gave her a weary look. "Aye, I suppose I haven't. We should remedy that soon. Today, give him the note."

She slid off the chair and started for the back door.

"Don't take your brother there. He'll get into something dangerous and put it in his mouth."

Emma swiveled around and tiptoed to the front door.

"Em, are you alright? I've not seen you so skittish in years." Mama's curiosity gave way to a smile of understanding. "Oh, it's Nan's business about that monster, isn't it? Poor Hannah."

Emma grasped the doorknob, afraid to turn it. "Do you believe Nan?"

"Whether or not I do or don't, the story says it doesn't come out during the day." Mama made a shooing gesture at her. "It's a tale to scare children inside at *night*, isn't it?"

"Yeah." Emma blushed, feeling foolish for being afraid of stories. "'Tis."

THE ROAD CURVED DOWNHILL, PAST OPEN FIELDS AND A FEW SPARSE huts. Early summer winds carried the smell of meadow flowers and warmth across the road. Emma returned the smiles and waves that greeted her from passing windows. Her house seemed out of place at the edge of the village. All the other homes this far away from the town proper were simple dirt-floor affairs, while hers had a living room, a loft, a pantry, and a back bedroom for Nan—not to mention wooden floors. She grinned, remembering the story of how Mama had insisted they stay here where she was born. Nan loved telling of how Da had expected his 'peasant wife' to jump at the chance to live in the big city. Like Emma, Mama loved the touch of the earth on bare feet. Her family had lived in the Village of Widowswood since Nan's Nan was Emma's age. Mama would have been miserable cooped up in a big city like Calebrin.

Emma paused, digging a toe into the dirt road and hugging the pouch. Mama said his choosing to stay out in the sticks proved he loved her. She closed her eyes, happy to have good parents. She sighed and cast a forlorn glance at the town, wondering why the 'gods' the townspeople always spoke of couldn't or didn't protect Kimber from having a bad family. The rustle of wind in the trees soon chased her guilt to the side, replacing it with worry. She crept to the edge of the path until she reached grass, gazing into the dark shadows among the shifting pines. At this hour, that poor girl would be off alone in the woods gathering apples.

She thought of Hannah and backed away from the forest, heart racing. Her favorite dress had nothing resembling a belt from which to hang the pouch, so she clutched it to her chest and ran. Wind pulled at her hair as she picked up speed, driven on by a strange sense of something chasing her. She stared at her feet hitting the path, as if not looking behind her would make the monster go away.

The dull thuds of her footfalls became sharp claps once dirt gave way to cobblestones in the heart of town. The scent of roast beef, chicken, and stew floated thick from a tavern at the corner, mixed with the flicking strums of a mandolin. Her eyes opened at the change in the ground, a second before she collided with a man in armor. He caught her by the arms before she could crack her head into his chest, and took a knee to bring himself closer to eye level.

"Belephir protect you, child. What are you running from? Is something the matter?"

Emma tried to say something, but had no breath. While she gasped, he craned his neck to peer over her shoulder. She lowered her hands, hanging onto the pouch by one finger hooked through the cord. Warmth rushed over her face with a blush.

"It's nothing, Kavan," rasped Emma. "One of Nan's stories got the best of me." She glared back the way she came at a scrap of forest visible between buildings. "I'm too old for such silliness. I thought something was in the woods, watching me."

Guard Kavan let go of her and brushed a few strands of hair out of her face before he stood. "Aye right, lass. Way too old. What're ya, ten now? Almost ready ta marry off. Definitely not a child." He winked. "Be walkin' with a cane in another week, ya will."

She stuck her tongue out and sputtered. He ruffled her hair, chuckling, taking a step before he turned back. "You sure you didn't see anythin'? We've 'ad reports of bandits nearby. Keep away from the woods."

"Yes. I'm fine. Just fetching herbs for Mama from Marsten." Emma looked down, picking at her dress.

"What is it, Em?"

"Is Kimber missing?"

Guard Kavan coughed. "What makes you think something's happened?"

"Umm…" *The Banderwigh let Hannah go, and Kimber runs around alone all the time in the woods. The monster would…* Emma's face scrunched up. *Now I sound like Nan.* "She seemed 'fraid of her da."

"Aye." Kavan glanced down the street. "Right mess, that. I'll go 'ave a look."

Guard Kavan stood up to his full seven-foot height, making her feel tiny. She curtsied to him and jogged deeper into the town center. On the next patch of street, she shuffled all the way to one side to avoid the tailor's shop. Monsters she didn't believe in, but no sense risking a jinx. A passing merchant in a blue silk doublet covered his coinpurse at her approach, until he saw her face.

"Good day, Emma." He flashed an embarrassed smile. "My word, girl. I mistook you for a filch."

"Allo, Mister Valis." She smiled and curtsied at him, unaware of the meaning of his gesture.

"Your old man really ought to bring you to my daughter-in-law's shop. That rag is unbecoming a young lady of your station."

Emma's face reddened and she looked down. *But, Nan made it.*

"Well, I suppose you're little yet. No sense you ruining silk by running around in the weeds. Might as well enjoy youth while you have it."

She forced a smile as the wealthy merchant tipped his hat at her and walked away. Like Da, he came from Calebrin, but still lived there. Whenever he ran wagons, he'd ask Da on as a guard. For a few minutes, she stared down at her dress. Every little hole she could stick a finger into and every smudge of dirt that refused to wash out had a memory attached to it. Emma hugged herself, as if at any moment someone would attempt to force her to wear something nicer.

The town square bustled with activity: traveling merchants, a skald, a great fat man in a brown robe shouting to everyone in an effort to sell his ale. Emma watched him, smiling at the silly faces he made while waving a wooden stein at anyone who came close. She crept up to his table, peering over the lip of a wooden mug. The stuff inside smelled nasty and she wrinkled her nose. He seemed about to yell at her to get away, but relaxed at her disgusted face. Emma lost interest and ducked around a flower cart—and bumped into the side of another man selling sweet breads.

"Sorry, sir." She took a step back.

"Oh, you poor dear!" He handed her one of the pastries. "Here. Take it."

A little black cloud formed in her mind. "Thank you, sir. But… I'm not a beggar."

"Don't worry yourself, girl. It's fine." He took her arm, twisted her palm face-up, and set the roll in her hand. "I insist."

The fragrance of sweet cinnamon and spice was too much to resist, and she took a bite. The flavor rid her of any sense of insult at his thinking her a street waif, and she flashed a smile of genuine thanks. The treat was half-gone by the time she reached the far end of the square and darted down a winding, narrow road. Clusters of old women paid her little mind as she weaved among the adults on her way to where the cobblestones faded back to dirt.

Beggar. She appraised the half-roll. *I should give this to Kimber.*

Marsten's shop made her house feel small: two stories tall, with a great porch that beckoned her toward a pair of double doors with square-paneled glass windows. She grasped the railing, leaving sticky handprints on the way up. Creaky rocking chairs on either side moved in the breeze, stalling her as soon as she set foot on the last step. Emma again felt silly for thinking anything but the wind could be responsible.

The door on the right stood wedged open, allowing her to walk into the choking stench of dozens of herbs and plants. Bins of Beauflower, Amethyst Moss, Azurevine, Faeberry, and Goldleaf lined the first row of shelves. Pungent Rotweed dangled out of a low-hanging bin; she could almost see the fumes wafting from it. She craned her neck, taking several steps on tiptoe to peer at the strange plants, wondering if Mama would ever teach her what the apothecary did with each one.

"Oi, careful, girl. Donnae get too close to that. Is Satyrsroot, will make ya sicker'n a mule in the rain."

She shot Marsten a confused look, letting her weight back onto her heels. "How sick is a mule in the rain?"

He huffed. The sudden blast of air made his wispy, white moustache jump. "Just a figure of speech, girl. That stuf'll make a woman sick. Probably kill a little'un for sniffin it."

"You're lying." Emma walked up to the counter. "You want to scare me away from touching things. Mama makes tea with it for Da sometimes."

Marsten turned bright red and coughed. She cringed at the harshness of his dry, wheezing chuckle.

"Aye. Should'a figured you'd know an 'erb or two. What's yer mum need?"

"There's a list." She reached up and set the pouch on the eye-level counter. "In there. With money."

Marsten upended the pouch, spilling copper coins and a few silver bits onto the wood with a clatter. Emma covered her nose with both hands in an effort to tolerate the overwhelming mixture of scents in the air. He plucked a strip of paper from the coins and pressed it flat, lifting his head to stare down his nose at the writing. She tapped her foot, waiting while he slid the money between two piles, glancing at the list every few coins.

"Aye. Be just a moment."

She folded her arms and nibbled at the last half of the sweet roll, unable to taste it in here, so powerful the aroma of various plants. A twinge of guilt made her stop. Kimber needed it more than she did. Marsten shuffled about behind the counter, gathering the supplies her mother had requested. Emma kicked at the floor, shifted her weight back and forth, and swiped her foot to draw arcs in the dust.

In the corner, where the counter met the wall to the left, a large wooden drawer held a number of mushrooms that caught her eye. Wide, flat tops ranging from eight to ten inches across sparkled in the weak light, some beige, others golden, and one bright orange with a white middle. Their stalks were almost a foot in length, causing them to droop over the front. Emma crept up to the bin. Wide-eyed, she reached to touch one with unsteady fingers, curious, but afraid of being yelled at.

When the tip of her finger came within an inch of contact, Marsten let his weight fall on the counter above her with a heavy *slam*. Emma recoiled from the bin and pulled her arms to her chest, a gasp shy of screaming. He stooped over and leaned on his elbows. Realizing he grinned at startling her, she scowled.

"Pretty, aren't they?"

"You could have asked me not to touch them. You didn't need to be mean."

"Oh, the look on your face." Marsten laughed himself coughing. "Your Mum's goin' to be cross with me, but it was worth it. Did she teach you what those are?"

She shifted to look at them once more, making a series of faces. "Mushrooms?"

"Well, in general terms, yes. Do you know what they're called?"

"*Big* mushrooms?" She poked one. Firm, dry, springy. "Flat-headed orangecap?"

"Creative, but not quite." He stood. "Those are Faerie's Throne."

Emma forced herself not to sigh at him out of politeness. "There's no such thing as faeries."

"They use 'em as chairs out in the woods. Sleepin' on 'em, takin' breaks from their endless days of playing. Sometimes they even"—he coughed, cheeks reddening—"uhh, dance on them."

"I'm too old to believe in faeries. It's a story for little kids."

"And old Nans." He winked.

"They're just stories."

A clamor at the door announced the arrival of a man burdened with packs and bundles. She glanced at him in passing, paying him little mind as he trudged up to the counter, clattering and bumping bins. Something he carried stank worse than the herbs. When she caught wind of it, she leaned into the shelf behind her, trying to get away. He struggled, shrugging weight off his back. The largest cloth bundle over his shoulder came undone from the sharp motion. Bright green spilled out from it, flying toward her. A spider with a body bigger than Emma and legs that spanned six feet to either side collapsed to the floor. The most ghastly smell of rot blew past her nose, making her long for the reek of herbs.

She screamed and wedged herself against the wall as the beast landed looking right at her. Eight milky white eyes, resembling wads of spun spidersilk, stared lifeless from a face six inches away from her foot. Emerald hairs covered the critter, matted with goop from an obviously fatal wound. Nightmares flashed in Emma's mind, memories of a dozen horrible dreams caused by the sight of one of these spiders lashed to a wagon years ago.

Whimpering too soft to hear, Emma glanced left and right at furry legs as thick as her shins. They'd fallen around her like a spilled wagon of fire logs, trapping her in the corner. She couldn't go anywhere without touching one to move it. Trembling, she clutched her arms to her chest, unable to stop staring at its eight dead eyes. Any second now, it would come back to life and sink its dagger-sized fangs into her.

"Got a fair wad of silk," said the man, ignoring her imminent death. He dug a shimmery pearl-white wad from his pouch, about the size of Tam's head. "Nabbed a trophy as well, biggest one I've ever seen."

Emma pressed herself against the wall, up on her toes. She managed to break eye contact with the giant spider and stared, pleading, up at Marsten. Fascinated by the wad, he didn't notice her, and plucked a strand of thread away from the mass to appraise it. He held the fiber, as thick as twine, up to the light and studied it for a moment before setting the whole wad down. It took some doing to get his hand off the sticky thing.

She whined and fidgeted, but neither man noticed. Marsten flashed a broad smile while examining another pack the trader had dropped on the counter. The spider's left foreleg slipped forward two inches. Emma let out a brief, high-pitched squeal.

The visitor shook his head at her. "Nothing to be 'fraid of, child. It's already dead." He jostled its rear end with his boot, and the entire spider undulated, its huge mouthparts waving at her.

That made it appear too close to alive, and she screamed.

Eyes closed, she tried to push the memories away. How many times had she woken in the middle of the night bawling? She remembered Mama's sleepy reassurances of being safe at home. Emma whispered to herself, the same words her mother had used.

"Shh, Em. It was just a dream. There are no spiders."

"Is this all you could get?" grumbled Marsten. "I'm willin' to offer forty kingscoin for this, but I have half the traders in Calebrin wantin' more."

A scrape made Emma's eyes snap open, fearing the emerald creeper had returned to life. The creature had shifted, slumping further to the ground. Pale green ichor leaked out of its front end, creeping toward her unprotected toes. Her chest tightened. She couldn't breathe. The room started spinning. She had only to kick a spider leg out of the way, a hairy stick as big around as her leg. She raised her foot, trying to step over it without touching. Rigid bristles scratched at her calf. Emma emitted a faint squeal and recoiled into the corner, shivering.

Neither man moved.

"The damnable things are getting more aggressive. They got Finlay." The trader bowed his head. "I never even saw where he went. One minute, he's at my side with his bow ready, then I hear a scream and turn, and he's just... gone."

"So," said Marsten, palms flat on the counter, "does this mean you'll not be hunting for more?"

"I reckon it might be a while, but I'm willing to go back. Need to find some men to help first. I've no interest in going back there with less than six blades behind me."

"Hey." Marsten tapped the counter twice. "Mind movin' the critter. Can't ya see it's scarin' the child?"

"It's dead."

"Would ya, look at 'er?" Marsten gestured at Emma. "Me sis was the same way with spiders. She'd be climbin' the walls to get away from a wee one. That thing would'a killed her from fright."

The visitor hauled the corpse from the corner, bundling the legs and tying them with twine. As soon as the leg moved out of her way, Emma darted along the wall and hid among the shelves. She held onto a box full of metallic blue Shimmerweed while trying to remember how to breathe. Conversation between the men murmured in the distance; she didn't care to listen in. Panic faded, and she went limp on her feet, forehead to the wooden bin, focusing only on taking long in and out breaths.

"Em?" yelled Marsten. "Are you alright, girl?"

She peered around the edge of the row, one eye, four fingers, and five toes visible to the man behind the counter. When she saw no trace of the trader, or anything even resembling an enormous spider, she approached.

"I don't like those things."

"Aye. I'd not want to meet one alive either, and I'm too fat to be carted off by 'em."

Emma glared at him, aghast he would say such a thing. Now tonight would bring a nightmare of being wrapped in silk and carried away into the woods. If the thought didn't terrify her so much, she'd have been angry.

"Here's your mum's order." He reached down, handing her a burlap bundle.

"Thank you, Mister Marsten."

She retrieved the dust-covered half of a sweet roll from the corner where she had dropped it. No amount of puffing on it made it look appetizing anymore. Not even Kimber would want it now. Well, maybe Kimber would, but she couldn't let the girl eat dust. Once outside, she tossed it to some birds pecking at the road. Emma gave herself a once-over, wiping evidence of her terror off her cheeks and putting on her usual stoic face. She twisted left and right to check her dress, and almost fainted at the sight of a few emerald hairs stuck like quills in her right calf.

"Marsten!" she cried, limping through the door. "It got me!"

Despite feeling no real pain, she moved as if her entire leg had gone numb. Marsten lifted a section of hinged counter and shuffled over.

"What happened, Emma?"

She turned, showing off the back of her leg and whining.

He suppressed the urge to laugh and scooped her up by a hand in each armpit. After carrying her to the counter, he set her seated upon it and held her leg up by the ankle.

"Them critters have stiff hairs. When somethin' scares em, they throw 'em like daggers."

Emma huffed and sniveled. "Are they poisoned?"

"No. Just sharp." He grasped each one in turn and gingerly worked them loose. "And barbed."

"Barbed?" Emma's knuckles whitened on the counter.

"The way they're shaped, they stick in easy, but tear on the way out. Too small to see." He held up the removed bristle, a green stick somewhat thinner than an arrow shaft that gleamed like a gem. "Rub your finger over the top."

It took a minute of staring, but Emma finally gathered the courage to set one finger on it. Sliding left felt like a smooth knitting needle. Sliding right seemed more like a nail file. She pulled her hand back.

Marsten knelt, pushing her foot up higher and easing the last two hairs out one at a time. He rubbed her calf afterward, smiling, and let her leg down.

"There ya are. Only but a wee stab. They dinnae go in far enough to do much. Hardly grazed ya."

"It hurts," she whined.

The pudgy apothecary struggled upright off his knee, gasped for breath, and meandered to a nearby bin. He took a small green leaf, crushed it, and rubbed the fragments around her leg. The area went numb and tingly.

"There. Good as new."

"Thank you."

He helped her down and handed her back her mother's order. "Go on now, Em. Your mum'll be worried if you take too long."

Emma waved and ran for the door.

5

APPLES TO WINE

*E*mma guarded her bundle of dead plants as though all the bandits in Widowswood wanted to take it from her. Clinging to it made her think of Mama and not of enormous spiders with swords for fangs waiting in every gap between buildings. She smiled at the man who gave her the roll, and walked dutifully across the square on the most direct path home.

A few of the town watch greeted her. Any close enough to touch her invariably patted her on the head. Every one of them asked what had scared her, as she evidently still 'looked frightened.' She told the story of the huge spider four times. Da was their superior, and she felt grateful they all looked after her. The Village of Widowswood counted as somewhere between a huge hamlet and a small town. Everyone knew the daughter of Guard Captain Dalen.

She frowned, unable to get rid of the worry something bad would happen to her leg for having spider-hairs stuck in it. Despite seeing nothing wrong, she couldn't put a feeling of discomfort out of her thoughts and paused every few steps to rub the spot.

A high-pitched shriek made her look up during one such pause. When the voice screamed again, she recognized it—Kimber.

Caution to the wind, Emma sprinted along an ever-narrowing

street that went into the north part of town where the poor congregated. An incoherent man reached for her from where he had fallen against a hovel, babbling in a drunken stupor about copper bits. She paid him no mind, running faster when Kimber screamed again. Emma rounded a corner, dashed past a few houses, and skidded to a stop by a fence.

No one else seemed to notice the commotion occurring in the dirt lot in front of a pathetic wooden shack, the whole house smaller than Nan's bedroom. Kimber, hair wild and full of thistles, positioned herself on the far side of a horse trough near the door. Arms held out to her sides, she trembled like a beaten dog, eyes locked on the wretched figure of a thin, wasted man towering over her. The girl's dress had ripped, exposing one shoulder and a new bruise.

A round bottle with a thin neck in the man's left hand sloshed when he used that arm to point at her. "Fink you kin sic the guard on me? Ungrateful little brat!"

He lunged to the left. Kimber went the other way, evading a grab and using the trough to keep her distance.

"Pa, I dinnae do 'et! No' me!"

Emma squeezed her bundle. Her fear of old man Drinn rooted her in place, while guilt at being responsible for Guard Kavan paying him a visit prodded her in the back. Kimber jumped right when her father faked left. He pounced and snatched a fistful of her hair, hauling her across the yard by it. Kimber wailed, grabbing onto his fist while scrambling to follow him across the yard. Old Man Drinn sat on a stool by the tiny house's only door. Once seated, he pulled the girl up and over his knees. Kimber shrieked and pleaded, clamping onto her tattered garment, trying to delay the beating as much as she could.

"Ungrateful little whelp!" He yanked at the fabric, trying to expose her backside for a spanking. "Can't find any decent apples, so you lie to the guards?"

"Stop!" Emma yelled, running over to the gate. "Don't hit her!"

Kimber's father squinted at the new voice intruding on his world. His left eye didn't seem capable of opening more than a narrow slit, while his right had widened to the point she expected it to fall out of his head. His thin, wiry body appeared every bit as starved as his daughter, though he didn't have her paleness. Kimber lapsed into sobs once he ceased trying to pull her dress up.

Old Man Drinn stared, awestruck, at Emma. "Who d'you think you are talkin' ta me like that?"

"I sent the guard. It wasn't Kimber's fault. Let her go!"

"Is that right?" He stood, carrying the weeping redhead over to the trough.

The way he held her, head down, made Emma afraid he was going to dunk Kimber under and drown her. Emma dropped the herbs and shoved the gate out of her way, storming into the yard.

"Been ae month since yer last bath, wee." He dangled her over the water, shaking her. "Best do a right lot of sellin' today, mebbe I'll forget it's time to—"

Emma swiped a rotten apple off the ground and hurled it. The foul missile splattered over the back of the old man's head. He yelled in surprise, losing his grip on the flailing girl. Kimber fell face-first into the filthy water. She surfaced seconds later and sloshed to the far side, shivering. Emma stood defiant, another apple in her hand ready to throw.

"If you don't stop hitting her, I'll send the watch again. You've no right to be so mean. Kimber's only a child. *You* should be the one earning money."

He wiped a hand over the back of his head, studying the ill-smelling brown smear. From the look on his face, it seemed he wasn't sure if he had spoiled fruit or brains on his fingers. He licked it and spat, setting his bottle on the stool. Shaking, he pointed a thick, yellowing fingernail at her.

"Too mean, huh?" Old Man Drinn stalked at Emma, reaching. "I'll show ya mean."

"Papa, donnae do et!" screamed Kimber.

He rounded on her with a glare that made her cry and duck half underwater. Emma hit him between the shoulders with another rotten apple.

"Leave her alone!"

Drinn went still for a few seconds, then turned about with a growing sneer. His big eye narrowed to match the other, his upper lip twitching. The glare he levelled at Emma froze her in place.

Seconds passed, the stillness broken only by the lapping of water in the horse trough and Kimber's sniveling.

Emma drew a breath to speak, but before she could think of what to say, Old Man Drinn let off a roar like an animal and ran at her. She ducked under a swinging fist and darted around him. He got a hand on her long hair, yanking her over backward onto the ground. She grabbed at the back of her head with both arms, screaming as he dragged her close and grabbed a fistful of her dress in his left hand. He leaned down hard, crushing her into the ground and forcing a wheeze out of her.

"Papa! No!" Kimber clutched the edge of the trough, casting hopeful glances at the street, seeming terrified of what would happen to her if she screamed for the guards.

"Little brat!" He slapped Emma back and forth across the face, then drew his hand high, this time making a fist. Breath laced with the sweet stink of faeberry brandy watered her eyes more than the pain in her cheeks.

Despite trembling, Emma stared at him. Sweat dripped from his nose. Distant water sloshed from Kimber climbing out of the trough. The girl ran over and grabbed her father's poised arm. She got an elbow in the face for her effort, which knocked her on her rump, crying.

Infuriated at that, Emma squirmed, grabbing his wrist and trying to shove it off her shoulder. Old Man Drinn looked down at her. The bones in his hand creaked. He took a sharp breath; ready to whomp her in the face.

Bwawk!

A large raven landed at the corner of the hovel's roof, fluffing its feathers. It cocked its head, staring at Drinn. The bird leaned forward, wings wide, threatening, emitting a noise like shale scraping on stone. Even Emma had to admit something about *that* bird didn't feel right.

He hesitated. Drunken rage faded to worry. When he looked back at her, his cheeks had become ashen.

"You... You're Emma." He lowered his arm and took his weight off her.

She scooted back along the dirt and gathered her legs under her. "Yes. You know who my Da is," Emma whispered.

He had the far-off stare of a man who'd just ensured his own death. "Aye."

Old Man Drinn stumbled back to his stool, stooping to retrieve his bottle along the way. He sat and took a long swig. Emma fixed her dress and walked closer, hands balled into fists. The raven settled its feathers. Kimber sniffled, making no move to get up from where she had sprawled.

"I'll make you a deal." She pointed at Kimber. "You stop being mean to Kimber, and I won't tell my father you hit me."

He sputtered in his booze. The raven tucked its beak under a wing.

"If you hit her one more time, I'll tell." She went over to help the younger girl up. The start of a black eye showed evident. Emma touched the spot gingerly. "I'm sorry. I asked Kavan to check on you. He visited because of me. I thought the bandits in the woods might've grabbed you."

"Bandits? Bah," grumbled the old man. "She'd be e'ery bit o' useless ta them as she is here."

Emma shot a disgusted glare at him before her expression softened toward Kimber. She whispered, "Tell me if he hits you again."

Kimber's green eyes stared off into nowhere. She trembled, afraid to look at her father or say a word. Emma wanted to cry. The same motherly feelings she had toward Tam reared up, and she gathered the other girl in a hug. Kimber didn't seem to know how to react.

A whispering breeze arose out of nowhere in the woods. Emma twisted to look. The raven faced into the wind, squawking at the trees. Though nothing appeared out of the ordinary, something about the forest worried Emma. For a moment, she couldn't peel her gaze away. Kimber's hand on her cheek startled her at how much the light contact hurt.

"'E hit ya, too," whispered Kimber. "I'as sorry."

"Don't go in the woods today," said Emma. *That banderwigh stuff is rubbish. I shouldn't say anything about the woods. It'll only scare her more.*

"Nonsense!" roared the man. "She needs ta sell apples or we'll starve."

Emma glared at the bottle. "You don't buy food with it anyway."

He wobbled to his feet and staggered at her with a menacing fist. Emma thrust her chin out.

"One more step, and I'll scream for the guards." She squinted. "You're an awful man. I'll not let you hurt her anymore."

Kimber ran into him, wrapping her arms around his legs as if to hold him back. "Papa, no. I love ya. I's 'kay. I's sorrys if'n I's been bad an' lazy. I'll go pickin'."

The girl pushed him back until he tripped and fell, seated, on the stool. She picked up the bottle and handed it to him. Emma shook her head and collected the bundle of herbs from where she had dropped it.

Kimber found her basket and went for the gate. "Wha's wrong wif 'a woods?"

Emma ducked out of the yard, waiting for Kimber to follow and close the fence. "Bad feeling. It's just a made-up story from Nan… and Guard Kavan said there's bandits nearby."

Kimber stared at her with an unreadable expression for a moment, then set off in the direction of the apple trees, head down. Emma didn't like the eerie feeling in the woods, but she couldn't believe a monster lurked out there. *Only a silly story.* Bandits wouldn't bother with a girl like Kimber. She didn't look like her family had any money.

Old Man Drinn stared at Emma. Something in his eyes sent a chill down her back. He swigged from his drink again, the slosh of wine and *pthunk* of his lips breaking the seal at the narrow neck seemed far louder than it ought to have. He smiled at her and raised the bottle in toast.

A man like that might not feel any guilt about making a girl like her disappear to save his life.

6

EYES IN THE WOODS

*M*ama whirled at the *slam* of the door. Emma leaned against it, eyes closed and out of breath from running the whole length of the dirt road between the town and home. As if Old Man Drinn hadn't been scary enough, she couldn't help but feel *something* watched her from the woods.

"Em!" Mama ran over. "Did you get into a fight with that Cooper boy again?"

Emma winced at the finger poking her cheek. "No, Mama."

"His mother promised me he wouldn't tease you anymore."

"It wasn't Rydh, Mama." She cringed away from the examination. "I bloodied his nose. He doesn't bother me anymore."

Mama pointed at a chair and took the herb bundle. Emma hung her head and trudged to the indicated seat, swinging her legs back and forth for a short while as her mother puttered around by *the cabinet*. Emma looked up a few minutes later when Mama stepped in front of her and placed a gentle hand atop her head, twisting her sideways to get a clear look at the bruises. Emma grabbed the seat of the chair, emitting a long squealing whine as a freezing cold, slimy cloth pressed over the hurt. The scent of earthy moss made her cough.

"What happened," asked Mama. "Your whole face is bruised."

"I promised I wouldn't tell Da."

Mama pressed into the soaked burlap, ensuring it sat evenly over her face. "You promised not to tell Da. You can tell your mother."

Emma stared at the ceiling, relieved that the dull pain had gone away. Mama did have a point, she *had* only promised not to tell her father. "Old Man Drinn hit me."

The look on her mother's face darkened to the point of frightening. She had never seen such anger in Mama's eyes.

"He did what?!"

Emma grasped Mama's wrist with both hands. "He was hittin' on Kimber. I told him to stop." She explained everything. "I told him I'd not tell if he'd stop hitting her."

Mama cradled Emma to her chest, stroking her hair. "Men like that don't listen to what women say, and they certainly don't like threats from little ones."

Emma sniffled. "He's gonna hurt her, isn't he?"

Mama kissed her head. "I'm proud of you, Em—however, you made a promise you shouldn't keep. He's going to be angry with Kimber for what you did."

"She didn't! That's stupid! But—"

"Don't worry. Your father won't be involved."

Emma looked up, confused.

"Your promise won't be broken. Now, go fetch your brother. It's almost time to eat."

Mama released her hug and peeled the now-dry cloth from her cheeks. Emma thought it odd that the slimy paste had dried to crumbles so fast, but paid it little mind and scampered off the chair for the back door. She caught herself on the doorjamb by the rear alcove and snuck a glimpse over her shoulder. Muttering to herself, Mama stomped over to *the cabinet*, intent on something. Any trace of kindness had fled from the woman's face. Most of the words loud enough to hear other than 'daughter' made Emma blush.

Emma slipped out the door, enjoying the cool evening breeze and the fragrance of hyacinth. Her cheeks no longer hurt, even when she touched them. She crept up to the well, squatting by a puddle to use it as a mirror—no bruise. The oddity of that added to the eerie feeling emanating from the distant forest. Something still felt as if it watched her out of the dark. Fear made her stand straight.

"Tam?" she whispered.

Fireflies zoomed about the meadow grass between the house and the woods, but she couldn't find any sign of her little brother.

"Tam?" she asked, almost at normal speaking volume.

Worry for her younger sibling pushed aside her irrational fear of Nan's faerie monsters, and she ran into the field, looking left and right.

"Tam!" she yelled with building desperation. "Tam? Where are you?"

Grass whipped at her legs as she sprinted in the direction of a weak cry. It sounded like Tam yelling for help. Had she been wrong? Was Nan's creature real? Had it released Hannah only to take him?

No! It wasn't after Kimber. Tam's even littler.

"Tam!" She kept shouting for him, her voice a barely recognizable screech by the time she reached the tree line. "Tam?" *I'm being silly. There are no monsters. He's just lost.*

She kept sight of home over one shoulder, but stepped with caution out of the meadow into the forest. Her toes sank into cool, moist dirt that somehow reassured her despite the oppressive dread in the air. Fear made it impossible to run.

"Emma!" shouted Tam, his voice seeming to come from everywhere. When he cried out again, she moved in that direction as fast as the knee-deep brush would allow.

Hands cupped to her mouth, she yelled. "Where are you?"

She found a narrow trail and jogged along it. Tam's yelling grew quiet again, and she slowed, walking in a gradual spin.

Snap!

Emma whirled around, half-expecting to see Old Man Drinn coming after her with a sword. That had to be it. He'd kidnapped Tam to lure her deep into the woods where he could kill her.

"Tam!" she shrieked, shaking from worry.

A group of five huge wolves emerged from the darkness, pale

yellow eyes unblinking. She went stiff, too frightened to tremble. The lead wolf sniffed at the air; he looked large enough for her to ride like a horse, with fur that shimmered from pale grey to charcoal as he moved. To his right and a little behind, a jet-black wolf almost as large locked eyes with her. For no reason Emma could understand, she knew the black wolf was female. The other three darker grey wolves sniffed at the air.

The sight of the predators made Tam's silence terrifying. Had the wolves gotten him?

She'd put too many trees between her and home to see it anymore —or even which direction to go in. Everywhere around her looked the same. If she ran the wrong way, the wolves would catch her. Even if she went straight home, they still would overrun her. She backed up, gasping when her foot sank into a cold patch of water. The lead wolf kept her pace. Two others circled to the right, emitting a keening cry only loud enough for her to hear they made a noise.

Emma kept her hands low, trying to act non-threatening while continuing to edge backward. She bumped into a tree, stumbled around it, and lost her balance after scraping her foot on a sharp, unseen rock. Her rearward crab-walk couldn't outrun the big wolf. He stalked after her as she scurried against another tree, and approached close enough to bite, but waited. The other four swept around in a circle, stopping less than an arm's length from her. The black wolf came up alongside him, and the pair seemed to stare right through her.

Hot breath washed over her neck and chest. His cold nose touched her throat. She clenched handfuls of dirt, bracing for the end of her life. The wolf snorted and turned away. Emma sat stiff as a headstone against the tree, paralyzed with terror and confusion as the wolves receded.

After a minute of silence, she risked moving enough to look around.

She curled up, knees to face, and let herself shiver away the energy her body summoned in response to fear. Darkness shifted to the right —something seemed to lurk there, watching. Careful not to make a sound, she stood. The largest of the wolves emerged from a shadow twenty paces away, still staring at her. Emma leaned back, eyes wide.

He playing with me. Does he want me to run so he can chase?

The big wolf sent a pointed glance in another direction, then backed out of sight.

Nothing but trees waited where he had looked. She swallowed, crossing her arms over her chest in a futile attempt to stop shaking. When she didn't move, the large wolf leaned into view again, baying at her and snorting in the same direction. Emma stopped trembling, confused by the odd way the animal behaved. She looked again, seeing nothing but trees and shadow. When she turned back, the wolf had gone. Emma thought his behavior too strange to ignore, so she went in the direction the animal seemed to be telling her to go. Expecting the pack to be on her heels, she ran hard. Trees flashed by. She held her arms up to shield her face from low-hanging branches, and called out for her brother again.

Not far from where a huge wolf had almost devoured her, she collided with her little brother, who burst out of the undergrowth coming toward her at full speed. Both tried to stop, but neither managed it in time. They slapped together, chest to chest, her greater size knocking him flat before they went rolling on the ground. As soon as he stopped, he burst into red-faced wailing.

Emma sat up, shook off her dizziness, and crawled to him. He looked as though he'd gone for a frolic in a thistleberry bush. She picked half-inch prickly spheres out of his tunic and hair, wincing whenever the needles bloodied her fingertips. As soon as she cleared him of thistles, she clamped him in a hug, patting his back and rubbing until he stopped crying.

"Tam, you know better than to go into the woods alone."

He sniffled. "You scared too? 'Fraid of da Bandy-wee?"

"Of course not." She grumbled. "Come on, get up. We're late for dinner."

She took him by the hand and pulled him along. The narrow trail led to the forest's edge, and the welcome sight of home on the other side of a meadow full of fireflies. Mama's silhouette filled the back door. Coldness fell over Emma from behind. This time, even Tam shivered and held on. Emma glanced over her shoulder at the pitch-black woods. Branches waved in the breeze amid the rustles and snaps from what she hoped were animals moving around. She backed up, finding herself scared to turn away from the trees.

"Emma, Tam!" shouted Mama from far away. "Where've you been? Come in this instant."

Trusting her mother, Emma broke her stare with the trees and ran for the house, almost dragging Tam off his feet. Hair flying, dress whipping, she tried to outrun the feeling that something chased her.

7

NOCTURNAL URGE

With her parents added to the bed, Emma had little room to move. She lay on her side, pressed into the wall below the windowsill with Tam at her back, his breaths warm upon her neck. Mama's arm covered them both. Blue moonlight filtered in the window, creating a patch on the wall that lit the room enough to see every lurking shadow. Sleep had come in short stints, though she hadn't yet dreamed of giant spiders. Tree-shadows clawed at the glass, occasionally startling her. Tam didn't notice—or didn't let on—how frightened she was while they ran home. Could Old Man Drinn have been hiding in the woods, waiting to get her back? Perhaps an emerald creeper?

It certainly couldn't be a banderwigh.

Da had talked on and off for months about building on to the house, adding a new room for her and Tam to share. The idea of having her own room, like Nan, had made her feel grown up and important. Tonight, she was happy he'd forgotten about it, and adored having her parents *right there.* A shadow darted by the window, like a man creeping around outside. Emma shot upright, gripping the cold wood by the wavy glass. She peered left and right at the dark, moonlit grass, but saw no one, nor any trace of footprints.

There's no such thing as monsters.

Emma exhaled out her nose, steeled herself, and settled back down. Tam whimpered in his sleep. Minutes passed in silent stillness. Nan's tale of the creature filled her head with worry.

She grumped, arms folded, chiding herself for letting such a foolish story get under her skin. No matter how angry she tried to make herself, the feeling of a dark presence watching her remained, as though something had crept into the room behind her, staring. Nothing else could better explain why she'd awakened in the middle of the night. She squeezed her mother's arm, unconsciously trembling. Mama muttered in her sleep, pulling her children tight to her. Emma felt silly all over again for believing in such tales, and closed her eyes.

EMMA FOUND HERSELF AWAKE, BUT IT WAS STILL DARK. SHE SIGHED, stretching her legs and trying to get comfortable. Tam prodded her in the back, explaining why she'd woken up. The little one poked her in the ribs again. She ignored him. After another few pokes, a wet finger found her right ear.

"Tam," she hissed over her shoulder, wiping her ear. "Go to sleep."

He shifted closer, his breath puffing over her cheek as he whispered, "I haveta pee, an' I'm not s'posed to go outside alone. Da's too sleeped."

"Use the chamber pot," mumbled Emma.

"You dropped it, 'member." Tam simulated a disgusting splatter noise. "Down'a privy."

She'd been too eager to help Mama, offering to take the awful thing out back and dump it before she realized how bad it really smelled. In her haste to be rid of the mess, she'd lost her grip. Da had yet to buy another one. They didn't really *need* it anyway, at least, not until winter when no one wanted to go outside in the middle of the night.

Emma squirmed around to lie on her back, wedging herself tighter between her brother and the wall. She eased Mama's arm away and sat up, wiping crumbs from her eyes. Da's usual snoring had quieted, and a pleasant smile on Mama's face hinted at a wonderful dream. Tam stood on the bed and walked to the end, climbing over the storage trunk to the floor. He went to the back door and waited there in his skivvies, unable to stand still.

After another breath, Emma crawled to the edge of the bed with care, so as not to disturb her sleeping parents. The instant her toes touched the icy floor, she shivered, wondering how her brother could stand there with nary more than a strip of cloth around him—or how it had become so cold in summer. Her nightgown was longer than her favorite dress, down to her shins. In better shape than her favorite dress—no holes or rips—the thick, white cotton also offered more warmth.

She climbed up on a stool to reach a lantern, setting it on the table before lighting it. After closing the little glass door, she gathered her brother's tunic and borrowed Nan's shawl, which she wrapped around herself, again perplexed at the unusual chill for the time of year. Tam raised his arms as she pulled his tunic over him and tugged it into place. He bounced with urgency. Emma opened the back door, held his hand, and raised the lantern over her head.

A path of irregular stones led in a twisty curve to the privy shack. The dark forest ringing the meadow behind the house gleamed with patches of white-azure in the unearthly light of a full moon. The edge of Widowswood flickered with strange spots of glow. Nan called them Faerie Lights. Emma figured they were bugs, like fireflies, only bigger and afraid of people. She hesitated, watching the pale green light orbs drift back and forth with motion quite unlike insects. After Nan's story, and with the strange mood in the air, she didn't quite know what to think of them anymore.

Tam tilted his head up to look at her. His thick, brown hair almost covered his eyes and touched his shoulders. He gave her an inquiring stare, then bounced a few times and grabbed himself. Emma brushed aside her fear and extended one tentative foot toward the path.

"Gah," she whispered, as she found out just how cold the stones were at night. "So much for the start of summer."

She pulled him along by the arm in an ungainly run intended to minimize how long her feet had to touch the freezing rocks. A few seconds later, they halted by the small outhouse. Emma let go of his hand to open the rickety door. Tam leapt through and tugged at the handle. He put a hand on her chest when she went to follow him in. She cast an uneasy glance at the woods. Her pure white nightdress glowed in the moonlight, a beacon that left her feeling vulnerable.

"Pi-vate," he said, pulling the door shut and locking it in her face.

Never mind that three or so hours ago, they had shared a bathtub, as they had their entire lives so far. Emma squinted, not wanting to show fear of being out alone at night. Nan's story had gotten to her. She held the lantern up, free arm across her chest in a vain attempt to stifle the shivering. The old one only wanted to scare her. Nan played a game, trying to make brave, suspicious Emma believe in nonsense. There was no such thing as child-stealing monsters that came out of the woods at night. Still, she would have rather been inside a space with a locked door.

"Hurry up," she whispered.

"It's cold. Can't start."

"I know it's cold. That's why I'm telling you to hurry up. I thought you had to go *bad*."

"I does."

"The wind is too cold. Let me in."

"No. Pi-vate." The privy shifted with his shuffling around inside. "You scared of a Bandy-wee?"

"Am not." She scrunched her toes in the grass. It had gotten quiet. "Okay, maybe a little."

He giggled.

A twig snapped.

Emma gasped, raising the lantern. She peered around the side of the little shed, finding nothing.

"Please, I won't watch. I'll keep my eyes closed."

Silence. She imagined him blushing.

She realized the night sounds had ceased. No crickets chirped. No birds tweeted, and no distant animals moved about—not even the low moan of the wind.

Snap. Louder. Closer.

She whirled to her left, light held high. A shadow slid over the ground as though someone crept behind the privy. Emma slapped her free hand on the door. "Tam, I'm not joking. Open the door, now."

"Peeing."

Emma cringed. *Okay, maybe I only saw a cloud drifting by the moon.* She stared at the patch of grass, finding no sign of anything moving.

Crunch.

She flattened herself against the door, her breaths reduced to short rasps. Too terrified to risk a peek around the side again, she shivered. She wanted to scream for her parents, but only a soft whimper came out of her. Staring at the woods, Emma eased her hand up, feeling around blind for the handle, and rattled the locked knob. She looked down past the glowing lantern in her other hand over pale moonlit legs. The grass wavered in the breeze. The stone footpath waited three paces away. She considered running for Da, but couldn't leave Tam out here alone, locked door or not. Distant wind howled louder, hissing in the trees and chilling her through the thin garment.

Snap.

She didn't look. *Only a chicken, maybe one of Hadrath's pigs got loose again.* She turned to face the outhouse, straining up on her toes to speak into the crescent moon hole.

Her voice wavered, close to tears. "Please, Tam. Let me in. I'm really scared."

The shadow of an enormous axe blade stretched over the glinting wood. The icy hand of fear scratched down her back. Darkness fell upon her as something big blocked the light of the moon. Emma jumped and spun around, staring up into pale, glowing yellow eyes. A shaggy man-shaped shadow loomed past the corner of the privy, a long-handled axe balanced over one shoulder.

Emma leapt back. The lantern flew from her hand.

She screamed.

8

FAERIES AND MONSTERS

*D*izziness spun around in Emma's mind. An overwhelming sense of vertigo mixed with the fragrance of pine and a hint of floating. Her right foot dangled in the path of a gentle breeze. The surface beneath her was hard and cold. She pulled her right arm up, bracing her palm against smooth metal and propping herself seated. Squinting revealed a dim space split into slivers by bands of black. As her eyes adjusted to the dim light, the bands sharpened from blur to jagged bars. Emma spun in a panicked flurry.

She sat in a hanging cage with irregular metal shards for bars, nothing any man crafted with forge and hammer. Here and there, 'thorns' protruded, as though some demonic sculptor had attempted to make roses out of black iron. Above her, the bars bent together in a dome shape, then curved out to angry points. A metal ring bundled them at the narrow part where they all met. Thick chains covered in rust and dirt connected the ring to the ceiling. The angular bars were too thick to get her hands around. The cage appeared big enough to let her stand up inside it, but only barely.

Her first attempt to get up sent her falling on her backside when the little prison moved, like trying to balance upright on a tree swing.

She stared past her knees at the mortared stone walls of a cottage swaying back and forth.

In time, the sway came to a halt. She grabbed from bar to bar, spinning to look around at her surroundings. The space appeared to be a small one-room cabin with walls of mortared, stacked stones. The only window sat high on the wall, within an inch of the roof, too small for even a child to escape through. Overgrown with shrubbery, it offered a narrow view of trees and blue sky, and gave her the impression the room was more underground than not. Roots invaded cracks in the mortar here and there, some with tiny black insects crawling over them, some with not-so-tiny insects. None of the walls had doors, and the only furnishings consisted of a single chair fifteen feet away against the opposite wall, and a plain wooden table with a small, grey brick at the center.

Da had used a similar brick to sharpen his blades. When she shifted to keep looking out from the cage, something soft came between her foot and the floor. She raised her leg and glanced down at a crude burlap doll missing one of its button eyes. Having no interest in a toy at the moment, she brushed it to the side and continued looking for a way out.

Seven similar cages of varying sizes hung beside her, three to her left and four to her right, all but two empty. The one next to her on the left held a girl a year or so older, grimy as a beggar and probably blonde. So far completely silent, the other girl came to life the moment Emma looked at her, and began muttering what sounded like an old nursery rhyme in a whispery rasp while clutching a petrified, half-eaten muffin she picked at and spun in her hands. Her primitive burlap dress had burn holes in places where patches of red, blistered skin peeked out. Smudges of char marked her cheeks, arms, and legs.

Emma's heart thudded in her chest at the sight of blood trickling down a dangling leg with cracked, red skin. Red droplets gathered on the older girl's big toe, falling to the floor with a *clap* as loud as blocks of wood striking stone.

She shied away, whispering to herself. "I'm having a nightmare."

The sing-song chant grew louder. Emma raised her head, staring past a curtain of disheveled black hair at the strange figure. Her voice flowed upon the melody of an old rhyme Mama had used to lull her to sleep years ago, but the words were quite different.

"Wrinkle, crinkle, burning bright.
Flame disport, a dancing light."

The girl gazed off at something far away. She twitched, then cracked an innocent smile. Smoke seeped from her lips as she spoke, filling the air with the scent of burned wood.

"Hither, thither, rush and churn.
around them all, reave and burn."

Emma held on to the bars, afraid to breathe for the sound it might make. The other girl rocked, cradling her pitiful morsel of bread as if it were a doll.

"Ashes, ashes, o'er my bed
Ashes, ashes, many dead"

Her voice fell to a whisper. Emma covered her mouth to hold in a gasp.

"Broken lantern, fallow dry
No one wakes, no warning cry"

Her somber rhyme became a fevered shout.

"Runs and hides, the girl her shame.
For now I know who to blame!"

The unexpected yelling startled Emma. She leapt back from the bars and fell against the opposite side, sending the cage swaying back and forth. The other girl fell quiet again, rocking and mumbling the same melody into the pittance of food she held close to her lips. Emma curled against the frigid metal, knees to her chin, trembling at the sight of a girl who'd gone nutters.

Her brother whined in his sleep behind her. Emma twisted around. Tam lay curled up two cages right, still asleep. One empty cage separated them. She cried at the sight of him trapped, and knelt in an effort to reach between the bars toward him. Face mushed against iron, she could barely get her fingertips to the next cage over, falling far short of his. She shifted, searching around the bottom of her cage for any sort of latch or keyhole, but found nothing. She knelt upon a simple, blackened metal disc, wedged in the curve of jagged bars that had no seams, no hinges, and no way to open.

She sat, knees tight to her chest, trembling. This cage was impossible. She couldn't fit between the bars, and it had no door. Emma felt like a ship in a bottle. Eoghn, the innkeeper, had one of them on the bar. That had mystified her with its impossibility at first, until Da explained how they build them inside, piece by piece through the neck. The cage had to be similar, a trick. She traced her fingers down the bars as high as she could reach without standing. The metal reminded her of blackened iron, like a fireplace poker. *This is a dream. Monsters aren't real.* Emma chanted *wake up... wake up...* in her mind for a few seconds. She pinched herself, and opened her eyes.

Still in the cage.

The older girl broke into fits of giggling, spraying crumbs out of her teeth.

Overcome, Emma pitched her head forward and sobbed on her knees. Tears ran down her legs as she called out for Da, Mama, and Nan. Her pleas echoed in the underground room, answered only by the wheezing snickers of the girl to her left. When she had cried herself out of tears, she lifted her head, sniffling and wiping her face. The older girl stared at her, anger glinting in hazel eyes. She leapt closer, a rapid lunge against the bars, startling a yelp out of Emma. The left half of the other girl's face was blistered and oozing, with much of her hair on that side missing.

Emma swallowed. "Why are you looking at me like that?"

The blonde girl's lips quivered with an inaudible growl. Emma pressed herself into the cage wall, as far away from the malice radiating from her neighbor as she could get. The hateful stare remained unblinking—without cages separating them, she believed the girl would hurt her. The other child reached a scalded left arm into Emma's cage, her hand past the bars to the wrist. Emma stared, paralyzed, until warm, slimy fingers groped at the top of her foot, leaving smears of bloody ooze. She squealed and yanked her leg away, huddling in a ball.

Snarling, the older girl thrust one red hand forward, pointing at

Emma's face. "Runs and hides, the girl her shame. For now I know who to blame! You killed them! You killed everyone!"

Emma whimpered.

"You killed them," the girl hissed. "And look what you did to me!"

Fear turned to confusion. "Killed who?" Confusion became anger. "I haven't hurt anyone. We've been kidnapped! My Da is the Captain of the watch. He'll find us."

The blonde grinned, pressing her head to the bars. "Your father's dead."

"No!" wailed Emma.

"Your mother's dead."

"No!" shouted Emma.

"Everyone you know is dead," sang the girl, smiling.

"No!" yelled Emma, tears rolling down her face.

"You been sleepin' for days." The older girl grunted and growled, trying to reach farther into Emma's cage, slapping bloody handprints on the bottom. Clear liquid seeped from blisters on her skin. "You threw the lantern. The whole village burned. Everyone died." Her eyes lost focus. "Ashes, ashes, o'er my bed."

"That's not true!" screamed Emma, cowering away.

"Your Nan, your parents, your sad little friend with the red hair, too. All dead." She hissed a croaking giggle past grimy hands. "No one wakes, no warning cry. Dead."

"No, no, no!" Emma sniveled.

"Your parents didn't know you were outside. They went back into your house looking for you while it burned. They died because of you. Your Nan, too. She was too old and slow to get out of bed before the fire took her!"

The older girl ceased her attempts to grab Emma, pulling her arm back and clinging to the bars of her cage with an unsettling, emotionless expression. She shifted, revealing more of the burned-bald side of her head.

"I watched my Mum and Pa die. Pa pushed me out the window, but the roof fell on him before he could get out, and covered me with fire." The girl tugged at the bars in a futile effort to rip them apart. "Look at what you did to me! I used to be pretty! Now I'm ugly!"

"No! I don't believe you," screamed Emma, covering her eyes.

She shivered in silence for a moment before the memory came back. A dark figure loomed around the outhouse. She shrieked, and threw the lantern into the air. Emma couldn't remember anything after that. Still cringing against the unforgiving metal, she curled up and bawled. Sorrow gripped her tighter with each breath. Her mind tormented her with images and sounds of what must have happened. She knew Nan's time was short, but the actual moment of loss still came with more pain than she could bear. On top of that, Mama and Da, too?

"It's gonna keep us like that other girl. She's dead inside." The blonde hissed, trying once more to reach in and grab Emma. "I'm gonna remember. When he lets us out of our cages, I'm going to kill you."

Emma slumped down, curled sideways on the bottom, trying to stay as far away from the sinister girl as she could. Breaths snuck past gaps in great sobs. Her cheek rested in a puddle of tears. The eerie melody of the awful rhyme echoed off the walls, too faint to make out words, but enough to mock the memory of her mother singing it. After some minutes, she looked up again at older girl. The burned waif had shifted to her knees close against the bars, staring with an evil, eager expression, adoring Emma's agony.

Tiredness gripped Emma. Her crying waned. Energy seemed to leech out of her like a physical presence, drawn toward the bloody figure in the other cage. She considered Nan's story again, unable to believe it might be true, and closed her eyes, trying to picture the silhouette of the shaggy man at the edge of the privy. Hand against the metal plate, she pushed herself upright, sitting and sniffling. The other girl twitched, white flakes peeling from her blistered cheek. She pointed, shaking an accusing finger.

"Gonna kill you. Soon as I'm free."

Emma grabbed at the thorny bars, pulling herself to her feet.

Warm tears splattered between her toes as she forced herself to look at the awful girl and stop thinking about her family being dead.

"He doesn't feed us much, but you can sometimes grab a bug on the wall and eat that," said the other girl in a casual, almost friendly tone.

Emma shied away from a demonstration, cringing at the *crunch* of a bug bitten in half. She looked back too fast, catching sight of a small black leg sliding past the girl's lips. Emma gagged, covering her mouth to keep from throwing up.

"You'll be hungry enough to eat them soon." The girl giggled for a few seconds, falling cold and serious in an instant. "Not so nasty when it's all you have."

Scratching drew Emma's attention to dozens of roaches, beetles, and centipedes on the wall behind her cage that had, seconds ago, been clear. Their sudden appearance made her jump, but she didn't scream at the sight of bugs.

The older girl snarled.

"Did you expect me to be frightened?" Emma scrunched up her nose. "They're just bugs."

"They're the only food you'll have sometimes." The older girl combed with her hands at what remained of pretty, blonde locks, pulling a clump loose. She held her arm out to the side, fluttering her fingers until the hair fell.

"It won't kill us," said Emma in a calm whisper, ignoring the discarded piece of skin. "It wants us sad, not dead."

The girl stuck out her tongue with a petulant noise. "*I* want you dead. You killed my parents and made me ugly."

Emma couldn't recall ever having seen her before. She studied the other child's face, trying to imagine her without the burns. As best she could remember, eight or nine girls around twelve lived in Widowswood Village. Only two had blonde hair, one of whom was chubby. The wretched person in the next cage couldn't be Julianna, the blacksmith's daughter—she was far too sweet to ever say such nasty things.

Emma thought and thought, staring at the bloody finger marks on the bottom of her cage. She huddled against the sharp metal, careful not to let even one toe get close enough to where the other girl could reach her. The burned child went back to her bread, licking and turning it like a squirrel with a prized acorn while humming her rhyme.

Minutes passed until an idea formed. Emma squinted.

"I'm sorry I killed your parents, Mary."

"Hah!" shouted the blonde. "Saying sorry won't bring them back!"

As sad as she had been, she became furious.

"You're lying!" Emma leapt to her feet, flinging herself into the bars with enough force to send her cage swaying. "My family isn't dead! There's no one named Mary in town. You're not Julianna! You just wanna make me cry."

"Dead, dead, dead like rats. Dead like rats in the river," sang not-Julianna, switching to an unmelodic screech that forced smoke out of her mouth. "Burned to a crisp!"

Emma lunged at the older girl, pointing. Her body hit the bars hard enough to rock her cage back and forth, spinning. Each time she spun past, Emma raked in an effort to scratch her tormentor. When the swinging slowed, she pointed at the burned child's face. "I don't believe you!"

"Dead like rats!" Cackling, the older girl clapped and rocked, but made no effort to touch her. "They all died screaming, crying out for you. 'Oh, dear little Emma! Where are you?'"

A tug of sadness gnawed at her heart, but watching this awful girl so happy about her misfortune enraged her. "Liar! Liar! Y-you're trying to make me sad so it eats my tears instead of yours!" Emma stood, pointing, breathing hard. Eventually, the wretched sight of the scorched girl made her feel pity. She lowered her arm to her side and gazed downcast.

"I dunno what village you're from, but I'm sorry you got hurt." Anger gone, Emma sighed down at her feet, pale against the black iron disk. The other girl might be mean, but she didn't deserve to be locked up in a cage.

Not-Julianna's expression of dire mirth fell to a flat line, then a sneer. The burned girl leaned back and closed her eyes. With a rattling hiss, her skin dried like paper before she burst into a waterfall of maggots. Emma screamed. A swarm of tiny, white worms writhed in a collapsing mass that melted away to a vaporous fog. Thick and clinging, the smoke pooled at the bottom of the cage, slipping through the bars in a gradual pour. Emma fell seated, heels sliding on the bare metal as she scrambled to back away as far as she could. She covered her nose and mouth with her elbow, trying to block the overpowering stink of burning meat. The vile fog cascaded to the floor, billowing out into a cloud that blanketed the hay scattered about the dirt. For a few seconds, she felt grateful the cage hung off the ground.

Lies, all lies. They're not dead. It just wants me to be sad. I never told her my name. She was the monster!

Heavy chain links overhead squeaked in time with her prison shifting back and forth. Emma glanced at where the burned girl had been; not even a single maggot remained. She got up, grabbed the bars, and shook her cage, bouncing and twisting in an effort to break it. When that failed, she climbed to the top again in search of anything she could move or that seemed loose enough to wiggle. One of the metal thorns bit her, and she cried out. She stuck her cut finger in her mouth and glared. Never had she felt so trapped.

"Da!" Her shout echoed into silence. "Da!"

She spun in place, searching the room for anything of promise, studying every place where roots had cracked the mortar between the stones. No doors, one tiny window, no way in or out. It was impossible for her to be in this room. It was impossible for her to be in a cage with no way to open. She let her arms fall slack to her sides, standing in the center of a tiny cage, her gaze focused on her sleeping little brother. The creaking of metal became quieter and quieter as the swinging came to a stop. Only two possible explanations made any sense.

Emma had fallen into an awful nightmare.

Or, Nan didn't make up stories.

There really *were* faeries and monsters.

9

ONE SUMMER'S DAY

*E*mma wiped the last of the tears from her face, exhausted from her sadness. She squinted, trying to recall what Nan had told her. The thing had fed from her. The sight of Hannah, so pale and wasted, sent a chill down her spine. This creature wouldn't kill them, but to do so might well be a kindness compared to what awaited her and Tam. She remembered Hannah stumbling out of the forest, clad in nothing but leaves. In her mind, the face changed. Hannah became Emma's older self.

Frantic, she crawled around in a circle, pulling and banging at the metal in hopes of finding some way to get out. She squatted and grabbed the edge of the disk, tugging. It didn't move. She reached up and yanked at the spot where all the bars curved together into the ring.

Maybe it opens like a flower. She prodded everywhere she could think to prod, but the enclosure felt solid, one single piece of iron with no hinges.

Impossible.

Emma sagged to the bottom, somewhere between kneeling and sitting. She tried to rub cold out of her feet while forcing herself not to cry. Her lip quivered, her face grew warm, a lump swelled in her throat. She drew her knees to her forehead and breathed. *I'm acting like a five-year-old. I need to stay strong for Tam. Da can't find us here.* The last thought proved to be a mistake, and she fell into sobbing again. Something tugged at her soul, making her tired. Her head popped up. She squirmed, not liking at all how it felt to be something's food. Her brother muttered, still asleep.

"Tam, wake up."

He mumbled.

She wanted to hold his hand more than anything, but didn't even try, knowing she could never reach so far. "Tam!"

The boy yawned and sat up, bonking his head on the side of the cage. He looked around, startled, rubbing where he had hit. Once he took in his surroundings, he lapsed into a red-faced screaming fit—wailing for Mama.

"Tam, be quiet. Don't feed it."

He continued bawling.

Emma scooted to the side of the cage closest to him, reaching. "Tam, shh, shh, it's okay. Don't cry."

He screeched even louder, yelling, "Mama" over and over. By the fifth repetition, his attempt to call for her didn't resemble a word anymore.

Emma hummed a melody her mother used to sing to them until his screaming lessened. The song made her want to cry too, but she held on to her need to protect him. She went through a full verse, in hum, before he stuck his thumb in his mouth and stopped screeching.

"Tamrin Brae, Tamrin Brae, went to the well one summer's day," she sang.

Tam sniffled.

Emma let her head lean against the cold metal, her musical voice echoing in the small chamber. "Clear water, clear water, the dear, darling daughter."

Tam wiped his face.

"Did fetch by the noonday sun," she sang.

He frowned. "Tam's a boy's name."

"Mama likes that song," said Emma, sitting back on her heels. "If you were a sister, she'd have named you Tamrin. Maybe Mama will let you grow your hair as long as mine and we'll put a dress on you."

His face reddened again, and tears fell.

No…

"I hadda dream they died."

She slapped the bars. "No, Tam. It's a lie. It lied to me, too. They're alive. The Banderwigh wants to make us sad. We can't be sad."

"B-Bandy-wee? You said it wasn't real!"

Emma shivered. "I didn't believe it before. I think… maybe I was wrong."

He wiped his eyes and glanced around. "I wanna go home."

"Me too, but you can't be sad. Did you see Hannah?"

"No."

"The lady with leaves on like clothes? Did you see her?"

Tam wobbled his head. "Yeah. She looked sick."

Emma giggled at his exaggerated nod. "The monster won't kill us, but he'll turn us like her if we let him. We can't let him win. It's not going to hurt us. It wants us to be sad all the time."

The boy crawled around in a circle, grabbing and prodding at the bars. After a few minutes of not finding a way out, he pouted and sniffled.

Murmuring voices outside brought her attention to the tiny window. The sound of men talking mixed with the squeak of wagon wheels and the bray of a horse. Emma flew to her feet, pressed against the bars nearest the window.

"Help!" She shook her weight back and forth, rattling and making noise. "Help us! We're trapped in here!"

Tam joined her in making noise and screaming. After a moment of frenzied shouting, she stopped so she could listen. Whoever went by outside had kept going. The voices quieted with distance. Emma set her feet against two thick bars and tried to swing her prison to the point of breaking. It careened around, striking the wall and both adjacent cages with ringing metallic *clangs*. Tam covered his ears from the noise, but the people outside either failed to notice or failed to care.

Or maybe they hadn't been real either.

Out of breath, Emma fell on her hands and knees, feeling a tad sick from the motion of her cage swaying and spinning. Walls went by, one after the next, each without openings or doors. She put a hand over her mouth to calm her stomach, and clutched the small burlap doll. *Was this Hannah's? Did she have this when it took her?*

"I'm hungry," whined Tam.

Emma dropped the toy, careful to ensure it didn't slip to the floor. "Me too."

He pouted. "Sorry I played in the woods. You shouldn't be in jail, too."

"Tam." She scooted toward him. "This isn't punishment. We've been taken by something bad. Mama and Da won't be angry with us if we get out."

He curled up on the bottom of his cage, back to her. Emma raked her fingers down her hair, clearing fragments of mulch and pine. She leaned against the bar with the fewest thorns, staring at the distant rock wall. Trembling set in when she thought about Hannah, taken at Tam's age, sitting in the same cage and not being let out until old enough to be a mother. If Nan didn't die in a fire, she would surely be gone by the time the monster released Emma. What scared her most was the look on Hannah's face.

Hannah didn't even recognize her parents. Would there be anything left of me then? Would I know who I was? Would I care? No. There's got to be a way to get out.

She swallowed her fear and stood again, squinting at the walls. "A secret door."

Tam sat up and peered at the room with her. Everywhere she looked, roots and dirt cracked the ancient walls. Not one place seemed intact enough for a hidden opening. With dread clawing at her heart, she stared up at the roof of the cage. Despite the eerie, burned girl vanishing into fog, Emma considered for a moment that Old Man Drinn might be responsible for putting her here. He was certainly mean enough, and she had given him reason to want her to disappear. She daydreamed about what Da would have done to him if she'd told him the old man hit her.

Da had once muttered something about him and thieves. *Thieves know about secret doors and locks and stuff.* She pulled herself off her feet, reaching into the upper parts of the cage where everything linked together. Something had to be movable. There had to at least be a keyhole. She poked her fingers around, exploring the knot of iron in the ring for almost an hour. All thoughts of the old man's involvement died with her hope of escape. Her prison appeared to be one solid mass of black metal.

She plopped down, gathering her arms around her legs and shaking. Drinn couldn't have made that awful girl vanish. No, nothing she believed in before could have done that. Unless, of course, she had been dreaming. *Yes, that had to be a dream. Someone's taken us to get money out of Da.* She sniffled. Impossible. An impossible cage in an impossible room.

Could the Banderwigh be impossible, too?

Hannah's parents never found her. Emma's throat tightened. But, Hannah's father wasn't the captain of the town watch. She risked a smile. Surely, Guard Captain Dalen would save them. Emma glanced up at the tiny window. For her to have heard passing travelers, they would have had to be close. They should have noticed two children screaming, but the people outside didn't hesitate. Emma traced her fingers down one of the bars, dreading how cramped it would be when she grew up. Her lip quivered.

Is this place enchanted?

Sensing her deteriorating confidence, Tam burst into tears, calling for Mama. Emma closed her eyes so she didn't see his face; that sight would have made her cry too. A rush of energy came past her like a warm breeze radiating from Tam and flowing into the wall, reminding her the monster feasted upon their sadness.

She slid her legs out the bars, sitting on the edge of the disc, singing and swinging her feet. "Tamrin Brae, Tamrin Brae, went for a walk one summer's day."

He gave her a pathetic stare, but curled up to listen, his tears slowing down.

Fear slipped from Emma's thoughts as she lost herself in the memory of Mama singing them to sleep. "She pranced upon the meadow grass, where faeries danced and faeries laughed."

Tam leaned on the bars, a trace of a smile on his face.

"They found her there, Tamrin Brae, and bid her stay a month and day..."

Emma closed her eyes, remembering the puffs of Mama's breath on her face whenever she held her and sang.

Her eyes grew heavy and her limbs leaden. Her voice mixed with her mother's in the back of her mind, trailing off into silence.

A SONG IN THE WOODS

The scent of soil filled Emma's nose, and she gradually became aware of cold wetness all along the front of her body.

Startled, she shoved herself up from the ground and gaped at the trees of Widowswood. Sunlight filtered down from gaps in the wavering pines, creating a dancing patchwork of light everywhere. She leapt to her feet, advancing a few steps in a whirling stride to take in her surroundings. Still in her nightdress, wet down the front and dirty, she shivered from the early-morning chill. The soft rush of wind in the treetops carried the calls of birds overhead. Emma swiped her hands down her dress, brushing away dead pine needles and clumps of bark. Freedom from the tiny cage made her feel better, but not so much it stalled her involuntary trembles.

"Tam?" she yelled to no response. "Tam!" she shrieked.

Emma balled her hands into fists, and stomped a footprint in the dirt. Angry, she snapped her gaze from tree to tree, searching for that overgrown window. She had no way to know how far away it had taken her from that place. Would it even look like a building from the outside? Perhaps it was an earthen mound with a tiny hole she'd never find. She looked around again, memorizing the area. Tam was still there. The monster had let her go because she could outwit it. Amid her singing, she had forgotten where she was and broke free of the sorrow it so urgently wanted. The Banderwigh still had Tam, and alone, he wouldn't be able to protect himself.

She had to go for help and come back.

Emma squatted and scratched an X in the ground. After digging a deep enough mark, she patted a pair of crossed sticks into it for good measure. A brief search yielded a sizable length of wood, one too heavy for her to lift all the way off the ground. Emma dragged it over to the mark she made, then squinted at the treetops. If she remained in Widowswood—which she felt certain of—the sun would be coming up in the direction of home: east. She wrapped an arm over the fallen branch and dragged it behind her, creating a trail as she marched off. It pained her to leave Tam behind, but it would be silly to go looking for the monster alone. She would only get lost, and probably wouldn't even find him. No, she would come back with Da and half the town guard. They could defeat the monster.

Strange chattering noises, snaps, and a sporadic pulsating thrum of unseen insects emanated from the trees around her as she walked east. The forest seemed different, as if every shadowed patch stared at her. Emma shivered, clinging to the branch, and tried to take her mind away from what had happened by singing.

"*Tamrin Brae, Tamrin Brae, went to the well one summer's day.*
Clear water, clear water, the dear, darling daughter.
Did fetch by the noonday sun."

Tam's smile came to mind, but she steeled herself against feeling sad. She would not leave him there. Emma sucked in a breath and pictured her mother singing. Dragging the stick, she kept walking.

"*Tamrin Brae, Tamrin Brae, went for a walk one summer's day.*
She pranced upon the meadow grass, where faeries danced and faeries laughed.
They found her there, Tamrin Brae, and bid her stay a month and day.
"*The Faerie King, the Faerie King, smiled and flew on emerald wing.*
Around this girl, Tamrin Brae, his fancy she had caught.
She danced and sang until the night, a feast they did then bring."

Her wavering voice didn't do as much as she had hoped to soothe her nerves. The urge to drop the branch and run as fast as she could go battered at her resolve, but her little brother depended on her. Emma would not allow that thing to turn him into a wasted wretch.

"Tamrin Brae, Tamrin Brae, so young and filled with life.

He bade her drink, Tamrin Brae, the wine of faerie's draught.

To sleep she fell, a month and day, awoke the Fae King's wife."

Emma swallowed hard. The song, meant to be calming, told the story of a girl who had vanished forever into the faerie kingdom, never to be seen again. Tears streamed down her cheeks as she thought of being separated from Tam forever. She caught herself a moment later, refusing to give in. If the monster still watched her, she didn't want it to smell her sorrow and take her back.

No. She figured it out. It wanted to basically eat her, so she'd make herself into something it would spit out like Tam and green vegetables. As soon as she felt sorry for the burned girl, the horrible fake child disappeared.

She stepped over rocks and roots to the edge of a stream and hiked up her nightdress to keep it dry while wading across thigh-deep water, cold to the point it made her shriek. The ground on the far side soon became an uphill grade. Emma looked again at the treetops, trying to figure out where the sun went. East. She had to walk toward the sun in the morning. Finally, she caught a glimpse of it.

Good. I'm going the right way.

Before long, the ground grew thick with grass, cold and wet. Trees thinned out, and soon, the edge of the forest gave way to open fields, the darkness between trees replaced by grass. Emma grabbed her heavy hunk of wood in both hands, dragging it behind until she hit the meadow. Once she reached the grass, she dropped it. The huge stick was itself a marker. She had emerged from further south in Widowswood than her parents had allowed her to go before, putting a long field of rolling hills between her and home.

Filled with hope, she ran as hard as she could, unable to resist the urge to cry out for Da.

ASHES, ASHES

*E*mma crested one hill, darted across a depression, and scrambled up the side of the next incline. At the top of the mound, the shape of buildings shrouded in early morning fog came into view far ahead. The sight of home gave her the strength to keep running, despite her exhaustion.

On a downhill slope, she slipped in the wet grass and tumbled out of control until she skidded to a halt, flat on her chest at the bottom. She sat up, clutching a scraped knee, unwilling to cry over something so trivial. Emma growled and got back on her feet, moving in a limping run to the next hilltop.

The sight waiting for her made her wither back to the ground.

What Emma had thought to be fog was smoke. Every hut had burned to the foundation. Dark grey trails wisped into the air from piles of still-smoldering rubble. A few of the more robust dwellings, like her home, remained as little more than stone walls outlining the ghosts of buildings. Emma glanced back at the woods, trembling, wondering how she hadn't seen any of the smoke before. With little life left in her legs, she plodded down the hill along the same dirt road the leaf-clad woman had taken into the village.

The destruction made her feel like Hannah had looked, drained and without hope. Instinct led her home, and there, she found a gutted mess. The back wall, nearest the privy, had collapsed outward into loose stones. She crept up the stairs, onto a charred porch she had swept so many times. An ash-covered stick with a small tangle of burned bristles leaned against the wall. The bottoms of her feet turned black crossing to the front door. Inside, the raised wooden floors had become white ash at the bottom of a shallow pit formed by the remaining walls. She climbed down, covering her face with both hands while tiptoeing around the debris. The fireplace, and Mama's cauldron, remained intact. The family bed had disappeared entirely. She couldn't find *the cabinet,* nor everything else that hadn't been made of stone or metal.

Overwhelmed, with tears streaming from her eyes, Emma ignored the wreckage and moved to where Nan's bedroom had been. Some of the thicker parts of wood from her bed frame remained as a loose arrangement of what could pass for half-burned fire logs. She squatted and clawed at the silt, coughing and sneezing. When she found no bones, Emma hugged herself and shook. Her home had burned, but her family didn't die here. Hope brought her standing. At least some pieces of bone would have survived a fire. Emma swallowed back her tears, and wiped her face with her forearms since soot coated her hands.

What strange things Mama talks about sometimes.

She searched the wreckage of the house, sifting among the dirt and ash until her arms blackened to the elbows. Not one tooth, no skulls, and nothing even close to a bone turned up. Emma let out an uneasy laugh, and made her way to what was once the back door. The townspeople would have all gone to the same place. Emma had only to follow the road northeast. She climbed the rear foundation wall, narrowly avoiding a splinter in her foot, and walked out among the scattered rocks.

There, on the ground by the water pump, lay the stick-knight and shrub-dragon.

Wind lifted her long, black hair to the side and carried tears off her cheeks. Arms slack at her sides, she fell to her knees and closed her eyes. She didn't sob anymore, having become too sad to cry. The toys reminded her of the little boy still stuck somewhere in a cage.

"Emma?" rasped a croaking voice from the remains of the house.

She looked up, staring between her fingers as she pulled hair out of her eyes. Nan's hunched-over figure balanced on her cane in the shadow of what little roof remained.

"Nan!" Emma jumped to her feet, running toward her grandmother. "You're alive!"

Nan raised her head. Beneath the shawl, her face had turned dark green, eyes aglow with deathly yellow light, and her teeth had vanished. Open wounds on her face leaked blood. The bones of her right hand showed through holes in the skin as she reached out.

Emma skidded to a halt on her heels, screaming her lungs empty. Nan moved toward her, cane above her head like a sword, far more nimble than the old woman had been in life. Emma scrambled backward, falling on her backside. She rolled over on all fours and crawled into a run, headed for the town center. Clattering cane and crunching twigs chased close behind her. Raw, animal panic seized her. The scent of death surrounded her.

Bodies lay here and there. Guard Kavan, Guard Filner, Old Man Drinn, Marsten the Apothecary. Emma raised her hands and closed her eyes, terrified she'd see her parents or Kimber among them.

Her foot squished into something cold and slimy, taking her legs out from under her and sending her into a tumble that ended against the wall of the miller's house. The scent of rotten apple mixed with that of burned flesh. Emma clambered upright at the same instant undead-Nan ambled around the corner and pointed the crooked cane at her. Emma grabbed the wall on either side of her, trying to press her body through the rocks like a ghost. Foulness oozed between her toes, but she dare not look. She edged away until she stepped on something rubbery and cold.

Emma looked down. Her foot had found Julianna's arm, dead and half buried under the caved-in wall of the blacksmith's shop.

She sucked in a breath to scream again, but stopped. Her heart pounded. Her breathing surged in erratic gulps. She leaned away from the horrible image of Nan, the cold of the stones seeping into her skin through her nightdress.

Her mind rose above the panic. *Tam's toys didn't burn. They're wood. And flimsy.*

"N-Nan." Emma tried to sound confident. "You're not Nan. Y-you're the Banderwigh." She swallowed hard, taking a step toward it. "You are not real. I'm dreaming again. I'm not afraid of you."

The old woman lowered her cane, balancing on it with both hands. The wounds and death receded, and the green tinge faded from her skin.

"Ahh, thank you, Em. I needed a little help to reach you. Tea leaves and incense can only do so much."

Emma blinked, stunned. Of all the things the monster could've done, she hadn't expected this. She pointed at Nan's face. "What lie is this?"

Nan grinned; her teeth had returned. "I'm in your dream now, Emma. The creature is making you see things, but I am trying to help you. Remember when you thought I was asleep?"

"Why should I believe you?" Hands flat against the stone, Emma crept to the side.

"The village didn't burn. Everyone is fine, but very worried. Your father still doesn't believe. No matter, your mother and I can handle him."

She's trying to make me feel better. This can't be the monster.

"Nan…" Emma calmed, running forward into a hug. "Nan."

The old one patted her on the back, held her for a moment, and let go. "Listen to me. Your home is warm, safe, and waiting. Don't let him inside your head."

Emma cringed as a bony finger tapped her on the skull three times.

When she opened her eyes, Nan had disappeared. She knew she roamed within a dream, but still walked away from the village, not wanting to look upon such awful sights. The meadow behind her house had no butterflies, fireflies, or anything flitting about but melancholy. Emma set her jaw high and folded her arms. This would not bother her.

"I've never tried to wake up on purpose before." She raised a foot, hesitated a second, and stepped on her own toes. She yelped and hopped, but remained where she was. "I don't believe this. Do you hear me? I don't believe this."

"Emma, help!" Tam's voice drifted out of the woods.

She raised her foot to take a step, but hesitated, body rigid, eyes closed, fists balled. "No. That is not Tam. I am dreaming."

"Emma, it hurts!"

Lies. Emma focused on the lie of it, and made her desire to help Tam into anger rather than sorrow. She sank into a squat, clamping her arms around her legs.

Not real.

Emma let herself fall back enough to sit, and rocked, thinking of how happy her family will be when she sees them again.

Not real.

RUN RABBIT, RUN

*T*ime slid by in the darkness of Emma's closed eyes. The faint sound of wind in the treetops faded without her realizing. When she looked up, she found herself hugging her knees, once more trapped in a cage that couldn't be opened. She stretched her legs out and braced a hand on her belly to stall her emotions. Nan had been right all along about the Banderwigh. Nan was still alive.

Emma narrowed her eyes. *I will win.*

The scent of ginger wafted in the air, bringing her notice to the lone table. It sat beneath the empty cage between her and Tam, close enough for either of them to reach plates of sweetbreads set at the ends. *Something* had gotten inside the room to bring them food and drag the table over. *Something* had gotten inside a room with no doors.

It will never let us see it. It makes us sleep so it can bring food.

Emma frowned at her confinement. Any sadness ran away in the face of her anger. She snarled, half-considering trying to break her way out. Her fury waned at Tam crying. Emma squatted at the edge of the hanging prison, face pressed between bars.

"Tam, stop crying. Nan is alive. I saw her in my dream."

He raised his head, looking as though he could burst into tears at the drop of a hat. "I saw Mama, but she's a ghost."

"You had bad dreams. Don't believe them. Mama and Da are alive. The village is not burning. The monster is lying to make us sad."

Tam sniffed the air, leaning over to peer at the treats.

"No, Tam. Faerie bread is dangerous. Don't eat it."

"S'not faerie bread, it's bandy-wee bread."

She slapped a bar for emphasis. "Don't trust it."

"We'll die if we don't eat. It smells good." He rubbed his stomach. "It's too big to be faerie bread. Faeries are bitty."

"Nan's pie is better than those stinky rolls."

Tam smiled.

"Mama's bread is much better than some silly monster's baking. Like, when it's warm and just out of the oven."

He nodded. "Yeah." His mirth faded to a pout at his lap.

"Don't be sad. We won't be here long." Emma shifted from squatting to sitting, letting her feet dangle outside again. "Tam, you 'member that time Old Man Drinn had too much brandy an' he tried to get on his horse and the saddle fell off? Dumped him right in the water trough?"

"He used bad words," muttered Tam, a trace of a smile forming.

"Or when Hadrath's fence broke and all the pigs got loose?"

Tam giggled. "They's runnin' through town for days."

Emma laughed. "One got into Marsten's shop and started eating everything."

"He used bad words on the pig." He slid to the side of his cage, sticking his feet out. "An' the pig was sick for a whole month. Its poo kept catching fire!"

"Ugh, you would remember that part." Emma grimaced. "Da's gonna go to Calebrin in a couple of days with Mister Valis. He said he's gonna bring you back a real wooden sword."

Tam's eyes bulged. "True?"

"Yeah." She looked up, kicking her legs back and forth.

Tam mimicked her pose: legs dangling, feet swinging, and rocked his cage back and forth until he giggled.

"The Feast of Zaravex isn't too far away. There'll be cakes and sweets!"

He gasped, drooling. About to cheer, his happiness faded. "What if we're still in here?"

"We won't be. I thumped Rydh Cooper when he stepped on Stick Knight's horse. I'll thump the Bandy-wee."

Tam snickered at her deliberate mispronunciation.

Emma looked up at the creaking chain and kicked her legs harder. "Hey, these are like swings."

He rocked harder, also laughing.

"Tam, you 'member when Da tried to make us a swing?"

"Yeah," he cheered. "You broke it. Your bum hit the ground and you turned red."

Emma winced at the remembered pain. "Yeah. And the branch fell on Da's head."

They laughed, swinging higher. The swaying chains squeaked like birds.

She swished her feet back and forth, finding a steady rhythm, and took a great breath before she sang, "Run, rabbit, run rabbit, through fields of men."

Tam more shouted than sang. "Grey rabbit run fast, run fast to your den."

Emma added a twisting motion to the swing, giggling as she sang. "The hounds are a'comin', the hunters pursue."

"Run, rabbit, run, rabbit, or be rabbit stew," Tam sang, before he broke into fits of laughter.

She sang loud, her voice flooding the chamber. "Through hill and hollow, run, rabbit, run. Until the hunters and dogs are none." His expression gave away he'd forgotten the next line, but Emma kept going. "The men, they give chase with many sharp arrows." She slowed, lowering her voice as she drew out the last line. "Run, rabbit, run, rabbit, back to your barrow."

His laughter echoed off the walls. They rocked back and forth, twisting and laughing as though they played in their backyard. Emma started another repetition of Run Rabbit, Tam singing all the lines together with her. Emma stopped trying to be Tam's 'little-mother.'

With nothing in her power to do about their situation, she let herself be his sister—a child as well.

Tam's face flashed by as the cages swayed and creaked. Giggling filled the tiny underground chamber. Blurriness crept in, making sounds seem distant and watery, framing his smiling face with a nimbus of light. Her laughter seemed to slow down and echo inside her mind. Nan tried to find her. Mama was alive. Her family loved her. Emma didn't notice the walls oozing blood from the mortar, the protruding roots blackening, or the approach of sleep—until she fell backward and hit damp ground.

13

OUT OF THE PAN

*L*aughter faded to intermittent giggles, then a silent smile. Emma's stomach hurt from overdoing it. She opened her foggy eyes to the sight of trees reaching straight up into a clear, blue sky. Grass tickled her legs and arms from lying on her back upon the cool, damp forest floor. She found it comfortable, and didn't bother trying to sit up while last bits of giggles worked their way out of her chest.

Tam's giggle came from nearby.

Emma reached up and put a hand to her forehead. Unable to stop smiling, she forced herself to sit up. Tam lay on his chest a few feet away, grinning in his sleep. She crawled over and sat on her heels beside him while shaking his shoulder.

"Tam," she whispered, jostling him until he moved.

He pushed himself up to kneel, a bit of leaf stuck to his lip. Emma plucked it away and dusted him off. She looked around at the woods, eyes narrowing in distrust. *The Banderwigh's trying to trick us again.* Contagious cheer surrounded her brother. His half-awake 'where am I?' expression set her off giggling again. After a brief annoyed glare, he pounced on her, dragging her to the grass and tickling wherever he could get a hand past her defenses. She squealed with glee, overjoyed that cold iron no longer separated them.

Emma rolled around with him in a tickle fight until they both ran out of breath and wound up face-to-face, gasping for air. His huge grin made her think he'd forgotten all about being taken and put in a cage. She decided not to remind him of it, and rolled on her back to rest.

He cuddled against her side, arm over her chest. "Em?"

"Tam?"

The boy whispered with his mouth an inch from her ear. "Are we sleepin?"

He does remember.

"I don't know," whispered Emma.

Tam pointed. "Trees aren't scary now."

Wary, Emma sat up and gazed around, studying the woods. The boy had a point. More light came down from the branches above, making the forest less eerie than it had been the last time she woke up out here. Having Tam with her also made her happy. Except for the change in brightness, this looked like the same spot where she dreamed the Banderwigh had released her before.

Nothing appeared different from the time she had found the village burned. Part of her dreaded this a cruel trick, and she'd take her little brother back to a heartbreaking lie—but sitting here wouldn't help either. *I'll go back but I won't let him see anything bad.* Emma gathered her feet under her, took his hand, and pulled him upright.

Fear she would find the trail she'd dragged in the dirt made her hesitate for a moment, but when she searched around—and didn't see it—she laughed. She considered hunting for that hunk of wood again to lead the guards back here, but decided against it. Getting home faster was more important.

She squinted at the sky, guessing it to be afternoon. With the sun at her back, she marched into the woods, leading Tam by the hand, heading in the direction she believed would take them home. A breeze whispered among the treetops, drawing her gaze upward. Birds flitted overhead, adding to her hope that they had escaped for real. While she couldn't say for certain, she mostly remembered a lack of happy chirping the whole time she'd been in the woods before finding the burned village. Signs of life reassured her that she'd escaped.

Tam tried to run off after small rodents or giant moths, or anything else that caught his eye. Emma kept a grip on his hand, grumbling at the occasional sound of cotton ripping while they waded into underbrush. Emma missed the dress Nan made—simple thorns never seemed to tear it, and it didn't snag in the woods.

As in her dream, she found a trail that allowed them to move faster until they stopped at the edge of a small stream. She crouched upon the bank, ankle deep in mud, and gathered a few handfuls to drink. Tam hovered at her side, doing the same. When she had enough, she eased one foot into the flow, gritted her teeth, and gathered her nightdress up to her thighs to keep it dry. She navigated the stream, her feet sinking into frigid ooze while the water crept up her legs. Emma kept pulling her nightdress higher to prevent it from becoming soaked. At the halfway point, the water edged past the middle of her thighs and her teeth chattered.

Tam, unconcerned with being wet, flung himself headfirst and splashed about, squealing with delight from the cold. Emma kept going until she stood on the mucky bank, and stood there flapping her nightgown to breeze-dry her legs, her teeth chattering. The boy kept swimming.

"Come, Tam. Mama and Da are worried. We need to go home."

He heaved a sad sigh, but his desire to go home overpowered his fun in the water. Without protest, he glided to the edge and trudged out of the water. "Are we in bads?"

"No. Nan knows what happened. We didn't do anything wrong."

Tam grinned, then darted off.

"Tam!" she yelled, running after him. "No."

He stopped short and turned around to look at her—and she ran straight into him. They fell together in a hug. He laughed; she gave him a cross stare. He tried to tickle her again, but she held his hands. He continued giggling at her stern face until she cracked up, too.

"Don't run off," she whispered, once the giggle fit ended. "There's wolves."

"Goblins too," he said. At first defiant, the thought of that scared him into a whisper. "Goblins will put us inna stew like Rabbit."

Emma got up and dusted herself off. "Goblins aren't real."

He ground his toe into the dirt, staring down. "Jes like there's no Bandy-wee?"

"I—"

Snap.

She whipped around, searching for what broke a branch or stepped on a bit of wood. Tam clung to her back. Several whispery voices chittered in high-pitched words—no language known to her. A moving patch of green caught her eye. Emma blinked at a four-inch long nose extending out from the side of a tree, attached to a potbellied body only a little taller than her. Stubby wart-covered fingers curled around the bark. The creature took deep sniffs, nostrils rimmed with wiry bristles flaring. Saliva squeezed between rotting teeth and dripped over a hairy chin.

That's... That's... Emma stared. *A goblin!* She clutched her brother's hand.

"Ow!" Tam yelled.

She bolted away from the goblin, pulling him behind her. Clambering boots chased them, crashing and breaking through the underbrush. Tam howled, but she kept going, dragging him several times when he tripped. Emma ignored the sharp rocks and painful roots punishing her feet. She stumbled twice, but fear gave her wings enough not to fall. Chattering drew closer. Emma tried to run faster, dodging low-hanging vines and weaving around trees.

Something fluttered overhead, its presence hardly registering in her mind. The woods blurred by on either side. A gurgling wail, fleshy *thud*, and high-pitched shouting behind her brought a grin to her face. She pictured a goblin tripping, and two or three more stumbling over the fallen one. Fleeting relief lasted only until lupine howls arose nearby, giving her another burst of speed. Seconds later, Emma skidded to a halt—the dark spaces between trees up ahead teemed with yellow eyes.

Tam ran into her back, knocking her forward a step.

A dozen wolves, including the huge one she had seen the other day, emerged from the shadows toward her, fangs bared, snarling.

She whirled around. Seven or eight goblins brandishing spears, their potbellied bodies squeezed into crude-stitched leathers, tromped out of the woods. They regarded the children with greed in their eyes. One looked at Tam and snapped its teeth at the air, drooling. The glint in its eye reminded her of Da with a steak in front of him.

Emma spun again to run, but only took two steps before freezing in place at the sight of the wolves creeping closer. The massive alpha fixed her with a gold-eyed gaze. Tam buried his face in her chest, shaking. Emma looked back and forth: hungry wolves in front, hungry goblins behind.

The Banderwigh's cage didn't seem like such a bad place after all.

14

BETWEEN FANG AND CLAW

W olves snarled. Goblins chittered, pointing spears at her and Tam. Emma had a feeling she now knew the goblin word for 'yummy.' She crossed her arms over her little brother, holding him tight while staring into the pale, yellow eyes of the largest wolf. His gaze held no malice, only urgency.

"I don't think the wolves want to hurt us, Tam," she whispered, patting his back.

He squirmed around to look. The lead wolf lowered his head as if in greeting. A twig snapped under a goblin's burlap boot. All at once, the line of wolves surged forward. Emma flinched and whimpered, eyes closed. Fur brushed past her. When she dared look, the forest in front of her was empty; the woods behind filled with awful sounds: growling, wailing, and goblin cries of pain.

She bolted across the sparse patch into thick woods, and kept going until the sounds of goblin slaughter grew faint. Emma slowed once her legs felt like pudding, and stumbled to a halt against a tree, gasping for air. Tam, panting, fell seated, wobbled, and went over flat on his back. He grasped her ankle, clinging to her leg while trying to catch his breath. Exhausted, Emma slid down the tree to sit next to him. The distant forest echoed with the snarl of wolves, the splinter of bone, and the shrieking of… goblins.

He sat up at the noises, hiding his face in her chest. Emma wrapped her arms around his head, kissing and staring over his hair into the trees, squinting in the direction of the fracas. She wanted to be ready to run if a goblin appeared and came after them, but she lacked the energy. Her attempt to stand succeeded only in causing one foot to slide forward until her leg lay flat on the ground.

"*Mahz-ba!*" A high-pitched voice let loose with a phlegmatic wail. "*Mahz-ba!*"

Distant, rapid footsteps followed, growing quieter. Emma imagined clumps of spit and drool flying from the creature's panic-stricken face. Despite being in a foreign tongue, the word repeated several times—an unmistakable command to run away.

She cradled and rocked Tam, giving him another kiss atop the head. "They're running away."

Tam looked up at her. "'Kay." He looked around before resting against her shoulder. His fear at being lost wavered his voice. "I wanna go home. Which way is it?"

"I…" She shivered, unable to answer as she had no idea. "Umm." *Don't cry. Just go east. We'll reach the meadow.* She stood, waited for him to get up, and took his hand. "East."

Minutes passed as she walked, occasionally looking up to guess where the sun had gone.

A large raven swooped by so close it startled a yelp out of her. It circled around before alighting on a branch a short distance away. She gazed at it for a silent moment. It looked like the same bird as the one that showed up at Kimber's pitiful home. *Don't be silly. It's a raven. They all look the same.* The bird hopped around, showing its back, and flew to the next tree. It twisted its head to peer at her and squawked.

It wants me to follow it. Emma blinked. *How do I know that? First wolves act strange, now birds?*

"Okay," she said, then swallowed. She eased one tentative foot forward into the grass before the raven flew to another, more distant, tree.

Tam looked up. "Wha?"

"I'm talking to the bird."

"Oh," said Tam, taking it in stride. "Mama talks to them too."

Emma shot him a look. "She does n—"

"She does. 'Member you called her sillyfeathers?"

An involuntary giggle slipped out. "Yeah… But she's only whistling back to them."

Emma, come, said a voice in her thoughts.

She tilted her head. The voice sounded like Nan. Hesitance gone, she broke into a run, following the raven. It glided ahead, alighting on a branch some distance away. Before she could catch up to it, the bird flew again, going from tree to tree. Soon, the shouts of men rang out, calling Emma by name. One of them sounded like Da.

"Da!" she yelled. "We're here!"

"There, that way," cried a man. "I heard a child."

Kavan?

Emma halted. Running in circles would only make it take longer. She remembered Da telling her that. Stay in one place. Wait.

"We're here!" She jumped up and down, waving her arms. "Da!"

"Papa!" shouted Tam, grinning.

"Emma? Tam?" called the same voice, closer, louder.

Definitely Da.

Branches and twigs crushed and cracked. Motion caught her eye to the left.

"Da, I'm here," she yelled again.

Six armored men dressed in the blue cloaks of the village watch emerged from the brush. Arnir, the eldest, had a smear of green ooze on his thigh. Emma's sprint toward them slowed to a stunned stagger. *Is that goblin blood? Not dreaming…?* Da scooped her off her feet into a crushing hug that squished her into Tam and jarred the thought out of her mind. She cuddled into his arms, crying tears of joy.

"Thank the gods," he said, kissing them both.

Emma hung there, happily enjoying being a child carried by her father. In his arms, the woods didn't scare her anymore. The search party collected in a line and trudged until they found a path, which they followed among the trees.

"Damndest thing I've ever seen." Kavan whistled.

"Indeed," said Arnir. "Wolves attacking goblins... What's the world coming to?"

"Aye." Kavan scratched his head. "An' they dinnae run at us!"

"At least we 'ave some stories for the Inn." Filner laughed, clapping his leg.

Emma smiled at Kavan, grateful for all their help. She let her gaze wander over her father's shoulder at the trees receding into the distance. The large wolf peered out of the foliage. No longer afraid of him, she waved. He bowed in acknowledgement and darted off. A yawn forced its way out of her. She draped herself over warm leather-covered armor. Da kissed her atop the head once more.

Her eyes half closed, Widowswood faded to a blur of greens and browns. She didn't know what to believe anymore. The Banderwigh was real. Goblins *did* exist, and for a reason she couldn't begin to grasp, wolves didn't feel like eating children.

Da carried them back toward town. Tam fell sound asleep before they walked out of the trees onto the dirt path. Emma stared at the receding woods. A light brown patch caught her eye amid the green at the side of the road. When she recognized it, she gasped.

In the grass, about twenty paces from the forest, lay an abandoned apple basket, its contents spilled.

15

THE CHILD SAVED

Despite Emma's protests, Da carried her down the trail to their home. A handful of people who saw their approach stopped what they were doing to rush over. The relief on their faces at her safe return created a warm spot in her heart, and deepened her worry about Kimber. One woman ran off, presumably to tell the entire village she and her brother had been found safe.

Da strode onto the porch and set Emma down first, but she stayed on tiptoe trying to climb back into his arms.

"Da, it's taken Kimber! It let us go, but it took her."

"Your mother would have had my head if I didn't bring you home straight away."

"We have to go back," wailed Emma. "It's got her! Her basket was by the trail."

He set Tam down and took a knee, brushing her hair around her face and leaving his hands on both shoulders. "Em, do you know where this supposed creature is? What do you expect to do if you find it?"

Mama ran out from the house, sliding to a stop on her knees with an arm around Emma and Tam. "Thank Mythandriel you're all right." She squeezed them each in turn before peering up at Da. "Did you happen to find my mother while you were out there? She's been gone all morning."

"Mama!" yelled Tam, clinging.

Da shook his head.

Emma continued staring up at Da, eyes brimming with tears, unable to think of anything to say. Frustration hurt as much as the guilt that hit her for being safe while Kimber sat in a little hanging cage.

Her best answer came out as a desperate whine.

Da stood. "Your mother and I were sick with worry. Nan thinks some critter got you." He chuckled. "Thank the gods you're safe."

Disappointment showed in his face, though he seemed too happy to have found her alive to scold her. Emma started to pout at her feet but wound up squinting at him with a determined expression.

"We didn't run off. Tam had ta pee in the night and the Banderwigh took us."

Mama squeezed them both tight. "You're safe now."

Da straightened. "Emma... You're rarely given to being false with me."

She folded her arms and frowned at the woods. The large raven overflew the house, swerving into a dive as if to land in the open space behind it. "I don't want it to keep her. She'll be like Hannah when it lets her go."

"It?" Da kissed her forehead. "I'm not angry with you, Emma. If you got lost in the woods, you can say so. I give you my word you won't be in trouble as long as you promise never to run off like that again."

"I didn't get lost. Why would we get out of bed in the middle of the night and go into the woods? The Banderwigh took us! It put us in cages that can't open in a house with no doors out in..." She blinked, realizing how nutters she must sound.

"You and your mother." Da shifted his weight back and glanced at Widowswood. "You both have some vivid dreams."

"Da. I'm not lying." She held her ground, not quite sure what to do with her hands. "I didn't believe it either before."

Mama shot him a look, then released the tight embrace to stand, but kept hold of Emma and Tam by a hand each.

He scratched at a few days' worth of beard.

Emma sulked. Da had to catch people doing bad stuff all the time. He knew lies. The unsettled look in his eyes said he didn't think she was fibbing. For whatever reason, he couldn't grasp the truth. She sighed. An uneasy smile was as close as he'd get to saying he believed such a story.

"Captain Dalen," shouted a guardsman as he jogged up.

"Yes, what is it?" Da pivoted to face the man.

Mama ushered the children inside and took a seat by the kitchen table before pulling Tam up into her lap. Emma offered a weak smile, staring down at her muddy feet. She crept over to the door to listen in on the men..

"Ol' Man Arden's dead," said the guardsman. "Was found in 'is bed this morn."

"Arden Drinn?" asked Da.

"'Ow many Arden's we got in the town?" The guardsman made a dry chuckle.

Emma swallowed, eyes wide. *Kimber's dad?* The man who bruised her face, beat his own daughter, and forced the girl to sell apples to buy wine was dead?

"Em, come here," said Mama, waving her closer. "Why do you look so sad? You're home."

She ran into her mother's arms, sniffling. "The Banderwigh's taken—"

Mama grabbed Emma with her free arm and pulled her close, kissing her atop the head. Seconds before it seemed she would faint from being unable to breathe, her mother relaxed and sniffled.

"Oh, Em. I thought—" Mama squeezed her again, fighting sniffles.

Voices outside grew quiet. Da and the rest of the watch went by the window, heading away down the street. Emma stared at the floor, ashamed of herself for being safe while the little red-haired girl suffered.

Nan emerged from the rear alcove, hurrying into the house

brushing her arms, sending a handful of black feathers fluttering. Emma gawked. Nan walked without her cane—or any trace of a limp —over to a side table where a small glass bottle sat in a bowl of herbs, beside a dagger and two half-molten candles.

"You're getting careless, Beth." Nan plucked the glass bottle from the bowl, dashing its contents into the cook fire.

The room flared with a rush of warmth and the smell of sweet, fermented fruit. For a few seconds, the fire tripled in size and turned purple.

Mama stroked Emma's hair. "You should've seen the poor girl. Em told her she could come by for food. He would've killed her eventually. Probably soon. If not from hitting, from not feeding her." Emma gurgled as Mama's hug tightened. "The wretch laid his hands on Emma. Left a bruise on her entire face."

"Yes, yes. Reckless, but deserved. All things considered, she handled him well enough." Nan put her fists to her hips. "Well, he won't hit anything anymore, now will he?" Her tone came off almost teasing, at the same time scolding. The old one set about cleaning the contents of the table, clucking her tongue.

"It's fine, Mother," said Mama. "The wretch had too much wine. He just drank himself to death."

Emma glanced from one to the other as they spoke, barely breathing.

"Must have been some strong brandy." Nan sniffed the bowl, eyebrows up. "Faeberry?"

"Nan," said Emma. "The Banderwigh got Kimber."

The privy door slammed outside; bad memories made Emma jump.

"Easy, Em. Why so twitchy?" Mama fussed with her hair.

She hadn't yet found anything to say by the time the back door creaked open. Kimber crept in, eyes downcast, shaking as if afraid she'd be yelled at for making the slightest sound. Purple covered half her face, one of her eyes had swollen closed. The red-haired girl took a seat at the table by a plate full of crumbs, and managed a smile. She looked like a horse had kicked her in the face.

"Hi, Miss Emma," said Kimber in a small voice.

Emma couldn't believe her eyes and blinked at her mother, at Nan, and at Kimber. The half-starved girl shivered when a group of townspeople walked past the window—and cringed seconds later when a loud knock came from the door. She edged forward in her seat, as if preparing to crawl under the table. Emma twisted in her mother's arms to peer out the window at a crowd congregated outside.

"They've come to see you, Em," said Nan.

"They're going to ask me what happened." Emma took in a breath and let it out slow. "What should I tell them?"

"What else?" Nan smiled with a wink. "The truth."

Emma turned her head to look at her grandmother. "No one will believe me."

"Do you believe what happened?" asked Nan.

"Umm." Emma stared down at her toes. "Yes."

Nan patted her on the head, guiding her toward the door. "Then it is the truth."

16

LIKE MOTHER, LIKE DAUGHTER

*V*illagers crowded up to the house. Emma stood at the top of the porch steps, graciously accepting pats and hugs. Mama hovered at the door, whispering thanks overhead as each person came by. Emma's tale of being taken drew pitying looks and whispers about bandits getting too bold. Most thought she'd been grabbed in the middle of the night by a brigand looking to hurt her father. She felt smaller and smaller as they drifted off, consumed by gossip and the idea that the Captain of the Guard should not live so far from town. Others sounded worried that such a brazen crime could have been committed against the daughter of the town's best swordsman without so much as one witness.

"No… it wasn't bandits," whispered Emma. She glanced back and up at Mama who offered a knowing nod. "It wasn't."

"Aye, Em." Mama moved up behind her, grasping her shoulder. "I believe you."

Emma smiled and clasped her mother's hand.

When all who had come to wish her well had walked away, Emma trudged behind Mama back into the house. Kimber crawled out from under the table, where she must've been hiding the whole time, and climbed into a chair. She sat for a few minutes with her face hidden behind her thick, curly hair. Nan wandered by, giving Emma a squeeze on the shoulder before she checked on Kimber. The pale girl lifted her head, and the old woman pulled her hair aside like a curtain.

"Oh, my." Nan blurted as she got a good look at the child's bruises. "Beth, I hope you used a pinch extra Banewillow."

Mama bit her lip. "I might have."

Nan rushed over to *the cabinet* and whipped both doors open. Much to Emma's surprise, the old one made no effort to keep the contents hidden from her. Glass containers full of various colored liquids as well as bowls, feathers, herbs, and strange stones lined the shelves. Nan moved like a woman possessed, gathering bottles and bits of plants in a flurry of activity. She threw everything in a large bowl and stirred it, muttering the whole time.

A moment later, she hurried back to the table and set a wooden bowl in front of Kimber. "Here, child. Drink this."

Mama cringed, covering her mouth. "I could've tended to her. You don't need to make her drink that mess."

Nan bugged her eyes and shook her head at Mama, gesturing at their guest. "That mess indeed."

Kimber made a face at the milky-white concoction. It reeked of plant matter and mint, and looked far from appealing. Emma scrunched up her nose and held both hands over her face.

"Well look at you two," snapped Nan. "You're the same person in two different sizes."

Mama rolled her eyes. "You never did make very good potions."

"They work, don't they? A *good* potion is one that does what it's supposed to do." Nan ruffled like an old hen, gesturing. "Your mother makes 'em *taste* all sweet. What matters that as long as they work?"

"It's more than taste." Mama ran a hand through Emma's hair, drawing out brambles. "My, you need a bath. Mother's been jealous for years of my potions, you know."

"Bah." Nan waved at her. "You still haven't learned how to change."

Emma giggled, cuddling with Mama and grinning ear-to-ear at Kimber, who still hadn't touched the odd drink. Nan gave her a stern look, as if to remind the child she had no choice in the matter. Kimber took the bowl in both hands, choking the mess down in one long series of gulps.

The expression that followed made Emma glad she didn't need to have any. Kimber coughed and gagged, tongue sticking out. She clutched the edge of the table, making gurgling half-coughs as if preparing to retch. Emma lost her appetite. Kimber swooned in the chair, her coughs quieting. The swelling and redness on her face faded and the bruises on her legs disappeared. Her black, swollen eye receded to a mild bruise. Kimber swayed around in a circular wobble, dizzy and looking about to fall asleep where she sat. Finally, the girl emitted a tiny burp that came with a wisp of green light.

Speechless, Emma stared.

Nan wandered about, pulling a chair up to the end of the table. She eased her weight down and glanced back and forth between the two girls. "Well now, Em. I reckon' you gave that ol' Banderwigh more than he could handle."

"What?" Emma shifted to face the table, leaning back against her Mama.

"Well, you see. The ladies of this family carry the gift. A critter like that can't be hurt easily with swords. You gave him a wallop, you did. If he comes back, it won't be 'til you're a Nan yourself." The old one winked.

Emma giggled. Tam pouted.

Nan lifted him up. "Maybe you too, boy. But'cha can't pass it on." She sniffed at his hair. "Maybe Uruleth."

"The bear spirit?" asked Mama.

"Well, he's always runnin' around bare," said Emma.

Mama groaned.

Nan set Tam in a chair by some bread, which he attacked. "So, child. Do you still think my faerie stories are nonsense?"

Emma drilled a guilty stare into the table. "No."

Tam gave her a raspberry and a shower of wet crumbs.

With a faint grunt, Nan settled down in a chair and leaned back, the wood emitting a soft creak. She threaded her gnarled fingers together in her lap and gave Emma a serious nod. "Good. Now, I think you are ready to learn. Believing is the first step."

Emma glanced up at Mama, her eyes full of questions.

Nan flashed a mischievous grin. "Your mother was a stubborn one, too."

17

WILD SPIRITS

*a*n hour of running about in the meadow behind the house ended with Emma, Kimber, and Tam laying in the grass and picking out shapes in passing clouds. Da had put his foot down that morning, dragging the girls into town to the tailor's shop.

With no choice but to get *something*, Emma had taken all of five minutes to pick out the plainest white sundress she could find. Kimber, on the other hand, must have tried on everything in the shop close to her size before settling on her current attire: a frilly, berry-pink outfit that made her look like an enormous doll. Da also purchased a plain dress for Kimber and a fancy one for Emma, which remained tucked away inside.

Emma laced her fingers behind her head, crossed her ankles, and smiled. Her 'nice' outfit would stay safe in the house until they forced her to wear it.

"Cow," said Tam, pointing skyward.

Kimber giggled, indicating a different cloud. "That one looks like a mouse."

A four-winged longfly buzzed about before landing on Emma's big toe. It shifted to face the wind, twitching in response to brief gusts. Kimber cringed at the sight of an insect the size of a dinner fork, and crawled behind Tam. Emma paid no attention to the bug, knowing longflies didn't bite people—they hunted other bugs. She couldn't picture shapes in the clouds anymore. They didn't resemble much more than blobs. At least none of them looked like a Banderwigh.

Kimber laughed at a silly face Tam made.

Too many questions bounced around in Emma's mind for her to enjoy gazing at the clouds. Da hadn't spoken again of her 'wandering off' in the middle of the night. He gave no indication of being upset with her, so she stopped worrying that a 'talking to' and punishment waited at any moment. Still, she would rather he believed her. The longfly shifted, walking over her toes. She giggled at the sensation of tickling. A moment later, it flicked its wings out flat, and took off with a heavy, droning buzz that sent Kimber into the grass with a shriek. Emma tapped her foot against the air, attempting to sort things out between the world she thought she knew and the one she'd just escaped. As much as the Emma of a few days ago would have agreed with Da about it being all a dream, she knew it wasn't.

Tam perked up. "I'm hungry."

"Dinner's not for a while," said Emma.

"C'we have fruit?"

Kimber stopped smiling. "I don't want apples."

Emma got up. "I'll ask Nan for some cherries."

She swatted bits of grass away from her dress on the walk to the house. The fragrance of candlewax and herbs swirled around in the warm air on the back porch. Emma made her way inside, eyeing Nan who stood by *the cabinet*, puttering around. Mama had gone out. Emma headed for the pantry, slowing as she passed her grandmother to peek at what went on.

"Done playing?" asked Nan.

Emma tapped her big toe into the floor. "Tam's hungry, are there any cherries left?"

"Come here, child." Nan turned to let her see the counter, where various herbs and a bowl of dark green powder sat.

Eyes wide with curiosity, she tucked up and grasped the edge of the wood. Dried berries, leaves, stalks, bottles of liquids in different colors, jars of animal parts, and odd powders filled *the cabinet*. Nan had never allowed her to see inside before. It looked like a much smaller version of Marsten's shop.

"Gather a few strands of that," said Nan, pointing at a bowl containing thin blue filaments. "Put them in this." She tapped a well-worn three-legged stone pestle.

Emma reached, but hesitated before she touched it. "What is it?"

"Nymph's Hair." Nan laughed herself to coughing at the face Emma made. "No, girl. It's a plant."

"Oh." Emma took some. As soon as she felt it, she flung it into the waiting stoneware and rubbed her hand on her dress. "It's fuzzy and sticky."

Nan took one more thread from the bowl, drawing it between thumb and forefinger in both hands. She held it to Emma's eyes, moving it so the light caught hundreds of fine hairs.

"The stickiness comes from small hairs. It won't harm you."

Emma touched one hesitant finger to the strand, poking at it a few times before finally grasping it. Nan let go, and the gossamer thread of plant matter draped over her hand, feeling a bit like a long, cold thread of snot. She scrunched up her nose in confused disgust.

"See, it merely feels odd. It is neither cold, nor wet." Nan motioned at the pestle. "You'll need five strands. You only took four."

"What are we doing?" She added it to the rest.

"Making an elixir to mend small injuries. Now, add a spoonful of that." Nan pointed at the green powder. Before Emma could ask, she winked. "Dried Liferoot, set to bask in the light of a full moon on the longest night of the year."

"Why?" Emma measured out a spoonful of the crumbling dust and dumped it into the mixing vessel.

"The moon gives it power. Perhaps you'll learn that ritual someday." Nan winked. "Now, add a bottle of water and stir."

Emma poured the contents of a nearby bottle in, grabbed the mortar, and began to work the mixture into an off-smelling paste. Once the threads of Nymph's Hair dissolved into the muck, Nan held her hand over the pestle and closed her eyes.

"Uruleth, hear me. Grant the boon of life to your children."

Faint green light surrounded the old woman's hand, falling as luminous vapor into the mixture. Strange symbols on the side of the stone vessel glowed in response. Emma stopped stirring for a few seconds, staring in shock until the light faded.

"Do not stop, child."

The symbols again flared to life as Emma grasped the pestle in both hands and ground the mixture. Within moments, the brown sludge turned white and thinned. The earthy smell grew herbal and, over the course of a minute, turned into the same substance Nan had given Kimber the previous day.

"Nan?" Emma peered up at her. "You turned into the raven, didn't you?"

Wrinkles deepened with a smile. "Yes, child."

"I'm sorry for not believing you."

"Oh, Em." Nan patted her on the back and set an empty potion bottle on the counter. "It is nothing to be sorry of. Many people go through their entire life without seeing such things. Beth was almost fourteen before she believed me."

"Beth?" Emma blinked. "Oh, Mama."

"Here." Nan gestured at the empty flask. "Pour it in this."

Emma poured the mixture in, marveling at how it slid out of the pestle without leaving any sort of coating. Nan took the bottle and twisted a cork into the neck before setting it on a shelf inside the cabinet.

"Can I turn into a raven?" Emma put together the ingredients for another healing elixir.

"I don't know." Nan tapped a finger to her chin. "It's different for all of us. It depends on your animal spirit. Mine is the raven. Your mother still hasn't found one. However, she has a gift for making potions." Nan elbowed her in the side and winked. "Why do you think your father is so brave and strong?"

Emma rubbed her side, eyebrows furrowed. "The pouch she gives him when he goes out?"

"Indeed. A little magic never hurt."

"He doesn't believe either, does he?" Emma stirred while Nan called upon Uruleth, adding the green-glowing magic again.

"The man makes excuses to explain everything he can't understand. He is from Calebrin, a big city two days northeast. They are removed from nature there. They think themselves above it with their big temples and important gods." Nan waved her hand about. "Too important for little old us. It's not that he doesn't believe. He chooses not to see."

Emma stirred until the substance turned white again. "I think I have a spirit, Nan. A wolf."

"Oh?"

"I've seen wolves twice and they didn't try to hurt me." She upended the pestle, filling the second flask. "The big one seemed worried about me."

Nan tapped a cork into the bottle. "Could it be you were just lucky?"

"They saved us from goblins."

"Perhaps you are right." Nan patted her on the head.

"What are you?" Emma scratched her left shin with her toes, peering up at her grandmother. "I mean, what are we? Am I like you and Mama?"

"I believe so." Nan caressed her cheek. "Some call us hedgewizards, others think of us as weedmages. A few think we are woodwitches, and some call us druids."

Emma made a face. "Druid doesn't sound as silly as the others."

"It doesn't matter what we are called, Em. We have a special bond with the natural world. Respect all things, and it shall be your ally."

"Does that mean we can't eat meat?"

"No, Em. Wolves and bears eat meat, as do cats and dogs. Mind you, be grateful to whatever animal gave its life. The spirits go around in an endless cycle of life and death."

"So we've eaten the same cow more than once?"

Nan cackled. "Not exactly, though..." She rubbed her chin. "I suppose it *is* possible. More likely, the cow came back as something else."

"Who is Uruleth?"

"Uruleth is the Bear Spirit, the guardian of life. We call upon him for healing and strength. Strixian is the spirit of the owl, a bearer of great knowledge. Ylithir is the wolf spirit, known for his cunning and guile. Loyalty as well, to his pack."

"Can I do... magic?" Emma glanced at the pestle.

"You are a little younger than your mother was when she learned her first bit of magic, but I think we shall start soon."

"Strixian..." Emma muttered.

Nan slapped herself on the thigh and snapped her fingers. "Why don't we start with something basic, see if you have the knack? Try this. You do believe now, do you not?"

Emma offered a weak smile. "Uhh, yes."

"Alright, Emma. If you believe Strixian is real, ask him to teach you the Whisper of the Wildkin. It's a spell that will allow you to talk with any animal."

"What are the words?" Emma tilted her head.

"What do you want them to be?" Nan winked. "Whatever you need." She closed her eyes, whispering. "Strixian, Spirit of Thought, grant me the gift of the wildkin."

Emma gasped with awe as tiny wisps of light wrapped around Nan and faded a few seconds later. The old one looked at the far end of the room and made a series of strange squeaking sounds. Two mice peeked out from under the bed, one of which ran over to her and sat up on its back legs.

"Go on, Em." Nan gripped her shoulder.

She tried to imagine the same strands of light around her arms, convincing herself what Nan told her was real. "Strixian, please let me have the wildkin whisper."

Emma swung her arms in a dramatic swish, like Tam's dragon-slaying wizard. She stared at her plain, somewhat dirty, and definitely not-glowing hands.

She pouted.

"Not bad, Em. But, you didn't want it enough. It's nothing to be ashamed of. Not everyone in our family has the gift."

Emma squatted and looked at the mouse. She found it difficult *not* to believe in magic, after everything she had seen over the past few days. After a few breaths, she gripped her knees and concentrated on the need to speak to the little rodent. "Strixian, please teach me the wildkin whisper."

A small tingle spread across her shoulders, as if something drifted close to check her out. Emma tensed, offering a momentary thought of reverence before calling out with desire. The strange energy flowed into her body. A tingly warmth entered the middle of her back, spread over her chest, and flowed down her arms. Threads of light wisped around her, circling and weaving among her fingers.

"No think no think she do it. Too young. Too young," squeaked a tiny little voice.

"Hello?" Emma asked.

The mouse jumped, doing a backflip. "Wow, wow. Worked!"

"How long does it last?" chirped Emma.

The mouse spun in a circle. "Don't know. Don't know. Ask old one."

Emma whirled on Nan. While looking at her grandmother, everything she tried to say came out as squeaks, which sent the mouse into fits of laughter the more panicked she became.

"You have to do more than talk while the magic is on you." Nan squeezed her shoulder. "Before you speak, focus on if you want to talk to a person or an animal."

She stared up at Nan, making a series of exaggerated determined faces. "How long does it last?"

Nan clapped. "Good. A little less than an hour or so." She stooped and squeaked at the mouse. This time, Emma understood it as, "Thank you."

The critter scurried off, hiding once more under the bed.

"I wanna learn more!" Emma bounced.

"All things in time, child. You should master that before going further." Nan tapped her on the head. "That is why boys have more trouble with it. They can't wait to learn everything all at once. They want to go straight to the lightning and think they waste time talking to mice."

Emma giggled. When understanding crept in, her jaw dropped. "Lightning?"

"That's many years away." Nan ambled over to the pantry, taking a sack of cherries down from a shelf.

"Can you show me what it looks like?"

"Not now, Em. This house is too nice to destroy."

Emma stared at her, horrified, eyes wide.

When Nan glanced back at her, she burst into cackles.

"Nan." Emma wandered over. "Would it break the house? What does it look like?"

"Have you seen a storm where the sky flashes?"

Emma nodded.

"Well, it's like that, but it goes where I want." Nan held up the bag of cherries. "Oh, don't look at me like that. I'm still your Nan. I'm not going to burn down any houses."

Emma pulled her dress up into a bowl. "Nan, what was the Banderwigh?"

Nan poured out a three-child portion of cherries, then put the bag away.

"I think they are men who have fallen victim to an old curse. Some believe them to be tortured souls, who suffered so much in life that they returned to take revenge."

"Revenge?"

"Yes, child. Revenge on anyone who would dare be happy while they suffered. Others may be distraught fathers whose children were taken away from them. Some, perhaps even by another banderwigh. They tried to kill the creature, or wandered in search of their lost family until they died. Some may have even succeeded in destroying one, but when they touched the beast's tainted weapon, the darkness devoured their soul. Or, maybe they're simply what they are—monsters."

Emma leaned away from the strange look in Nan's eyes and swallowed. "Is Kimber's dad gonna become one?"

Nan waved at her. "Oh, no. That man wasn't worth spitting on, but not the kind of evil that turns into such a creature."

"I thought it would take Kimber. She always went alone into the forest. Why did it take me an' Tam?"

Nan rubbed her chin and closed the pantry. "Why do you think?"

Emma stared at her dress full of cherries for a moment, considering. "We were happier. It would hurt more to be taken."

"Yes, yes, close enough I suppose." Nan shooed her toward the door. "Don't keep them waiting. Oh, and Emma..."

She glanced back from the end of the porch.

"Don't waste your time talking with any of the local horses." She huffed. "They're all such horrible gossips."

18

ONE OF THE PACK

No one had spoken of the Banderwigh for almost a week.

The village even seemed to forget about Old Man Drinn's sudden death. People mostly expressed surprise that it had 'taken so long' for the strong berry brandy to kill him. No one acted surprised at all that he drank himself to death. She couldn't figure out how long she'd been in the cage. Mama said she'd been missing for a whole day, but it didn't feel like that much time had passed.

Emma sat cross-legged in the meadow with her eyes closed and her hands on her knees. Head tilted back, she inhaled a breeze that brushed her face. She tried listening for the sound of spirits. However, every time she started to feel calm, a bug would land on her face or the grass would tickle her legs. Each distraction, insect or plant, broke her concentration and left her frustrated.

She leaned forward, raking her fingers at the grass and thinking about what Nan had said. Life took on many forms, each of them essential. *Does grass have feelings?*

After a while, the wind calmed and she tried again. Something buzzed past her ear. The noise ceased at the same time a light presence upon her cheek crawled up onto her nose. Emma ignored it, listening to the sound of the breeze and thinking of the big, grey wolf.

Silence. When she opened her eyes, they crossed to focus on a fat bee as big as a grape, all black, except one small spot of white hair between the wings. *A flyeater*. Emma thought about puffing at it, but didn't fancy having a giant, red nose for a week. It departed when the wind stirred again, letting her breathe. Once her nerves settled, she shut her eyes and thought about spirits and the strange green light fading into the pestle.

The feeling that wisped around her before she used the speaking magic had been, according to Nan, Strixian's first contact. At the moment she felt it, she tugged at her desire and the magic had worked. Emma focused on that feeling, but didn't think about any specific animal. Minutes passed, filled with quiet breezes and the occasional buzz of a passing insect. Out of nowhere, the world fell into a state of calm silence... and a presence filled in the void before her.

Hello? Is someone there? Are you my animal spirit?

Cold touched her forehead. She opened her eyes, finding herself nose to nose with the large wolf she had seen twice prior. Instinctual fear of such a big wolf set her heart racing. Considering their respective size, he could snap her neck with ease. She leaned back, mouth agape. He stood still, staring right through her. Before her fear sank too deep, she thought back to the wolves protecting her and Tam from goblins.

"Great Strixian, please grant me the wildkin whisper." The energy responded, wisps of light skimmed along the meadow swirled around her, and absorbed into her chest.

"Greetings, Emma. I am Greyfang." The wolf's jaw moved as though he had let out a howl too soft for human ears, but a man's voice created words in her mind, deep and confident, like Da. "It is good to know you."

"Thank you." She reached out and touched him, fingers combing the fluffy fur on the side of his face. Excitement filled her blood. She moved to kneel, and the wolf allowed her to wrap her arms around him. "Thank you for protecting me."

"The raven is friend. So shall you be. Come, little one." Greyfang turned sideways.

She glanced at the distant house. Everyone else had gone inside. Tam no doubt engaged in knight vs. dragon warfare while Nan watched. Mama took Kimber to see the magistrate.

"We will not be long." The great wolf lowered himself to the ground.

Emma stepped over him, sitting on his back and twining her fingers in his fur. When he stood, her feet couldn't reach the ground. She peered over the side at the distance separating her toes from the meadow, and gulped. He bolted into a run with such speed, Emma nearly fell. She started off screaming, but the sound turned gleeful before her lungs emptied. Meadow grass became a dull green blur, punctuated by the sporadic glow of fireflies streaking by. He ran up and down small hills so fast it felt as though she flew in dips and dives. By the time they reached the edge of Widowswood, she couldn't stop grinning and laughing.

"Lean forward," said Greyfang.

She gripped with her legs and bent forward, sliding her arms around his neck. He bounded over the brush and weaved among the trees. She looked around in awe as he trotted around a fallen log into the mist of a modest waterfall. The undergrowth on the other side thinned, and they cleared ground with such speed Emma's legs hurt from watching. He slowed to trot along the edge of a smaller waterway, perhaps the same one looped back, until it split around a tiny island. Greyfang approached the edge, then bounded across to the far side in a great leap. Emma crashed against the back of his head when they landed, but held on without falling.

She sat upright, relaxing and looking about at the woods. The entire forest felt different. No longer did she have any sense of fear or worry. The natural world embraced her, making her feel as safe as inside her home. Even the trees gave off a protectiveness that hadn't been there before.

He leapt another fallen tree, landing in a shaded grove where the wolves had made their den. A dozen adults and several pups perked up. The little ones raced over to greet the alpha, eager to gain his favor and show their respect.

The wildkin whisper translated the names of the adults into concepts: Runs in Shadow, Stalks the Wind, and Moonsong—the big all-black wolf—came forward to greet her. All the wolves approached to sniff at her. Wet noses roamed her legs, arms, and neck. The pups licked and nipped at her toes, making her giggle.

The moment had every making of a nightmare. Emma knew she was a defenseless human child surrounded by carnivores, but felt no fear. For no reason she could explain, she trusted them, and they returned her lack of fright in kind.

Moonsong remained after the others wandered off. "Human... Please, follow."

Greyfang stooped to let Emma jump down to her feet. She walked after the female, past a cluster of curious pups who kept yapping "hi." Moonsong stopped at the end of a row of stacked stones, a long-forgotten ruin of human construction. The wolf swung her head back and glanced up at her with sad, yellow eyes.

Emma crept around the broken wall and gasped at a wounded, light-furred wolf, lying on its side and wheezing.

"Howls at Rain. He is of my womb," said Moonsong. "The metal fang of a goblin will soon take his life."

"I'm..." Tears welled up in Emma's eyes. "It's my fault."

Howls at Rain snarled, baring fangs. "Human... bad." His aggression trailed off to a whimper when she stepped closer, gasping air in his nostrils with short breaths. "You..." He flicked his tongue at her leg. Once he recognized her, he gave off a great sigh, and relaxed.

She knelt at his side, picking at blood-matted fur a hand's width behind his right shoulder where a dagger wound oozed blood. The injury smelled foul.

"I'm so sorry... I'm just a child. I don't know what to do."

The mother wolf bowed her head.

The potion. Emma blinked hard, clearing her eyes of tears and her mind of helplessness. She placed her palms flat on either side of the wound and tried to remember. What did Nan say? Greyfang moved up alongside his mate; Moonsong nuzzled him.

"She is still a pup," said Greyfang.

Moonsong padded over and touched noses with the hurt wolf. "We have given our son to save the life of the humans' pup. Is this the will of Ylithir?"

Emma choked back a sob, guilt overwhelming. She offered an apologetic look to the wolves for a moment, before resolve filled her heart. "Uruleth, Spirit of the Bear, I call on your power to heal." She gritted her teeth, straining as if she needed to force the effort out of her own body.

When she opened her eyes, the wolves had vanished, and the trees appeared different. Her mouth hung slack at the sight of spectral pines, their trunks wider around than a house and too tall to see the tops. Overhead, the sky held the dark of night, yet every surface shimmered with an unearthly glowing outline that fluttered in wisps.

She looked down at her hands, still held as if over the wound. Her mind raced, searching for some explanation for what had happened.

"Uruleth—?"

"I am here."

A voice rolled like a tumbling boulder over the woods, shaking her bones. Emma shivered at the powerful voice flooding this strange reality. A ghostly mass in the shape of a bear advanced out from the trees toward her. If it yawned, its mouth would have been large enough for her to walk into without ducking her head. Such a massive creature should surely have scared her, but a sense of reverence overtook her.

Emma bowed her head. "Thank you for visiting me."

"You ask me to restore a child of Ylithir. He who is known for cunning. He who is known for taking advantage of the weak. I do not know you, daughter of Bethany Dalen, daughter of the Raven. For what reason should I provide that for which you ask?"

"Great Uruleth…" Her voice wavered, unsure. "I am Emma. I believe the wolf is my spirit, and Howls at Rain got hurt saving my life. If not for him, the goblins would have killed me and my little brother. Isn't Ylithir also known for loyalty to his pack?"

Uruleth exhaled in a huff out his massive nose, blasting her with a torrent of hot, wet air that made her hair flutter back. "You have the taint of darkness on you, child."

"A banderwigh took me."

"Ahh yes." He exhaled on her again, a faint green light upon his breath. Tiredness she didn't notice she'd been carrying faded away. "And yet you are here."

Emma held her chin up. "I didn't let the monster make me sad. It set me free. Nan—The Raven—said I banished it."

"You possess remarkable strength for one so young, but your fight is not yet at an end." The enormous bear flickered bright for an instant, then faded away. "You have managed to find nobility within the opportunist. Your desires are pure. I shall grant your request."

Emma opened her mouth, but couldn't come up with anything to say, her heart swollen with gratitude.

Far off in the distant wood, the shadow of an ethereal wolf raised its head to look at her. The grand animal stood statue still, a transparent figure outlined in threads of pure white light. His blue eyes shimmered, conveying acceptance. Emma smiled. Amid a great rushing sound, the other-forest vanished. Soft green light pooled in her hands. She stared into it, feeling energy drain from her as the mass of glowing magic grew in size and brightness. A part of her knew she held pure life, flowing around her fingers with a vibrant, yet cool tingle. The din of yapping wolf pups rushed in to fill the silence and fur swelled up beneath her hands. Gradually, the color of the normal world returned.

She startled at the coldness of a nose at the side of her neck. The wolves all crowded around to get a better look at the cloud of emerald light wrapping her arms. Hope filled her as she watched it swirl. Howls at Rain's wound didn't close. Alarmed, Emma started to panic, but remembered what Nan had said about desire. She took a determined breath and tensed.

Focused on the want to help, she forced the life energy around her hands to flow into the creature before her. The glow diminished and the wound shrank to a small scab. Howls with Rain made a soft noise somewhere between a sigh of canine relief and a growl, then lapsed into sleep. Moonsong sniffed at where the wound had been, and rubbed her head against Emma's.

The gesture made Emma cry again, this time from joy. She thought of Mama's reaction when she had seen the bruise on her face. Moonsong nudged at Emma's side, nosing her way under her arm into a hug, then licked at her face.

"Emma," said Greyfang. "Your mother is searching for you. It is time I return you to your family."

She spent a few seconds giving 'goodbye for now' pets to the swarm of pups and letting them lick her hands. At an insistent grunt from Moonsong, Emma stood and climbed onto the large wolf's back once more without a trace of hesitation. Greyfang wheeled about to face back the way they came, then bounded into a run, racing into the woods, leaping thick bundles of roots, and swerving around dense trees. Emma let go of his neck and raised her arms, calling out with delight at the wind in her face.

"Emma!" Mama's desperate shout echoed in the forest.

He steered toward the sound, trotting out onto a clear trail. A few paces away, Mama spun about at the sudden appearance of a wolf of that size, quarterstaff raised. Seeing her daughter riding it stunned her mute—but the sight of her mother shocked Emma just as much. The woman looked like an entirely different person in a dark green robe and darker cloak, with enough fierceness in her eyes to give any bandit pause. Emma had never thought of Mama as anything more than a warm, loving townswoman, but the way she held the staff proved her family was full of surprises.

Greyfang crouched so she could dismount. Emma hugged him about the neck, then ran into Mama's embrace.

"I'm sorry to frighten you. One of the wolves got hurt when they saved us from the goblins. I spoke to Uruleth!" Emma bounced.

Mama bowed at the alpha, who bowed his head in acknowledgement before zooming away into the dark.

"I see Nan has taken to teaching you some things already. I would like to know what happened." Mama smiled and ruffled Emma's hair.

She drew a gasping breath upon noticing a trickle of green liquid working its way down her mother's weapon.

"It is nothing to fear, Emma. Just a few goblins."

She clung to her Mama's side as they walked home, and told of her meeting with the spirits.

19

SIBLINGS

$\mathcal{W}$ ind howled outside, driving a storm into the walls and filling the air inside with the scent of rain. Emma, Kimber, and Tam lay on the floor in the loft upon one of Nan's quilts. The area didn't have separate walls and ceiling so much as two angled surfaces that could be called either. Storage trunks lined the sides of the small space, and one tiny window above a bench let in grey light. Rain pattered heavy on the roof, surging in waves with a gusting wind. Tam lay flat on his chest, his stick-knight and shrub-dragon locked in mortal combat before his eyes. The girls lay next to each other, propped up on their elbows. Kimber dug her feet into the quilt for warmth while Emma crossed her ankles in the air and gnawed on a cookie from the plate between them.

Emma smiled at the memory of baking them a few hours earlier, with Nan's help. The cookies had come out lacking in sweet, but Nan saved them with a brushing of molasses.

Tam made roaring noises, distracting her from her daydream. Shrub Dragon wanted to devour all of the cookies before the children could get any, but Stick Knight had the upper hand. Kimber fussed with the yarn hair of a cloth doll Emma had bequeathed to her; she had not much bothered with her dolls since she had taken to looking after Tam.

The new member of the family looked so different with her hair clean and combed—not wild, frizzed, and matted with dirt. She was still too scrawny, something Nan promised to remedy. No one in the village seemed the least bit upset at the death of Old Man Drinn, though Kimber sometimes became sad about it. Emma couldn't understand how the girl could have any feelings for that man. She tried to imagine how she would feel about Da if he treated her like that, and snarled, biting off half her cookie in one chomp.

Emma stared at the bite mark while grumbling in her head, wondering how an entire village could whisper in secret, lamenting how bad poor little Kimber had it. All the while, no one did anything to help. Of course, with the man dead, they clucked like hens about how the gods always took things to rights.

A twinge of unease crawled across her gut at the thought of him. The look in Mama's eye when Emma admitted how she'd gotten bruised frightened her. The staff-toting woman in the woods didn't seem anything like the happy mother who smiled and waved at everyone in town at least once a day. Emma shivered at a surge in the wind, wondering if Mama might have played a part in the man's death. She remembered the flash of purple fire, and Nan always going on about Mama's skill with potions.

Could she have killed him?

Emma glanced into the armhole of Kimber's dress at her prominent ribs. The girl would have starved if he didn't hit her to death sooner. Emma felt uneasy at the idea Mama might have taken a man's life, but… maybe for the best.

Tam tugged the cookie plate away as Kimber reached for one, moving it closer to him and Emma. Kimber's smile vanished and her eyes reddened. She let the doll slip out of her hands and looked away from both of them.

"Tam!" Emma handed Kimber a cookie. "That's not nice. Why did you do that?"

He mashed his crude toys together, not looking at either of them.

Emma tapped her fingers on the floorboards until he looked up, giving her a pathetic stare.

"Tam?"

He sniffled. "I only get half your love. You gotta share it wif me an' her now."

Kimber crossed her arms and put her head down.

Emma shifted from lying on her belly to sitting with her legs to the side. She leaned forward and ruffled his hair. "Tam, love isn't like cookies. I don't have any less for you because we got a new sister."

"Mom didn't have her." Tam pointed.

Kimber mumbled something. From the sound of her voice, she'd started crying. Emma crossed her arms and gave him a stern look.

"What?" asked Tam.

"Be nice, Tam. He might have been mean, but she's just lost her father."

"He was bad," said Tam. "I know he was bad 'cause he made her go in the woods alone. We're not 'llowed to do that 'cause Papa says we'll get hurt." He thought for a moment. "Did her papa want her to get hurt?"

Emma cringed. She hated lying to her brother, but he was only six. "I... don't think so, Tam. Just careless and stupid... and mean."

Kimber curled on her side. "Yer Ma an' Pa don' really wan' me. They bein' a nice 'cause I donnae 'ave a home na more."

"You didn't have a *home* before." Emma put a hand on the girl's shoulder. "Kimber, Da and Mama want you to be part of our family. Me an' Tam, they *had* to keep 'cause she had us as babies. They chose to keep you."

Tam gave Emma a raspberry.

Sniffling, Kimber rolled over and sat up, unable to look Emma in the eye. "I's a so scared 'a him. He always hittin' on me, no ma' how good I tried ta be."

"Mama was mad at him for that. She protected us both, like a mother should."

Kimber smiled despite tears, and wiped her face. "Tha' be nice, if she wan' me."

Emma took Kimber's arm. "Grab my wrist." She took Tam's arm. "Grab her wrist."

The three children sat, forming a circle by a grip on each other's arm. Tam held Kimber, who held Emma, who held Tam.

"Great Strixian," she intoned, closing her eyes. "Make us one family." Emma dropped her voice to a faint mumble that neither Tam nor Kimber could hear. "Please grant me the gift of the wildkin whisper."

The magic of beast-speech came to her in the form of the wispy white lights. Kimber and Tam went wide-eyed at the glowing threads circling them before flowing into Emma's arms. She raised and lowered their combined grip twice and made a show of breaking the circle with her hand held up, fingers apart.

"There," said Emma, with a matter-of-fact nod. "Now we're real siblings."

Her brother looked at her as though she'd poured cold oats in his skivvies. Kimber cradled her wrist and sat with her mouth open. She looked from the quilt at Emma's knees to her face and back again.

Emma folded her arms across her chest to settle the matter.

"W-what was that?" whispered Kimber.

"Magic," said Emma. "You saw it, right? You're our family now."

Tam gazed down, guilt all over his face. He bit his lower lip and pushed the cookie plate toward Kimber.

Nan shuffled into view at the bottom of the loft ladder and gave Emma a conspiratorial wink. "Em, Kimber, come help me start on dinner. Your father's going to be frozen when he comes home in this weather."

Emma leaned to whisper in Kimber's ear. "See."

THE TALL GRASS

*T*he week following Emma's 'ritual' in the loft, life took on a sense of normal. Nan occasionally whispered to her about magic, but avoided the topic more than spoke of it. Kimber had come out of her dark spell, and the house had filled with the giggles of children. Even Da had warmed up to her, despite his hesitation about taking on the burden of another child, especially after Mama and Emma had cornered him one night. Emma didn't let on she knew what Mama had done, but they both made it clear Kimber was there to stay.

Emma sat chest-deep in murky bathwater, running a soapy rag up and down Kimber's back. Tam sat on the other end, in front of Kimber, who scrubbed his hair. He amused himself by grasping at suds, closing his fists so hard white puffs shot into the air. Mama knelt beside the tub, using the space behind Emma to wash laundry. Nan wandered by, causing a break in bathing while she refreshed the bathwater from the kettle. Emma scooted away from the rush of heat at her back, squeezing Kimber into Tam. She swished her arm back and forth in the water to mix the not-so-warm with the near-boiling parts.

When the heat became tolerable, Emma relaxed and scooped

water over Kimber's head with a wooden bowl, rinsing the soap out of her hair. The fragrance of wildflowers surrounded them.

Emma sniffed the air. "Nan, why do you make your soap smell nice, but your potions taste like wet mud?"

Mama stifled a chuckle.

"Bah." Nan flung her hand down in a dismissive wave, and winked at Mama. "And bah to you too. The both of ya, indeed."

Emma handed the bowl to Kimber so she could rinse Tam's hair. Once the boy had been de-sudsed, they all rotated to face the other way. Emma sat cross-legged and helped Mama with the clothes in front of her while Kimber washed her back and hair. Tam, now behind Kimber, threw suds on her, the floor, the table, Mama, and Nan whenever she went by. Kimber grunted, trying to squeeze her leg between Emma and the wooden tub in order to sit comfortably. Emma scooted forward to give her more room, while stuffing one of Mama's dresses under water.

"How ma' time' d'we 'ave to do this?" whispered Kimber at Emma's ear.

"Do what?" asked Emma

"This." Kimber slapped at the surface. "Sit inna water."

"Have a bath?" Emma held up the dress to appraise a stained spot. "Once a week."

Kimber stopped scrubbing Emma's hair. "Neva hadda proper bath a'fore. Jes tossed inna trough when I'as real bad."

The old man had barely fed her, much less taken proper care of his daughter. Emma didn't want to dwell on such things. "I can tell. It feels like Tam is throwing soap on me."

He giggled.

"'E *is* throwing soap on us," said Kimber.

Mama left the last few pieces of laundry to Emma, and moved over to teach Kimber how to wash. Emma squinted at the bundle of wet cloth in her hands, jealousy rising. When the little fingers scrubbing her hair paused, she glanced back. The large smile on Kimber's face, and Mama's wink chased her envy away. Three of Da's shirts, and two full hair-washes later, the bath had become cool. Emma sank neck deep, slouching with her knees out of the water after she finished the last item—a cooking apron.

Mama stood, wiping her hands on her dress, and went to fetch towels. "That's quite enough. Come on, all of you out before you prune."

Tam leapt from the bathwater and ran off into the house.

Kimber climbed out of the tub, laughing at him. Emma pulled herself upright and stood there dripping.

Mama shook her head and draped towels over the girls. Emma pulled the cloth off her head and wrapped herself in it.

"I tell you, Beth. His patron spirit is the bare." Nan clucked.

Emma giggled. Mama seemed unamused.

"He takes after his mother," said Nan with a wink. "You know, girls, after baths, she used to run straight outside—"

Mama glowered, throwing the wet apron over Nan's head. "Mother!"

Nan laughed herself to tears.

"Hang the lot outside, will you?" asked Mama while the girls dried themselves. Then, she stalked off in search of the runaway boy. "Tam, come here this instant! Get down from there!"

Against the backdrop of running and laughing deep within the house, Emma, still mostly wet, tugged her less-than-favorite dress in place and gathered up an armload of damp clothing. Kimber took the rest, and they went out to the back porch, a less grand affair than the front. It stood off the ground at only the height of a single stair, and held a small table and three chairs, two of which rocked. The girls dropped the clothing on the table. Emma dragged the non-rocking chair over to stand on so she could reach the clothesline.

The mid-summer day brought warmth to an unusually strong wind, which lofted the fragrance of meadow flowers and made securing the wash on the line a chore. Despite it being over a month away, the town buzzed with anticipation for the upcoming festival of Zaravex. As far as Emma knew, it involved lots of cakes and candies for the kids and three days' worth of people making noise late into the night. For some reason, older girls always wore a lot of flowers in their hair around that time.

An orange and red sky settled behind Widowswood, bringing the fireflies to prominence over the grass in the wake of the setting sun. Emma ran her fingers through her hair, flinging water and letting the breeze dry it. She stepped down, slid the chair to the left, and climbed up again. Kimber handed her each piece of laundry in turn; soon, wet clothes filled the line.

Laughing, Tam bounded out of the house in a sky blue tunic and went off in search of glowing bugs. Mama leaned on the doorjamb, folded her arms, and smiled at the three of them.

The girls hurried along at their task, eager to finish before the sun had disappeared entirely. Mama walked over and shooed them into the field, taking over the rest of the chore. Emma and Kimber leapt off the porch.

"Time for bed soon," called Mama.

"Yes, Mama," replied both girls at once. They exchanged a glance and burst into giggles.

With at least a half hour left before dark, they dashed off into the waist-high grass chasing fireflies. The waning light seemed to vanish much faster than Emma wanted it to while they caught and released glow bugs before going off in search of more. Tam set out to find the biggest, best glow bug of all.

"It's dark," said Kimber. "We should go inside."

"Yeah." Emma ran over to her, then leaned her hands on her knees to catch her breath. "Tam?"

No answer.

Emma stood up on tiptoe. "Tam?" she repeated, louder.

"Tam!" cried Kimber.

Snap.

Both girls spun at the noise from the tree line. They had traveled rather far from the house and could see into the woods. A fleeting shadow leapt between trees. Kimber cupped her hands to her face and called for Tam again. Emma froze in place, searching for the creature she *knew* she saw. When Kimber touched her arm, she screamed.

The sudden loud noise made Kimber cry out and clasp her hands over her mouth. "W-what?"

Emma opened her mouth to answer, but the darkness moved again. She pointed, shouting, "Tam! Where are you! I'm not playing."

Snap.

Kimber gasped. She clung to Emma's side, shivering. "Wot's 'at? Somefin' movin'."

"M-maybe it's Greyfang," said Emma not really believing it.

"Who's 'at?" asked Kimber.

"A nice wolf."

Kimber scrunched her nose. "Wolfs in'nae nice. 'Ey bite."

Emma studied the tree line. The shadows held malice. Something lurked in the dark, but *not* a wolf.

"T-Tam?" She spun around. "Kimber, g-go home before it comes after us."

"Rawr!" roared Tam, leaping out of the tall grass with his hands like claws.

The girls both shrieked.

He fell over, laughing. Emma pounced on him, gathering two fistfuls of his tunic and shaking him. Her hair fell around her like a curtain of night.

"By the gods, Tam! Don't do that to me!"

He went pale, cowering away from the look on her face.

After a lingering glare, she pulled him into a hug. "I'm sorry. You scared me."

Crack.

She jumped, dragging her brother around to put herself between him and the woods.

"Why are you mad? You beat the Bandy-wee."

Emma backed away from the trees, seizing her brother and sister each by the hand. She wanted to run, but her legs wouldn't move. She couldn't even find words—only stare into the darkness. A presence watched her, and it gave off such evil she burst into silent tears.

"Tam? Kimber? Emma?" called Mama in the distance.

They tugged on her arms, but she remained rooted in place.

Tam yanked harder. "Em, Mama's calling."

Her mother's voice scratched at Emma's fear, breaking the spell. She blinked, shaking her head. "W-we should go."

Mama gathered her dress and stepped down off the back porch, looking worried. Emma squeezed her siblings' hands and pulled them into a run for home, not once daring to look behind her. Mama let her pass, lingering for a few seconds to peer into the forest before following the children back into the house, and pulling the door closed.

21

ARMOR

*E*mma shot bolt upright, grasping at the bars of a cage that didn't exist. Finding herself at home, in bed, she sat for a moment, shivering and clutching the blanket to her chest. When it sank in she was safe, she rolled over and squeezed Tam until he gave her a 'what are you doing?' glare.

Kimber had migrated into the spot where Mama usually slept, limbs spread every which way as though she'd fallen out of a moving wagon. Mama had rolled into the void left by Da, who was nowhere to be seen. *Probably in the outhouse.* Emma crawled out of bed, giving up on any chance she would she be able to get back to sleep.

Besides, it would be morning soon.

She rummaged the huge chest at the foot of the bed until she found the dress Nan made. Off came her nightdress despite the chilly room, and she wriggled into the beloved garment, clinging to it as if it would protect her from what she'd felt last night. Wearing her new dress for a while rather made this one feel too small on her, but she didn't care. Nan, also awake before the sun, was in the process of gathering fruit and bread for the morning meal. Emma scurried over to help. It didn't take long for the old one to notice the fear in her.

"Spiders in your dreams again, Em?"

"No." Emma lifted the great wooden bowl with both arms as if hugging it, the vessel too big for her fingers to touch on the other side. "I saw something in the woods last night."

"What was it?" Nan raised an eyebrow, following her to the table with a loaf of bread.

Emma set the bowl down and pushed it to the center of the table. "Dark. I didn't exactly *see* it, but I knew it was there. Something wanted to hurt me."

Nan picked at a few wiry grey hairs on her chin. "A boar perhaps? Certainly, the goblins wouldn't dare get so close to town."

"It wasn't goblins." Emma went back to the pantry for the cheese. "It sounded too heavy. I don't think it was an animal." She set the block down by the bread. "It felt like... hate staring at me."

"Hmm." Nan pursed her lips. "I suspect that's why Beth went out. I don't think she found anything." The old one shrugged. "If she did, she hasn't said a thing."

They set the table and laid out the breakfast meal. Minutes later, sunlight leaked over the horizon, the rays soon bright enough to make Emma's squinting eyes water.

Da thundered in the front door, stomping and clattering in full armor. He took the broadsword from his belt and leaned it on the wall before heading to the table. His boisterous arrival woke Tam, who sat up and stared blank-faced at the wall.

"I swear on Belephir's sweaty ba—" He glanced at Emma. "I swear... The next time Glinn and Dorran decide to get into a drunken punch-up at two hours 'til dawn, I'm going to charge them with destruction of property."

"What property did they destroy?" asked Nan.

"My sleep." Da sat and leaned his elbows on the table, tapping his gauntleted fingers on the wood for a moment before leaning forward. "Em, what are you doing wearing that rag?" He downed a half-stein of water in one swig. "I thought we agreed to keep it for sentiment only."

Tam crawled off the bed and trudged over.

"She had a fright, Liam." Nan ambled over and patted his brigandine pauldron. "To her, it's no different from this."

Da chuckled. "Must be something *special* about it... I can't imagine how it's not fallen to pieces, old as it is."

"Are you talking about her dress or your mother in law?" asked Nan with a raised eyebrow.

"The dress," he said with a note of whimsy.

Nan smiled.

Tam tugged on Emma's arm. "Pee."

Emma bit her lip, looking at the window. Early morning sunlight sparkled in the thick, uneven glass. She took him by the hand and walked him to the privy. This time, she scooted in behind him before he could slam the door in her face. She turned her back to him and secured the lock.

"You a'scared?"

She let her head sag against the rickety wood. "Yeah."

"Me too," whispered Tam.

THE FAMILY GATHERED AROUND THE TABLE FOR BREAKFAST. MAMA glanced at Da with worry in her eyes—he ate as fast as he could without choking. Tam poked Kimber in the side, starting a tickle war. Emma couldn't stop thinking about the way the forest made her feel. It couldn't be true. The Banderwigh was gone, not to return until she reached Nan's age. It couldn't possibly be coming for her again.

She stared over her bread at Kimber's bright green eyes, alight with joy. The girl raised a knee to block Tam's hand, and retaliated with a tickling finger to the armpit that made Tam squeal. No, the Banderwigh wouldn't come for her. It wanted her sister. It knew Emma wouldn't give in, and Kimber had been too broken before to be a tempting target. Now that she had become happy, it could hurt both of them by taking one. Emma scowled at her plate. She wouldn't let it win. She was ten years old now. Two younger kids needed her protection.

"What did those berries do to you, Em?" Da chuckled. "You look like you want to smash them flat."

She blushed. "Nothing."

He stood, leaning left to kiss Mama, and right to pat Tam on the head, then swooped around between the girls, wrapped an arm around them, and planted a smooch each atop their heads. Kimber looked up with adoration on her face.

"I've got to go on patrol."

Mama scrambled out of her seat, racing to *the cabinet*. Emma slid off her chair and ran to Da's sword where he had left it leaning on the wall. She wrapped her arms around the scabbard, grunting with its weight, carrying it over to him. The scent of weapon oil tainted the taste of her half-chewed mouthful. Mama handed him a leather-wrapped bundle: elixirs to keep him strong, awake, and fast.

He ruffled Emma's hair and went outside with Mama. Emma waited all of ten seconds before she scooted out of her chair and snuck over to the door, leaning the side of her head against it. Kimber soon appeared next to her, almost nose-to-nose. Emma held a finger up in a 'shhh' gesture. Kimber nodded.

"I don't like this, Liam," said Mama. "Something doesn't feel right."

"You worry too much, Beth. It's just local bandits. The man looked a lot worse than he was."

"The caravan lost two men. Bandits don't often kill the merchants. They want to rob them again the next time they come through. That man barely lived, and did you see what they did to the horse?"

Emma gasped.

"I don't know, Beth. Something's got them riled up. It might be pressure up north. Mercenaries from Calebrin and Andor are moving against highwaymen all over Andorath. Activity has been picking up as of late and it's got the king's ear. You know his favorite solution is to throw gold at a problem until it goes away. This poor sot might've just made the mistake of only having four guards."

"What if it's mercenaries from Namriel?" asked Mama, sounding worried. "The Talethians have been eyeing Andorath for a long time."

Kimber bit her knuckle, trembling. Emma held her hand.

"I rather doubt that. The Talethian Empire has already

overextended itself. You should hear all the stories that come out of that place. Faeries in the woods, indeed."

"Aye, strange thing about stories. Sometimes, they're true."

The sound of a kiss made Emma cringe.

"This is bandits, maybe something what strayed in from the north. We'll be fine."

Her mother sighed. "I don't like the idea of you traipsing about in the forest looking for trouble."

They fell quiet for a moment. Both girls made icky faces at the noises of an obvious long kiss.

Da grumbled. "I'll be fine. It's not as if I'm going alone, there'll be twenty of us. Braddon's insisting on it."

"Why doesn't he go with you, then if it's so important?"

Emma grinned at the look she knew Mama would be giving him at that moment: chin raised, eyes flaring, hand waving.

"Because he is the mayor, and it's his job to tell—"

"Nonsense. He's a coward." Mama dropped her voice to a near whisper. "Just... be careful. Em's riled up about something and you know how the ladies in the family can get."

"Well, then I'm not too worried. Small girl, small problem. If your mother was in a tither, I'd lock myself in the wine cellar at Eoghn's."

Mama laughed. "It's not a scale, you know."

The girls cringed at the sound of another kiss, and scampered back to the table. They looked too innocent when Mama walked in. Nan found the crumbs on her plate fascinating. Mama slipped into her seat, gaze down and hands bracing her forehead, thick curly hair falling onto the table.

"Don't be afraid, Mama." Emma slid out of her chair and hurried around to stand beside her. "It's not after Da."

22

FOREBODING

*E*mma came to a halt at the back door, leaning on the wall to catch her breath. She swept her hair out of her face and managed a half-hearted smile, watching Kimber and Tam running about in the meadow. The sky over Widowswood glowed with a dozen shades of orange and purple. It would be dark soon. Emma made it three steps into the house before her smile collapsed. Mama still sat at the table, arms crossed in her lap, staring at the front window. Little of her supper had been touched; most of it remained on the plate. To the right, Nan's muttering echoed out of the hallway leading to her tiny bedroom.

Mama hadn't slept the first night Da failed to come back from patrol. When another day passed without any sign of him, she'd donned her traveling clothes and spent the day searching the woods, finding only goblin blood, which Nan collected. The old one had asked every bird and critter she encountered, yet none of them could find the missing guards. It was as if the forest had swallowed them whole.

Now, three days later, Mama appeared to have given up hope. Emma knew what she felt out there; she sensed the hate in the dark.

Only fear that the Banderwigh had returned—for her—kept her from being as upset as Mama.

"Mama?" Emma tiptoed over, resting her hand on the woman's shoulder.

She said nothing, but reached up to grasp Emma's arm and stared at the front door.

Tears knocked on the inside of Emma's eyelids from the expression on her mother's face. Emma knew something was wrong, and moved in front of the chair.

"Mama, you didn't eat anything."

"What has become of your father? None of the men have been found. Not one. No tracks. It's as if they never were."

Emma drew in a breath to answer, but held still. A wash of heavy, frigid air rolled over the floor, growing colder without apparent cause. Numbness spread into her feet and crept up her legs. Dread left her staring without words for a full minute. Emma ran to the edge of the back porch, her sudden sprint startling a gasp from Mama.

A thick mist fell from the trees of Widowswood, surrounding their meadow in a standing wall of white. Her brother and sister ran about among tiny, dancing dots of light—oblivious to the mist approaching from the edges of the meadow. Emma leaned as tall as she could and held her hands to her mouth.

"Tam! Kimber! Come inside."

Kimber slowed her playful run to a trudge, and looked toward the house.

Tam stopped in place, waving his arms. "Did Mama say we hadda come in?"

Emma looked down, curling her toes over the edge of the wood. "No, but I want you to come inside."

He laughed and kept going.

"Tam, please!" She stomped. "Something's wrong. Look at the forest."

Kimber jogged up alongside her. "What's happened?"

It's got Da. Emma gulped and kneaded her dress. "Da's not returned yet. Mama's worried something's happened. I don't like the way the air feels. It's too cold. And that fog."

Kimber twisted to peer at the woods, went wide-eyed, and stepped back to hug her.

The wind picked up, lofting their hair together into a streamer of red and black. Kimber squinted into the breeze, out toward the forest. Emma stepped onto the dirt beyond the porch, but the other girl wouldn't let go. Fear was contagious.

"I don'ae see nothin," said Kimber. "'Cep 'a fog."

"It's not the seeing." Emma cupped her hands to her mouth again, shouting, "Tam! Now!" She took a step back. "It's the feeling."

Kimber squeezed her.

Tam held his arms out to the sides, waving them up and down. "Aww. Why? The sun's not down yet."

"I'm gonna put him in a sack," muttered Emma.

Kimber yelled over Emma's shoulder. "Tam, please come in."

With both girls against him, he hung his head and trudged back to the porch in a winding, unhurried path. At each turn, he balanced on one leg for a moment before nearly falling sideways into the next bit of walking. His expression would've fit being sentenced to a month of nothing but turnips and broccoli. As soon as he came close enough to grab, Emma seized his hand and pulled him into a hug. She pushed him past her onto the porch, and guided her siblings inside with a hand on their backs.

His grumbles stopped at the sight of Mama's forlorn stare. He flopped on the rug by the fireplace to reenact the slaying of Shrub Dragon for the hundredth time. Emma reached up, secured both latches on the back door, and tested it. Confident nothing could break in, she went to the table and cleared the dishes. Kimber helped, and soon, only one untouched plate remained.

Emma crawled into her mother's lap. Her presence seemed to snap the woman out of whatever daze had fogged her mind. Mama brought her arms up and wrapped them about her. Warm breath puffed into Emma's hair, making her smile and cry at the same time.

"Please eat, Mama, you're scaring me," whispered Emma.

Kimber crept closer with hesitant steps, glancing off to the side. Emma shifted to make room and gestured for her to climb up, too. They sat quiet for a while, Emma staring worriedly at her mother while Kimber closed her eyes, basking in the glow of a real family. Emma took a piece of bread from the plate and poked Mama in the lip with it twice.

"Please, eat."

Mama took the bread after stroking her hand over Emma's hair. "You're always trying to take care of everyone."

Emma clung to her, resting her head on Mama's shoulder. "I'm scared, too."

She held both girls close, and sang a few lines from an old lullaby, almost enough to rid Emma of her fear. She hadn't hidden it this time, hoping the instinctual need to comfort a frightened daughter would pull Mama out of her strange sadness.

Minutes later, Mama stopped singing.

Something bugged Emma. Her mother didn't act right, almost as if an unnatural force affected her mind. She hadn't eaten or drank anything unusual, though. Sometimes, she made a special tea for people who had a lot of pain that made them sluggish and drowsy.

Emma reached up and brushed the top of her head. "You got crumbs in my hair."

The fear had returned to Mama's eyes, but the unexpected complaint made her laugh.

"Mama, do you think the Banderwigh came back already? Did it hurt Da?"

"No, Emma. Those things run away from adults." Mama brushed crumbs from Emma's head. "They're only scary to children. Like goblins, they're cowards."

Emma's eyebrows drew together. "Why are you smiling?"

"I'm used to my Emma looking for boring explanations. Attacked by bandits, found someone that needed help, or maybe they got lost."

She stared into the dark corner, her voice a touch above a whisper. "I believe now."

Memories of being trapped in a cage that couldn't open, in a room with no door, unable to reach Tam, watered her eyes. The burned girl's laugh echoed in the back of her mind. Somehow, somewhere, that awful false child knew Da was missing and loved it. It occurred to Emma at that moment she hadn't done anything with the experience but bottle it up inside. She had to hide her emotions to protect her little brother. Mama kissed her on the forehead. Images of the burned village came back to her, and she buried her face against Mama's shoulder and wept, shaking from all the fear she'd kept locked away while sitting in a cage.

"Oh, Em…" Mama rocked her gently. "What's wrong?"

Kimber held her hand.

Emma mumbled past her tears, telling her about the cages and the dreams, about the horrible, evil girl, and about how scared she really had been the whole time. Kimber hid behind the folds of Mama's dress as the story unfolded.

"You were very brave, Emma," said Mama.

She sniffled, looking up. "I didn't believe it. I was only brave 'cause I didn't think it was real."

"No." Mama wiped the tears from her cheek. "You've always looked after your brother. You were strong for him. You're smart, Em. You knew, and you did what you had to in order to protect him."

She let her head down and closed her eyes. The gentle motion of her mother's breathing and reassuring whispers carried her off to sleep.

EMMA AWOKE STILL CURLED IN MAMA'S LAP. IT HAD GROWN DARK, AND without a candle or lantern burning, the house filled with a murk of shadows and moonlight. Not even Nan puttered about. Mama slumped in the chair, head back and mouth open. The arm that had cradled Emma lay on the table, her other limp at her side. Emma shivered and sat up, looking around.

Kimber and Tam had the family bed to themselves and seemed determined to use up the entire area. Both appeared sound asleep with contented expressions. The strange sound of Nan snoring came from the rear hall, and one of the mice had climbed up onto the table, helping himself to the half-eaten bread. He froze as Emma moved. She didn't bother trying to talk to him, too tired to think about magic. Instead, she smiled, hoping the gesture had some meaning to his little mouse brain. The rodent zoomed off the table, crust in mouth, vanishing into the dark. Emma settled against her mother's chest and closed her eyes.

A few minutes later, a metallic rattle broke the silence, like someone trying to break in the back door. Emma's eyes snapped open and she gathered her hands together under her chin, curling into a ball. Drifting curtains sent shadows scurrying about, the fabric glowing like specters.

"Mama?" whispered Emma.

Her mother continued to sleep.

"Mama!" rasped Emma a little louder, trying not to wake her siblings.

She patted her mother on the cheek to no reaction, not even a shift or sleepy mutter. Emma curled tighter, crossing her feet. The rattle again came from the small alcove at the back of the family room. Without the fog of being half asleep, she made sense of the sound—the back door must be open and blowing in the wind. Before any of this happened, she would have grumbled and assumed some*one* went to the privy.

Now, she feared some*thing* had let itself in.

Emma slid out of Mama's lap, seized her by the shoulders, and shook. Her head wobbled about, but aside from continuing to breathe, the woman did nothing. A wave of cold air slid over the floor. Emma shivered, curling her toes. *Nan said I'd be old like her before it came back.* She took a deep breath and smoothed her palms down the front of her dress. *Grow up, Emma.* She padded over to the cabinet, retrieved a small blanket, and carried it back over to cover Mama.

Rattle.

Hands clutched to her stomach, Emma crept to the small alcove by the back door. A shelf of Da's boots lay undisturbed to the right, several cloaks hung on pegs on the left, shifting with the gusts. The door flapped in the wind, creating an ever-changing shape of moonlight on the floor. She swallowed, unable to resist trembling.

A sudden gust whipped the door to the left with a loud *crack* against the outside wall. For a second, she had a clear view of the outhouse, then the house door blew back in the wind and slammed. She jumped and screamed into her hands, trying to muffle herself. Once the shock wore off, she eased forward, one tentative foot into the patch of moonlight, pale skin aglow. She reached out for the handle and took another step. Howling wind drew creaks from the rafters overhead. Emma froze in place, peering up at the roof. The back door rattled in its frame, the breeze trying to tug it open again.

She swallowed.

Another step, arm outstretched.

The shaking door bounced the latch open. It flew wide and clattered shut. *Just the wind. It's only the wind.* Emma slid her left foot forward, teeth chattering from the frigid air clinging close to the floor. Two more steps and she could reach the door. Groaning walls protested the air outside, but despite the solid wood, the chill seemed to blow right through the house.

A shadow to her right moved.

Thunk.

Emma leapt to the left and spun, up on her toes with her back pressed to the wall among the cloaks. Da's shortsword, in its scabbard, had fallen over. She sank flat on her feet, the warmth of a blush spreading over her face. *Only a darn sword falling. Grow up, Emma!* She stooped to pick it up, and leaned it back against the wall where Da kept it. She took a casual step toward the door and reached for the handle, but it whipped open as if avoiding her, and smacked against the wall outside.

She stared over her milky fingers, lit ghostly blue in the moonlight, still poised to grab the latch. Too scared to scream or even breathe, she stood still as a statue, waiting for the wind to slam the door. The winding trail of stones between the house and the privy made her remember *that* night. The frigid air swirled around her legs, freezing her from head to toe as though she didn't even have a nightdress on. A brush of chill reminded her of the outhouse's purpose. She pressed her knees together and pouted at it. The more she didn't want to walk outside, the more urgent her need to use it became.

The wind refused to close the door again despite a few minutes of determined staring. Emma let her arm down and scowled, then whined at having to pee. If she hadn't dropped the chamber pot down the privy, she'd have used it instead of leaving the safety of the house, but she had no choice. *The Banderwigh's gone. I'm being a scared little child.* Jaw clenched, she backed away from the door, stooped, and grasped the shortsword. The weight made it awkward and heavy, but far less so than the broadsword. Then again, grown men didn't often use swords longer than they stood tall. To her, the shortsword looked about the same size as the broadsword in Da's hand.

Emma tried to connect the feeling of the weapon in her hand with Nan's tale of Princess Isabelle. This thing seemed so unwieldy in comparison to the way Nan described the swordfight. Curious, she grabbed the scabbard in her other hand and pulled at the handle. The blade came free with a metal *scrape* that sent a shiver down her back and brought goosebumps to her arms. She let the sheath slip off and hit the floor with a surprising *bang* given the deep silence in the house. Emma jumped, even though she'd expected the noise. With both hands on the grip, she held the shortsword out in front of her. Moonlight from the open door flashed pale blue over the shiny silver blade. The edge glinted sharp and deadly. Da might give her a whack on the bum for taking it out of the sheath, but she would gladly suffer getting in trouble if it would bring him home.

Her lip started to quiver at how much she missed him, but she couldn't surrender to crying while something *creepy* roamed around. Emma put her sadness aside. Step by tedious step, she advanced out onto the back porch, whirling at every shadow with the little sword raised.

This is stupid. I shouldn't go alone.

She stepped off the porch and cringed the instant her bare foot landed upon the freezing stone path.

Mama won't wake up. She's exhausted. I can't bother Nan, and Tam and Kimber need to stay safe.

Sword held out, she crept down the path to the privy, wondering where the warmth of early summer had run off to. When she made it a little past halfway, a loud *crack* broke the silence behind her. With a shriek, Emma whirled to face the house, her foot slipping on wet stone. She sprawled in the grass, staring at the house door—slammed in the wind. Gasping for breath, she leapt upright, shortsword wobbling in her trembling arms. Terrified she would hear a twig snap or see the Banderwigh come out of the dark, she sprinted to the house.

The door opened easily.

Emma fell against the wall to the right of the door, back pressed to the house, still winded. She clutched the shortsword to her chest, her hard breathing puffing fog on the shiny metal. Eventually, urgency pushed her into motion again. She avoided the stone path, running over grass to the outhouse. She leapt in, slammed the door, and flicked the lock. Feeling momentarily safe, she let the sword hang limp at her side and spent a few minutes breathing hard. When her heart no longer hammered in her ears, she took a seat, keeping the sword nearby.

Soft *thuds* came from her heels tapping the front of the bench. The whole privy shack swayed in the breeze. She gazed up at the cobweb-infested roof, begging Uruleth in her mind not to let the thing collapse. Finally, her nerves settled enough and she tried to go as fast as possible.

Soon after she finished, the strangest sense that something stood on the other side of the wall came over her. A mere inch of wood between her and *something.*

Too scared to make a sound, she waited, still sitting, blade held high—for about twenty minutes.

Nothing happened.

Emma eased herself to her feet and crept to the door, peering out the gap between door and wall. Moonlit grass, a rocky path, and an empty porch waited for her. She teased her fingers at the lock. Her sense that something watched her hadn't lessened. Her legs hurt, her feet had gone numb a long time ago, and her teeth wouldn't stop chattering.

It's summer. It shouldn't be this cold.

She cried in frustration, unable to come up with any explanation for what was happening, other than the monster. Da was missing, Mama wouldn't wake up, and she doubted Nan would hear her if she screamed over the wind. Also, if Emma made too much noise, Tam or Kimber would wake. Frustrated and worried, she bit her fingers.

It wants Kimber. It wants me to scream so she comes to see.

Emma gripped the freezing iron latch. In her mind, she flung the door open and there stood the Banderwigh, ready to grab her. She grabbed the shortsword in both hands again, pointing it at the locked door.

"Da," she whimpered, afraid to even yell for help.

The back door rattled in the distance.

Emma cringed, eyes closed. *There's nothing between the monster and my family. I have to close the door.*

She flung the latch open and burst into a run. In seconds, she slipped in the wet grass, but managed to keep her balance, flailing her arms while skidding to an ungraceful halt. Emma stared down, wide-eyed at the strip of moonglow in her hands—the gleaming edge of the shortsword.

If I fall on this, I'll die.

She tilted the sword, using it as a mirror to look behind her, dreading she'd see a huge, hairy shadow looming over her—but nothing stood behind her but sky. Emma exhaled in relief and looked back at empty field and dark trees. With the sword held out to the side, she made her way toward the house in a constant spin, watching out for anything trying to sneak up on her from every angle. Step by agonizing step, she crept to the porch, slipped inside, and pulled the door closed. She stood there watching Mama sleep in the chair by the table for a moment before turning to lock the door. After a test rattle, she took a step back and exhaled.

The board beneath her shifted from something creeping up behind her. Her heart pounded. She squeezed the handle of the shortsword, preparing to spin with it...

"Haveta pee," said Tam, two steps behind her.

Emma whirled, leaping backward against the door. The sword tumbled out of her grip when she clamped both hands over her chest and gasped for air. Tam tilted his head at her in confusion. Once she realized what he said—that she had to go *back* outside—she shivered.

"Be careful." He pointed down.

She looked. The sword had stuck into the floor, an inch shy of her foot.

23

A PLEA FROM THE DARK

*P*oke.

Emma grumbled, barely managing to swat a hand at something prodding her cheek.

Poke.

Emma's eyes fluttered open and focused on a blurry shape in front of her face—Tam's foot. She scrunched up her nose and pushed his leg away. Kimber's arm flopped over her from behind, the girl's sleep-breath puffing at the back of her neck. The room remained dark. Emma snuggled into the covers, shut her eyes, and wanted this strange night to be over.

"Emma?" called Da, his voice distant and echoing.

At first, Emma thought she'd slipped back into a dream. She burrowed deeper into the bedding.

"I need you, Emma," said Da.

Shivering, she opened her eyes again, staring at the plain brown wall inches in front of her face. *I'm dreaming.*

"Emma?" called Da.

She bit her lip. Clearly, she heard his voice and couldn't be asleep. Gingerly, she plucked Kimber's arm from her side and draped it over the girl's chest before sitting up and rubbing her face. Mama still slept in the chair by the table. Nan's odd snoring continued from the inner hall. Emma listened to silence, dreading the rattle of a door opening at any second. A moment or four of being awake should prove the voice to be coming from her mind.

"Emma?" asked Da, sounding like he stood on the back porch.

"Liam?" muttered Mama, a soft moan in her sleep.

The air seemed warmer, as it should be in the middle of summer. She crawled out from under the blanket, then over Kimber as carefully as possible. Emma sat on the edge of the bed, toes not touching the floor, but close enough to sense the chill in the wood. She stretched and yawned. Her eyes wanted to close again. She wobbled back and forth for a few minutes, fighting the urge to fall over backward and pass out.

"Emma…" called Da, his voice urgent.

Trembling, she slid from the bed and wandered to the table. "D-Da?"

Silence.

She spun in a slow search of the room, looking for anything out of place.

"Emma?" called the voice. "I need you."

She rushed into the alcove and climbed up to stand on the shelf of boots so she could peer out the little window. The meadow behind the house appeared empty, not even fireflies moved about. Her breath fogged at the glass as she leaned close, gazing left and right.

"I'm dreaming."

"Emma, I need you," said Da.

The beckoning voice sounded as though it came from the distant trees, was too loud to be real, too loud to come from a man too far away to see. Emma climbed down to the floor and grasped the latch, but decided against opening the door. Outside, the wind gathered strength, howling and whispering over the forest. A thick blanket of cold air seeped under the door and lapped at her toes. She backed away, breathing faster and faster.

Don't be stupid.

She ran to her mother, grabbing her dangling arm and shaking it.

"Mama, Mama, wake up. I hear Da."

Emma pulled, shook, and whined, but her mother didn't wake.

"Mama!" Emma pushed at her shoulder. "Mama, wake up!" Emma trembled; she couldn't understand how the woman remained sleeping. Fear and desperation overwhelmed her and she screamed, "Wake up!" while slapping her across the face.

Emma recoiled, ashamed of herself for hitting her mother.

The woman lay limp as a corpse.

Mama didn't budge as Emma shrieked, stomped, and kicked at the chair. Neither did the other two children. The house hung in deathly quiet except for the moan of the wind outside and Emma's heavy breathing. She darted over to the bed and pulled Kimber up into a sitting position, then shook her by the shoulders, but her head wobbled about like a rag doll. Emma eased her back down and jostled Tam, going so far as to put her icy foot against his bare back. The boy didn't even mutter in his sleep.

"Emma, there isn't time," said Da. "Your mother can't help you now."

Tears gathered in the corners of her eyes as she shot a pained look at the door. She couldn't tell if the voice really came from Da or if some evil spirit wanted to trick her. *What if it is him? Does Da have a spirit animal?*

After a final pleading stare at her sleeping mother, she rushed to Nan's bedroom. It had only enough space for a modest bed and one chest of drawers. Black-feathered talismans hung all over the walls, mixed with wooden beads and shining polished stones on cords. Any one of them could potentially be helpful, but Nan hadn't taught her much of anything except how to talk to a mouse. Emma launched herself onto the bed, bouncing and shaking the old woman. Nan continued to snore.

"Nan! Wake up! Something's the matter."

Emma drew her arm back, but stopped. *I can't slap Nan.* She fell over her grandmother, shaking her and clinging at the same time.

"The old one cannot help you either," said Da, the ghostly voice no louder or softer than before.

"Nan, Nan, wake up! Please."

"…returned. Magical sleep…" Nan's arm lifted, clawed the air, and fell limp. "Too strong against someone so old."

"Emma… I'm dying," said Da.

Crying, Emma slid off the bed and went into the main room, wiping her face on her sleeve. She changed from her nightdress into the one Nan had made, feeling a bit braver and warmer for wearing it. Her favorite garment stopped above her knees, much shorter than the nightgown. It shouldn't feel warmer.

Emma's eyes widened. *Did Nan put magic in it?*

From the forbidden cabinet, Emma took the two healing elixirs she'd helped make, stuffed them in a pouch, and swiped Nan's dagger. A length of rope from the pile of stuff by the front door became a belt, from which she hung both items.

"Emma, hurry," said Da.

"This is stupid." Emma ground her foot into the rug. "It's trying to trick me."

Da whispered on the wind. "Em, please. You're my only hope."

She brought her hands to her face, covering her mouth and nose. Da sounded so desperate, it hurt to think about ignoring him. Mama didn't respond to metal pots banged together or a half-cup of water poured on her. Emma set the empty glass on the table and glared at the door. Her fright simmered into anger. The monster had hurt Da, and it did something to her entire family to make them sleep.

"Emma," said Da. "Hurry."

"Leave them alone," growled Emma.

She leaned up and kissed her mother on the cheek. "I love you, Mama." She went to the bed and tucked her siblings in, giving them each a pat on the head. "I love you, Tam. You, too, Kimber."

Neither child so much as moved. Emma gasped at seeing her brother so still. She grasped his shoulders and shook him, harder than last time. He had always been a light sleeper. Not until she leaned over him and warm breath caressed her cheek did panic shrink away to anger. He was alive, but something kept him asleep.

Magic…

Emma balled her hands into fists and glared at the nearest window.

With one hand on the dagger at her hip, she backed away to the alcove by the door and lingered in the corner, watching her family sleep. The soft howling wind gave way to quiet. Emma gripped the dagger handle and rushed outside before the dread of never seeing them again could change her mind.

An unrelenting wind blew sideways at her as Emma ran across the meadow. Patches of winter chill mixed with the summer air, until she entered the forest and everything became cold. Once inside Widowswood, she slowed to a brisk walk, keeping her gaze on the vines and roots crisscrossing her path. She knew enough to avoid stepping on the more painful bad plants. Every so often, her father would call out, keeping her moving.

"Emma, this way…"

Da's voice led her deep into Widowswood. Emma gazed up past shifting branches at scraps of starlight leaking between the pines. Small shapes she hoped were birds zipped back and forth. Each time he called out, she turned a little toward where the voice came from. A constant rustle of wavering branches came from overhead, though no wind reached her. Anger and fear seesawed in her heart. A fast-moving shadow on the left made her jump. She scowled at it, lost her nerve, and shied away from the darkness around her.

If the Banderwigh came back, it would have gotten me by now.

Emma's concern for her father had led her too far into the trees to see her way back home. In the night forest, every direction looked the same. A shiver ran down her body at the realization she *couldn't* go back. She could only follow a disembodied voice that might or might not belong to Da's ghost. If not the monster, what could've put her family in such a sleep she couldn't wake them?

"Emma, please hurry," said Da.

She startled at the sudden break in the quiet; the time between his pleas had grown longer and longer. The voice was louder—she hoped that meant she was close.

"Da!" she yelled, breaking into as much of a run as the foliage would allow.

Her pouch of potions bounced against her thigh as she cracked and crunched across the undergrowth. A glint flashed in the woods up ahead. She headed toward it, grabbing and pulling low-hanging vines and branches out of her way. After a short trek, strange shapes, rounded huts too small to be real, emerged from the darkness, as if someone had made a village for children. The tiny buildings tilted at odd angles, almost spherical with misshapen windows and doors. The area had too much light to be illuminated by the moons alone, given the thick trees overhead. An eerie glow hung in the air, a nightmare into which she had walked.

Awful smells blanketed the miniature village, burned meat mixed with the stink of an outhouse at high noon. Emma slowed to a creep, covering her nose while wandering among the squat dwellings. She followed a hint of a dirt footpath around a squat, rounded house, and stopped short at the sight of goblins—dozens of them—all dead. She stepped on something she mistook for a thick branch, but it felt squishy. She looked down.

A severed goblin arm.

Emma swallowed the urge to scream, backpedaling to get away from it, squealing after a few steps when she put her right foot down in cold, thick slime that squeezed between her toes. Her leg sank up to the shin in the foulest-feeling substance she had ever touched. The fragrance of rotting fruit and dead bodies rose up from a tiny pit full of sticky purple ooze that had been concealed with a dusting of loose grass and dirt. She shivered in disgust and tried to pull her foot out, but couldn't move it. The effort made her fall over forward, catching herself on her hands and one knee.

"Eww!" she wailed, clutching handfuls of dirt and coughing at the horrible stink.

A mass of flies, which had dispersed at the disturbance of her stepping on their meal, settled back down on the jelly, as well as her leg. The sensation of bugs crawling on her, combined with the glue-like ooze and the stench almost brought her dinner up. She tugged at her leg, gasping in pain when the substance refused to release its grip on her skin. Emma tried to hold her breath, grabbing the grass and straining to drag herself away from the hole, but no matter how hard she pulled, the gummy mess wouldn't let go of her foot.

She refused to shout, fearing more goblins might be nearby in the darkness. Her free foot slipped over grass as she tried to push herself away from the gummy snare. She wound up spinning all the way around in a circle, looking for something to grab. Growling, she clawed fistfuls of dirt out of the ground, still unable to overpower the awfulness that held her trapped. If there had been any goblins, they would have made short work of her by now.

Emma collapsed, out of breath, close to giving up and screaming for help. When she rolled onto her back to sit up, the dagger's handle jabbed her in the ribs. A wide grin spread over her face. *Ooh!* She wobbled as upright as she could with one foot in a pit, drew the ten-inch blade from its sheath, and held it in both hands over her head. After a confidence-building breath, she tried to jump forward, but the glue held her to the ground. She fell flat on her chest with the dagger buried to the hilt in the dirt at the end of her arms' length. Stunned by landing so hard on her chest, Emma wheezed and gasped. Once she caught her breath, she hammered the end of the dagger, driving it all the way to the hilt in the dirt. Then, she grabbed it in both hands and pulled. Grunting became yowling as the foul substance peeled away from her skin, but she kept pulling, determined to free herself.

Finally, the adhesive let go and she scooted forward with a sudden slide. Emma lay still for a moment, cringing in pain. Involuntary tears leaked from her eyes; it felt as if the goo had ripped all the skin off her foot. It took her a moment to build up the courage to look. Aside from bits of errant grass and a thin layer of purple slime from mid-shin down, her leg appeared unhurt. She stood, easing her weight onto the tender foot and cringing at the feeling of her toes stuck together. The awful smell followed her. She limped, trying to wipe the stickiness off on the grass.

A short distance away, a boot that looked like it belonged to one of the town watch stuck out of a similar hole. She wobbled over to it, relieved to find it didn't belong to Da. She knew better than to waste her strength trying to pull it out.

Traps?

Emma looked around. She decided to grab a stick and test any patch of earth with a poke before putting her foot down. Bit by bit, she walked around chunks of goblin. Most and been cut open and loose arms and legs lay scattered around. Her last meal churned and flipped in her gut at the fragrance of dead things in the air. A thought came to her on the way through the carnage, hitting her like a bucket of early morning river water. What if the voice belonged to Da's ghost? Had their patrol found this goblin village and been killed? Might he lay wounded somewhere?

The Banderwigh might not have anything to do with this at all.

Oh, no... Mama...

"Da!"

Her shout startled some birds airborne, but other than her voice echoing back, she received no reply. She repeated the call several more times while exploring the goblin village. Near a hut that still smoldered, a human's broadsword lay abandoned. She ran to it and squatted, unable to tell if it had belonged to Da or one of the guardsmen. Unlike her brother, she never had any interest in swords, and couldn't recall if his looked different from the others. Tam had rattled on to no end about how nice a blade Da carried. This one looked plain and functional—she wished for that to be a good sign.

Dread gripped her heart as she touched her fingers to the bare steel. The blade was unstained by green or red blood, dirtied only by a clod of soil. Several flies following the stink of the purple goo landed on her foot, but she didn't care.

"Da!" she yelled.

No voice responded.

I'm too late.

Crouched in the dark, alone and lost, Emma covered her face and wept.

END OF MISERY

"*W*hat your leaky eye?" snapped a voice, high-pitched and gurgling.

Startled, Emma jumped, and fell back seated. She looked around, wiping her tears. "Who's there?"

"Mealy bits talks," said a goblin-pitched voice behind a rotund dwelling.

She stood and crept to peer around the side of the crude building made of bundled sticks. About fifteen paces from where the broadsword lay, a goblin sat with his back propped up against a stack of firewood. Were he standing, the creature would have been about the same height as her. His potbellied body had to be twice or three times her weight. Uncountable wrinkles and swollen pustules covered his dark green skin. A brown leather sash crossed his chest, supporting an empty shortsword-sized scabbard dangling around a skirt made of animal furs. Green blood leaked from cuts all over him and one of his burlap boots was missing. More hair grew upon his eyebrows and toe-knuckles than atop his head.

The goblin sniffed the air, licking at his teeth. "Mmm. Smell like eats."

"I'm not food. I'm a girl."

He laughed, spewing green slime and blood between rotten teeth. "Girl food gooder." Evil gleamed in yellow eyes. "Sweeter is meat when it cooked scared!"

She cringed. "You're awful!"

The goblin raised his elongated, narrow nose and inhaled with a delighted smile. Nostril flaps puffed out with three distinct breaths. His voice weakened to a hissing half-whisper. "Smell scared. Smell tasty." He clawed a three-fingered hand in a beckoning motion. "Me die soon." He coughed. "Come, let smell tasty before go dark."

"No. You're horrible!"

She glared at the wounded creature, confident he couldn't even stand. Emma inched around the hut into view, clenching the dagger handle at her hip. The goblin waved his head back and forth, eyes sliding half closed while continuing to sniff the air. He bit his lower lip, inflating a blister. Tears of joy welled in his eyes, and he brought his bony, green hands together.

"Why are you looking at me like that?"

"So sweet! Me not ever see such yummy!" He squealed. "Best than maggotberry pie!" He poked one finger to his chin. "Even best than cowhorn custard."

The goblin struggled to reach forward, tongue thrust from his mouth in an attempt to lick her despite the distance. Emma cringed, halting a few steps away and yanking her dagger from its sheath.

"Hey!" He pressed himself back into the firewood, a trace of voice returned to his whispery rasp. "No sharp! No sharp!"

"I'll not let you eat me. I'm a person, not food." She furrowed her brow. "I didn't know goblins could talk."

The goblin grasped his cheeks, mouth agape. "Food! It talk!"

Emma fumed. She considered stabbing him, but didn't want to get close enough. Out of the corner of her eye, she caught sight of a spear and put the dagger away. The goblin-made weapon, much smaller than human spears, was the perfect length and balance for a smallish ten-year-old. She hefted the weapon, pointed the tip at the nauseating creature, and stomped over.

"No!" he wailed.

"You eat children!" she yelled. "You're horrible!"

"Not want!"

She let the point droop, giving the creature a distrustful glower.

"Have to! Bigs too hard to catch." The goblin offered a cheesy smile, shrugged, and chuckled. Bright green slime dribbled off his chin.

Emma pulled the spear back and closed her eyes.

"No! Begs. No sharp!"

"If you were not mostly dead, you'd be trying to kill and eat me," she snapped. "Why should I feel the least bit sorry for you?"

Not that she would admit it, but she *did* feel a sorry for the pathetic thing. He would have to make her much angrier to be able to kill a defenseless creature, even a goblin.

"Me hurted. No danger." He pointed at her pouch. "You brings magics. I smells."

The goblin reached toward her again and she slapped his arm aside with the spear. "Those are for someone else. Do you think I'm stupid? You'll just try and hurt me after."

"Promises!" The goblin clutched at the leather weapon harness across his chest. "Promises, no!"

She held the point to the goblin's chest. "I don't trust goblins. Da said only barristers lie worse'n goblins. You're only going to trick me."

He grabbed the end of the spear as she went to shove it forward, but her lack of conviction and his advantage in strength made the gesture futile. For a moment, they played tug of war. Emma's hair thrashed wild about her face as she struggled. She raised a leg to brace a foot on his chest, but leapt back with a high-pitched squeal when he tried to grab her ankle.

"You wants your da?" The goblin narrowed his eyes. "Me having the knows."

"What do you know?" She pulled at the spear, toes digging into the dirt.

He let go without warning, causing her to fall on her rear end. "Me knows where."

Emma scrambled upright, jabbing at the air around the goblin's head. "Where is Da? What happened here?"

"Not doing the saying." The goblin folded his arms. "Magics first."

She glanced down at the pouch, at the healing elixirs she had brought in case Da needed them. "He might be hurt. Tell me if he was hurt."

"You having the pigs?" The goblin's right eye widened into an amber pool. "Food's food?"

"I am not something to be eaten!" She swung the spear over his head, more to vent anger than hit him.

"Does you knowing one pig from da other?" The goblin coughed up blood. "Alls sames."

Emma trembled with anger. Her pity faded fast. "So, you're saying you don't know which one of the humans was my father?"

"Tasty smart."

She shrieked and charged with her spear aimed low. The goblin wailed and swung an arm sideways, deflecting the point into the firewood pile. Emma stalled in a forward lean, enough weight supported by her grip on the spear that to release it would cause her to fall onto the goblin. She let her knees go forward, dropping her on her backside into a roll. The goblin swiped at her, one fingernail claw tearing a scrap of cloth from the hem of her dress. Her heart pounded in her head as she sprawled wordless, watching him sniff and lick the tatter like an expensive chocolate. The pleased moans and whimpers coming from the hideous thing made her sick.

She grabbed the dagger, drawing it while the creature distracted himself with the scrap of fabric. Emma stood but managed only a single step before yellow eyes as big as her fist shifted to gaze at her.

"Wants da, gives magics." The goblin put a hand on the spear, pushing it to the ground. "No sharp."

Frustration, anger, and worry kept her silent. The woods chirped with the sounds of night: insects, birds, and the occasional rustle of something small moving about. Emma stared at the injured creature, bleeding from dozens of minor cuts.

"Promises. Give magics, me gives da. Me no cooks."

"You just tried to grab me!"

"Closes. Too tasty. Hads to. Me not promises then."

She squeezed the dagger handle. "Y-you w-won't cook me if I help you?"

"Food having the knowing!"

She scowled. "I am not food!" she screamed, voice echoing in the trees.

The goblin chuckled. Pea-green blood leaked around teeth the color of moldy butter. "Wants your bigs? Yes?"

Emma reached a hand into the pouch, grasping one of the two flasks. Against her instincts, she took a step closer. The goblin's eye twitched. Drool leaked from the corner of a widening smile. Another step. The goblin lunged forward, grabbing her with man-sized hands that looked out of place on such small arms. He pinned her elbows to her sides and lifted her on tiptoe.

"Me gots!"

"Y-you're not really hurt!" Emma screamed and squirmed, her kicks only made him laugh louder. "You said you wouldn't cook me."

"Me won'ts." He pulled her closer so she couldn't kick, and wiped his nose across her chest to inhale her scent. The shudder of joy in his body horrified her. His eyes flared open with a greedy gleam. "Me eats raw."

"You promised!"

He lifted her off the ground, bouncing her like a favored treat. "Goblin promise!"

She writhed, kicking at his legs. "You lied!"

The yellow grin widened. "Goblin promise!"

Emma grunted and gasped, unable to wriggle out of the creature's grip. He was as strong as Da, perhaps stronger, and his claw-like fingernails came close to drawing blood at the small of her back. Twice, she tried to stab him in the belly with the dagger still in her right hand, but couldn't reach. The goblin looked around, trying to figure out how to stand without letting go of her.

"Help!" she yelled.

The goblin cackled and tried to lick her face. Emma leaned back.

She couldn't get her foot up to push him away, and had nowhere to go. The instant dread won over disgust, she swung her head forward, smashing the flailing tongue against the goblin's four remaining teeth. She wanted nothing more than to wipe the horrid slime off her forehead, but he kept her arms pinned.

He wobbled, dazed, and let loose an eerie howl, trying to push his tongue up off the fang sticking through it. A single tear ran down his rough, green cheek while he strained. At long last, the writhing tongue popped loose and he sagged with relief, blood running down his chin. After two breaths, a terrifying anger warped his face.

"Now me eats legs first! Makes food watch!"

Emma wrenched herself to the left, stabbing sideways and sinking an inch of blade in the creature's forearm. He yelped and let go with that hand. She landed on her feet, and tried to pull away. The goblin held on, squeezing so hard she expected her arm to snap. She swapped the knife to her free hand and slashed in wild strokes at the huge hand still gripping her from armpit to elbow. The goblin recoiled in time to avoid a cut, letting go. She traded the dagger back to her right, backpedaling while using her dress to wipe tongue-slime from her forehead.

With a gurgling roar, the goblin grabbed the spear and lumbered after her. Emma backed up, casting hesitant glances at the ground, wary of another glue trap. After three steps, she found herself more afraid of stepping in another glue trap with a live goblin nearby than the idea of trying to kill one. He didn't even stand as tall as Rydh Cooper, and she'd thumped him good. Emma glanced at the dagger. Killing was a lot worse than thumping, but the goblin didn't give her much choice. She wanted to run, but one misplaced step in a glue snare would be the end of her.

She held her ground, raising the trembling knife out to the side. Her body shook, her mouth went dry, and the sound of her breathing drowned out the goblin's yowls. The urge to call for Da tightened the lump in her throat, but it gave her an idea. She took a deep breath and let out a lupine howl that sounded like a wounded pup.

The goblin raised the spear, tilting his head in confusion at her sudden aggressive pose. He smiled, and came storming up to her in an ungainly waddle, teeth bared and spear raised.

"Me likes stupid foods. No have ta runs."

Emma gripped the dirt with her toes and stared at the tip of the spear moving toward her. She'd let it swing first, duck, and get in close, like Da taught the guards. Her knuckles turned white on the dagger handle. She stopped breathing as the creature came within striking distance. At the last second before Emma flung herself into a desperate attack, a look of complete dread washed over the pudgy menace. Not a full second later, the goblin's skin went from green to grey. The spear clattered to the ground as he flailed his arms in an effort to shield his face. After a wheeze, his eyes rolled up into his head and he fell over backward.

Emma glanced at her dagger with a raised eyebrow. If not for the change of color, she would have thought the creature's inexplicable collapse another 'goblin promise.' She crept closer and poked him with her toe. The body had already become cold.

Dead.

Dead and nearly frozen.

Widowswood had gone quiet. Not a single bird or cricket chirped.

"Emma," said Da, right behind her.

Something did *not* feel right. The voice made her skin crawl. Too slow, too deep, too cruel. She squeezed and released the dagger's leather-wrapped handle. Even the wind seemed to hold its breath.

Her hair slid over her shoulders as she turned and stared up into the glowing eyes of the Banderwigh.

ANOTHER KIND OF TAKING

Goosebumps crept over Emma's arms. Scared mute, she backed away from the silhouette of a shaggy man, taller than Da, face shadowed save for two hollow eyes of pale amber. The silver-blue head of a giant two-handed axe strapped to his back gleamed bright. Old and weathered, the wooden handle looked like a thick tree branch worn polished by many years of use.

Emma glanced at her dagger, and put it back in the sheath hanging from the rope around her waist. It wouldn't help her. She stood as firm as her shivering body could, amazed at herself for the show of courage.

"I'm not afraid of you. You won't make me sad."

The Banderwigh slung the axe from his back, shining blade swinging in an arc past the ground with a heavy *whoosh* before his other hand caught the shaft by the head. Emma couldn't help but stare at the gleaming metal. He held the weapon sideways across his waist, knuckles creaking, and took a step closer.

"I won't let you hurt my family!" Emma leaned toward him, trying to project anger. "Stop making them sleep!"

Cold surrounded the once-man, a biting chill drawing all warmth from everything near him. He stopped close enough for the needle-like chill to rake over her front, and looked down at her.

"I know you won't hurt me. You just want to eat my sadness." Emma pointed at his face. "Go away!"

A noise welled up from within him, at first, indistinct from the wind, but it grew into a howl of pure hatred. He reared back, raising the axe. Emma's courage faltered—she scrambled away. A roar of fury ripped the air, chasing birds from trees. She shrieked and flung herself to the ground.

Skiff.

Mirror appeared in front of her face in the blink of an eye. Emma shuddered at her reflection on the axe head embedded in the ground four inches from her nose. The scent of moist dirt filled her nostrils. She flattened her palms on the ground, not moving until the shiny blade pulled away, rising into the air with clods of soil falling from the sides. Emma rolled over and crawled across mulch, too panicked to stand. A slow, ponderous *whoosh* preceded another loud *crack*, announcing the death of a small tree inches behind her.

"Eep!" She rolled over into a half-sit, pointing. "Y-you're j-just t-trying to scare—"

Her words became screams when he swung the axe at her again. She jumped back a second before the blade *thumped* into the earth between her knees, slicing the hem of her dress.

She put a hand over her heart, where the blade would have landed if she hadn't moved. The Banderwigh grunted; the obvious effort taken to dislodge the weapon from the ground said it all. He didn't want to abduct her again.

He wanted revenge.

Emma scurried away in a reverse crabwalk, then flipped over and crawled. After the axe *whooshed* over her again, she lurched upright and ran heedless of the threat of glue traps in her panic. At the end of the goblin village, she crossed her arms in front to absorb whipping vines and aimed for small gaps between trees. Forcing him to go around tight spaces bought her a little safety in distance, but he kept chasing her.

Trees shot by on both sides. Twigs, branches, and pinecones splintered and crunched behind her, accompanied by the occasional grunt and *swoosh* of a blade. A faint nip at her trailing hair finally pulled a scream free from her lungs and gave her a surge of speed. She hit a tree head-on, catching her weight with both hands and flinging herself around the trunk not two seconds before the axe dug into the wood with a *crack*. She didn't slow down to watch him wrest it loose, and sprinted along the path of an inch-deep creek until the tromp of heavy boots rushed up behind her, drowning out the splash of her feet in the water.

Blinded by terror, she veered to the right and raced toward a fallen tree, jumping over it. No air remained in her lungs to scream with when she found open space on the far side. Emma flailed her arms and legs on a brief fall, then hit the soft, wet earth, tumbling into a logroll down a steep, root-studded incline. Over and over she rolled, finding almost every gnarl or rock on the way. At the bottom, she curled in a ball with her hands over her belly.

"Owowowowow," she wailed.

Dirt fell on her legs. She flipped onto her back, staring up at the ridge she'd fallen from, some twenty feet up the hill. The Banderwigh stood on the other side of the dead tree, glaring down at her. Her pain vanished under a new wave of fear. Emma dragged herself over to a three-foot tall stump, which she used to pull herself upright. A roar echoed overhead. She spun to stare at the ridge, but the Banderwigh had vanished. Motion in the air drew her stunned gaze straight up.

The Banderwigh careened in an arc, axe over his head, falling straight at her.

Her legs gave out. She fell hard on her seat with her back to the dead tree. Tattered bear-fur robes awash with arctic cold surrounded her in time with a deafening *crunch* above and behind her. Emma slid forward, shrinking away from the axe, winding up almost lying on her back between the monster's boots. The blade had split more than halfway down the length of the ancient stump.

The Banderwigh stood over her, his tattered rags surrounding her like an impenetrable cage of magical ice.

"P-please, don't." Emma tried to force herself to move, but her body would only shake. "Y-you were a man once. You're not evil."

Uncontrolled rage seemed to dull, and the faintest trace of pupils appeared within the baleful yellow light in his eyes. Emma's terror lessened ever so slightly. *Nan was right!* She forced herself to flash a nervous smile.

"It's the axe. It's cursed!"

Emma extended a hand to touch him, but recoiled from the painful chill, cowering against the wood.

The Banderwigh tilted his head as if he no longer knew what to think of her. She held her hands up, hopeful. As if wounded by her hope, he screamed in anger. Rage warped his face, devouring the trace of humanity in his eyes. He thrashed at the handle, attempting to dislodge the axe.

Emma scrambled to her side and up onto all fours. With splinters falling on her from above, she fought her instincts and leapt at his cloak, swatting it aside like a heavy curtain. Furs brushed her skin, coating the backs of her arms in frost. Ignoring the burning cold, she barged past and sprinted in a random direction. The crunching of wood and loud growling grew distant behind her. Minutes later, her run staggered to a walk. Her chest burned from breathing so hard. The forest here looked little different from anywhere else. Cloaked in the thick of night, Widowswood offered no clues as to which way led home.

Sweat ran down her face. Exhaustion and terror wracked her with shivers. She reached out to grasp a tree, coming to a halt and leaning on it. *I should hide.* With a stifled grunt, she pushed off and trudged. Her legs ached and her feet hurt, but she forced herself onward. A clearing by a giant fallen tree contained the remnants of an abandoned campfire, long burned out, where a small pack sat propped up against the fetid wood. Emma hurried over and discovered the fallen log to be hollow, with enough room inside for her to fit. It seemed as good a place as any to seek shelter. She knelt by the pack and opened it to find a waterskin embedded in a mass of bug-infested beige mush that had once been some kind of food. The substance had rotted to the point she couldn't tell if it had been grain or meat. Maggots and beetles fell away from the leather when she lifted the waterskin out of the foul-smelling muck. She uncorked it and sniffed, jerking her face away from a pungent, sour smell. Despite being parched, she knew drinking this would make her sick. Still, the tainted water proved useful to wash the sticky residue of the goblin's trap off her leg. With that done, she gazed up at the stars, feeling lost and alone.

Before the Banderwigh could reappear, she crawled to the end of the dead tree and peeked inside. Termite grooves lined the interior, running among dozens of shelf mushrooms that also covered most of the outside. The fungus added an earthy fragrance to the wet wood. A hollow, damp log would be a far cry from her warm bed at home, but it would have to do. She would never find her way back in the middle of the night.

Emma got one hand inside the damp mulch before the snapping of twigs startled her chest full of air. Two glowing yellow spots approached in the dark. She wanted to cry, but couldn't. How could she hide from a monster that magically knew wherever she went? Emma forced herself up on protesting legs and scrambled off in an ungainly run.

"Da!" she wheezed, her attempt at a yell scratched out of her dry throat as a whisper.

The Banderwigh moved among the trees like a living shadow, unhindered by the dense growth that scratched at her legs and tugged at her dress. She grasped at low-hanging foliage, tearing it out of her way to navigate the thickening forest. The hiss of an axe slicing the air made her shriek and duck into a turn. A tough vine caught her across the instep, tripping her into a stumble that she barely prevented from becoming a pratfall.

Her body neared the point of quitting. She couldn't keep running much longer. *Maybe if it gets me, my family will be safe?*

Emma glanced over her shoulder, thoughts of sacrifice in her mind. The horrible stare he gave her tugged at a survival instinct more primal than reason, and she forgot everything, even her own name. Only getting away mattered.

A burbling noise ahead offered the promise of escape. Some of Nan's faerie monsters hated rivers. Emma couldn't remember which ones refused to cross running water, but the idea offered more hope than she'd had a moment before. She ran across a wide dirt trail, in her panic not realizing it until she'd gone six steps into the brush on the far side. Skidding to a halt, she put her back to a tree. The Banderwigh reached her in seconds, axe poised. Emma waited for the swing and flung herself to the ground, cringing at the resonating *crack* of metal on wood. She crawled under his arms and scrambled upright again. A few seconds' reprieve came as he worked the weapon free, giving her time to return to the clear path.

Without the hindrance of undergrowth, she pushed herself into a hard dash. It didn't take long for the Banderwigh to fly onto the trail behind her, billowy black cloak flaring on the wind. A brief panic-fueled spring later, the scent of water pulled her off the path. She whined, straining to run, unsure if she would make it to the river's edge before she passed out.

Ylithir help me!

No sooner had the thought formed in her mind than her next step came down on a thin layer of leaves that ripped out from under her. Emma shrieked as she flew across a four-foot wide hole and crashed chest-first into the dirt rim on the far side, armpit deep in the ground. She scrabbled uselessly at crumbling soil and some soft sticky residue, her fingers raking without gripping.

Emma slipped down and fell, screaming up at the hole of moonlight shrinking into the darkness overhead.

The Banderwigh's glowing yellow eyes appeared, staring down at her.

Everything went black.

NOT SO ITSY BITSY

*E*mma floated as if in midair. She knew her eyes were closed, but lacked the energy to open them. For some minutes, she didn't try to move. Her body demanded rest, and her feeble attempts to deny it failed. Sleep seemed to come and go in brief fits. Something furry brushed over her left calf. She dreamed of rabbits and smiled.

Legs like twigs scurried over her face.

Her eyes shot open to the sight of a cave ceiling covered in white strands. She tugged at her arms, finding them stuck and immobile. Lifting her head, she looked around at herself lying on a massive spider web, arms above her head in the position she must have landed in. Six bright green spiders as big as dinner plates crawled over her, working extra silk around her body to keep her secured. Only her head, hands, and feet remained free to move.

All the spiders froze in place when she screamed.

She stared down at the dagger on her belt, then up at her right arm wrapped in silk. Grunting, she tugged and squirmed. When the attempt to free her arm failed, she resorted to panic and thrashing. One of the spiders returned, baring its fangs an inch from her face. She screamed again, and fainted.

By the time she came to, the spiders had vanished, but she

remained stuck. In little patches, she could pull her skin away from the tacky substance, but whenever she worked one spot free, another became stuck. This webbing wasn't even half as sticky as the goblin glue—which hurt to peel off skin—but having it all over her body made it inescapable. Whimpering, Emma pulled with as much strength as she could summon, and managed to slip her right arm a few inches down. The effort exhausted her and she went still, breathing hard.

Twenty feet above, a round patch of starlight shrank as spiders repaired their trap door with webs, branches, and mulch. Emma clenched her jaw, straining again to get her arms free. Thick cords bunched about her elbow and wrist, refusing to let her arm move any farther. She gave up on her right and tugged at her left, looking at the hand she twisted and pulled. A previously meaningless lump of webbing tore open to reveal a withered man's face, little more than a skeleton covered by tight brown leather, face frozen in the shape of a final, terrified wail.

The trader's friend.

She huffed and gasped, trying to get away from the corpse. Side to side she thrashed, pulling at her legs and trying to sit up. Driven on by complete disgust at being next to a dead person, she fought until several sharp yanks got her shoulders loose and she leaned up a little. Her arms remained stuck from the elbow forward. She pulled her legs inward for leverage, and wound up tilting to the side, staring down through the gauze-like haze. The spiders built the web at an angle, tilted downward in the direction of her legs. She dangled fifteen feet above a cave floor covered in multiple layers of pillow-like webbing. Emma shivered, wondering how many unfortunate creatures had found themselves stuck like her after falling in that hole.

The sticky substance pulled at her hair when she turned her head. She gasped and whined in pain. A strand of web draped across her face, ignoring her attempt to puff it away. Emma peered past her feet at a cave tunnel leading away from the chamber, filled with oval web bundles of various sizes.

Some had antlers protruding from the silk while others looked like they contained goblins. Smaller ones, the size of boars and raccoons, formed perfect egg shapes, revealing nothing about what unfortunate creature might be inside. She looked up at her arms, as far away from the dagger as they could be. Another round of squirming succeeded only in pulling her hair.

Her struggles came to an end when she noticed a thread of silk climbing the wall to a cave opening three feet above the highest part of the tilted web. Eight large green spots in two rows of four loomed closer to the dark opening.

Spiders feel the web moving... That's how they know they caught a bug.

Her worst nightmare turned real—a massive furry green spider—extended four green-furred legs out of the hole and pulled itself into the weak moonlight. Four more legs dragged out behind it, uncurling one at a time to grasp cords of silk thicker than her wrist. The web shuddered under its weight, bouncing her in place as the monstrous spider ambled sideways in a wide circle. She'd never seen a spider that large, its body as big as a draft horse. Blind with terror, she rocked back and forth, kicking and thrashing. Screaming gave way to sobbing and crying out for her father.

Fur as stiff as broom bristles brushed her right foot and made her go still. Through tear-blurred eyes, she stared at it, whimpering. Fangs the size of Da's broadsword hovered over her, dripping with translucent green liquid. It swayed left and right, as if unsure what to make of its latest catch.

"Da... help," she mewled, so quiet perhaps the spider didn't even hear.

It shifted, leaning over her to inspect the silk holding her by the arms. She turned away from its underbelly, cringing at the sensation of silk tightening about her skin. Its most vulnerable spot hovered right above her face, but her dagger may as well have been on one of the moons. Her fear reached a point where it gave way to calm. As the spider tended to her other arm, securing her to the web, she wondered why the Banderwigh hadn't taken advantage of her helplessness.

Are banderwighs afraid of spiders, too? The ridiculousness of the thought made her laugh.

The sudden burst of noise startled the immense spider, and it swung itself around to hiss in her face. She screamed, shut her eyes, and strained to get away from it. The hiss faded to a bubbling rasp. It backed up, drew silk from its spinneret, and set to weaving sticky ropes around her midsection.

It's going to wrap me up!

"Da!" she shrieked, again startling the creature.

It can hear me.

Any progress she had made in freeing herself was gone; she felt more immobile than before. It wouldn't take long before she vanished entirely inside a giant cocoon. She screamed at it, trying her best to roar. It jumped and raised its fangs, but calmed when she didn't attack.

It knows I can't move. Her jaw dropped. *Is it smart?*

She swallowed hard and tried to find enough calm to speak. "S-Strix…" She coughed. "Strixian, *please* give me the wildkin whisper!"

If ever in her life she wanted anything, she wanted to talk to this spider.

Strands of white energy coalesced in the air, twisting in a spiral that settled into her chest, giving rise to strange whispery noises coming from the spider as it wound silk around her leg. The odd sounds became speech.

"Sssmall. Too sssmall," it rasped in a whispery, breathless hiss that trailed off to silence. "Won't keep. Eat sssoon. Babiesss didn't wrap it well."

"Hello," said Emma.

The giant emerald creeper whirled around with a sudden twist that made the web bounce and sway.

"Speaksss?" It reared back, raising four legs and its venom-soaked fangs.

"P-please, let me go. I'm too small to eat."

It lowered its legs to the web and spoke in a hollow voice with a feminine quality. "You are in my web. You will feed my children."

"But, I'm only a child, too. I have a mother. H-how would you feel if someone killed your babies?"

The spider rushed at her, stopping with its ever-moving mouthparts inches from her nose. Wetness sprayed over her as it rasped, "Humans *do* slay my babies! I should drag your dry bones back to them."

Emma cringed at the feeling of its bristles on her legs. The memory of the wagon covered in dead spiders, which had haunted her dreams for years, came back to her. She whimpered as the spider took little delicateness in lashing several strands of web tight around her chest.

"But, I didn't hurt any of your children."

"You think that mattersss?" It reared up over her. "My children didn't kill humansss."

She struggled to unstick her finger, and pointed at the dead man two feet away. "What about him?"

"Hisss companion killed one of my children."

Fear washed over her in waves; she closed her eyes, trying to keep her breathing even. The webbing around her middle made it hard to get air. "They said they were attacked first."

"I do not believe you," hissed the spider. "They have hunted usss for the all of exissstence."

"Humans are scared of spiders. They run away from even tiny ones," she whimpered. "I'll tell them to stop if you let me go."

The spider slipped to the side, circling. "You sssaid you are a child. They will not lisssten to you." It shifted to appraise her. "You are alssso an egg-layer. Humansss do not listen to their egg-layersss, even when they are not children."

Emma glared at it in shock. "Humans don't lay eggs!"

"You are trying to trick me!" it hissed. "You have soldiersss and egg-layersss, just like usss."

Her unconscious struggle against the web ceased, leaving her limp and out of breath. "It's not true. The town elders always do what my Nan tells them. They're afraid of her." *Now, I know why.* She flashed a nervous grin. "Believe me, I can help."

"You deccceive! You ssseek only to live." It moved to gather silk around her other leg.

She didn't even try to struggle since she couldn't move at all. "Please. Let me go. I know how I can make them stop killing your babies."

The spider pulled a strand up, wrapped it over her thigh and pulled it taut. It hesitated; eight eyes flicked up to look at her. A moment of consideration passed, and it resumed its work. At the point where it reached the hem of her dress, it wound silk around both legs.

"Wait, please!" Emma lapsed into sobs. "I can help you. They kill your babies for silk."

"Isss that ssso?" The hollow whisper turned her blood to ice. "Than I ssshall kill you for your juicccesss."

Emma snarled. "No. That's stupid! I'm the only one that can stop them."

"I do not believe you."

She ducked her head back as its immense abdominal orb swung overhead. The spinneret yawned, a cavernous, pulsating orifice wider than her head. Inside, white lumpy things embedded in pale green flesh swelled, about to spray her in the face. Emma rambled as fast as she could speak, ignoring the thread of viscous liquid descending onto her cheek and nose.

"How many humans can talk to you? I can make a deal. I can stop them. Please!"

The white bulges undulated and glistened with unformed strands. Emma shivered, trying to turn her face away, but couldn't. *Please, please, please, please.* After a moment, armored places closed over the orifice, and the spider whirled around. It lowered itself, face close to Emma's.

"How can I know you will not sssimply run away and hide?" Eight eyes narrowed. "I ssstill think you are deccceptive."

It took her a few breaths to regain the nerve to speak. "It is true I could run away and never come back. All I can do is promise."

The spider leaned away, the whisper trailed off to silence. "I have heard enough of promisssesss. The green ones always promissse."

"I'm not a goblin." Emma raised her head, whining as the webbing pulled her hair. "I'm a druid. Uhh... I will be a druid when I grow up." *If I grow up.* "Do you know the Raven?"

The spider stood taller. "Thisss one has heard of her."

"That's my Nan. I'm her grand... Uhh, I'm her baby's baby."

"Sssuppossse I releassse you?" It swayed side to side. "What do you propossse?"

A glimmer of hope she might've found a way out of the worst situation she could have imagined brought a nervous giggle. Emma tugged at her arms, shifting her hips in search of a way to escape the webs making it hard to breathe. "I will come back once a month to collect scraps of old web and bring them to the humans. I will tell the merchant I won't bring him more if anyone hurts your children. They are greedy and will not want that."

The enormous spider twitched its fangs, scraping them over each other as if sharpening knives. Agonizing minutes dragged while the huge arachnid leaned one way or the other, pondering. Emma squirmed.

"What isss wrong?"

"I can't move, and it's hard to breathe."

The spider's reaction, uncontrolled laughter, turned Emma's face red with anger. "It's not funny! I've had nightmares about big, green spiders since I was little. I'm so scared I'm not even scared."

"That makesss no sssensssse."

She cringed; the pitch of its whispery voice rattled her bones. "I thought you were monsters. I'm sorry."

The largest emerald creeper Emma had ever seen positioned itself over her and looked down. "You will be our emissssary to the humansss."

She trembled, her body rebelling at being immobilized so near to a creature so deadly. "What's that mean?"

"Your offer. To trade sssilk. Sssay you will do thisss."

Emma nodded, the only movement she could manage. "Yes. Yes. I will."

Its great mouthparts stretched out and swung down. Emma held back a scream, closing her eyes and flinching as the web bobbed and bounced. The tightness about her chest released, then her arms detached. She squirmed amid the stickiness as it slashed her loose from waist to toe, and lifted her in its forelegs. A wail came out of her as it began to rotate her like a chicken on a spit and wrap more silk around her into a cocoon.

"Hey! What are you doing?"

It stopped turning her and scuttled down the web to the floor. "Sssorry. Inssstinct."

The spider set her on the ground and backed off a few steps. She sat up, using the dagger to slice her legs apart and tearing the beginnings of a cocoon away, before plucking stray webs from her hair. After clearing her dress of as much webbing as she could find, she stood and put the dagger back on her belt.

"Is this the way out?" She went to leave, but stopped, horrified at the cave full of dead things wrapped in silk.

An immense green-furred leg as big around as Da's thigh appearing beside her almost stopped her heart. Something hit the ground behind her with a *splat*. Emma twisted and looked down at a big bundle of spidersilk. The spider, on solid ground, stood tall enough for her to walk under without stooping. Numerous strands of long, black hair adhered to the ball of silk. What had a moment ago immobilized her in the face of certain death had become a potential offer of truce.

She stooped to pick up the bundle, which despite its size, didn't weigh much. The sensation of touching the sticky mass made every muscle in her back tense.

"Thisss way." The big spider prodded her with a leg toward the cave.

Emma crept over webbing so old it had lost its stickiness, like clouds under her feet. A goblin-shaped impression in a silken wall twitched as she neared. She yelped and jumped sideways, crunching into a dry cocoon that sprouted a bony human arm and a puff of dust. Emma gulped and moved away from it, looking down at the pillowy ground so she didn't have to witness any of the horrors mounted on the walls. After quite a while of walking, the cushiony webs stopped, leaving her stepping on stone and dirt.

The great spider prodded her in the back here and there to signal turns, and soon, she came to a halt at the entrance to a cavernous space packed with silken orbs the size of wagons. Before Emma could open her mouth to ask why she'd been brought to this chamber, the spider chittered.

"Come, children."

A rush of fear made her light headed. Three caves led from the room, in addition to the one behind her. None of them seemed promising as an escape, and all teemed with sudden motion. Hundreds of emerald creepers appeared, scurrying closer. Most looked like the ones she had seen before, bodies about four to five feet long. Innumerable others emerged, some as small as a man's hand. The swarm rushed to within a few feet of her. Emma instinctively backed away, stopping at the insistence of a giant spider paw at her back.

"Be calm, child. Thessse are my children."

The smallest spiders scurried over her feet, spiraling up her legs and over her back. She shuddered, too afraid to move, even to blink. *I'm not going to be afraid of spiders after this.*

"Now that they have sssseen you, they will not harm you." The Emerald Queen clasped her by the shoulders and spun her around, eye to eyes. "Unlesss you betray usss."

Emma shook her head so hard she almost knocked herself dizzy. "I won't." She traced an X over her chest. "Swear."

One leg, bristles as thick as carrots, raised and pointed. Emma curtsied at the giant arachnid and crept toward the writhing mass of spiders. An ocean of shimmering emerald hair receded as she moved, parting enough to let her walk by before filling in behind her. She dragged her feet, afraid to step on one of the smallest and anger them. Numerous egg sacs vibrated with a high-pitched sound that made her skin crawl and tightened her jaw. No spider followed her into the passage at the far side of the chamber. Once the ground cleared of little spiders, she picked up to a run. After a brief sprint, she slowed and peered behind her, relieved at not seeing any spiders. Emma fell to her hands and knees and gasped for air. At the realization of how close she had come to death, she threw up. When puking stopped, she crawled away from the puddle and collapsed, shivering out the last of her terror. *The spiders can talk. No, I can talk to them. They're not evil, only defending themselves.* Her shaking faded to a mild tremble in a few minutes. She sat up and took a deep breath.

"I'm scared of them because they might kill me. I can talk to them and they promised not to kill me. I don't need to be scared."

Emma rocked back and forth.

"I don't need to be scared."

Drips in the distance punctuated the silence every few seconds. Emma convinced herself as much as she could not to be terrified of spiders, and stood. After collecting the wad of spidersilk, she marched onward. The cave continued for some distance, flooded with a scent of earth so heavy she tasted dirt. Mosses of green, violet, and blue grew around the walls, studded with tiny pink mushrooms. She held her arms out for balance, navigating patches of strange-colored jelly and gleaming slime that felt like walking on cold, raw egg. The cave had little clear rock to step on. She had to leap several times to avoid putting her feet in scary, unknown puddles. At the far end of the rainbow cave, water collected in a shin-deep pool around a spot where it bubbled out of the ground. She squatted at the edge, gathering several handfuls of the icy spring water, which she gulped down before wiping her face with the back of her arm.

It became harder to walk past the wet section, making her believe the tunnel curved uphill. At the scent of fresh air, she raced ahead for another few minutes until she reached a curtain of roots. The darkness of Widowswood waited on the other side. Emma looked over her shoulder, shivering at the memory of how many spiders she'd seen. She faced the roots, dreading the thought the Banderwigh would still be out there.

Stuck between her two greatest fears, she couldn't bring herself to move. She peered out past the hanging strands at the sky, wondering how long it would be until the sun came up. Though Mama said the Banderwigh only came out at night, her mother had never seen one up close. Not all legends wound up being true. Every tiny noise in the cave made her twitch, expecting a spider wandering up behind her. She almost found the courage to step outside until a twig snapped somewhere off in the dark.

Poison fangs or an axe... not much of a choice. She exhaled hard. *Standing here like a chicken won't help anyone.*

I talked to the spider queen and she didn't kill me. She'd had nightmares of giant green spiders for most of her life. Compared to facing one the size of a giant horse, a furry man didn't seem quite so bad anymore.

Emma closed her eyes, thinking about her family. She grasped the roots and walked out into the moonlight.

27

LOST IN WIDOWSWOOD

*S*naps, crunches, and whistles echoed over the whispering wind. Emma clung to the pillow of spidersilk as though it would protect her. A short distance from the cave, she found a trail wide enough for a horse. The night sky offered little clue as to which direction was east or west, so she stood at the edge of the dirt path for several minutes, looking left and right. After considering for a while, she decided to head to the right. The soft, cool dirt provided a welcome relief from stepping on the occasional painful twig or root gnarl.

Emma jumped at a crunch in the undergrowth to her left. She took two steps back, ready to run for her life, but a deer bounded out onto the trail. It stared at her, frozen for an instant, and scrambled off into the distance. Fear drained out of her, leaving her slouched and panting as she resumed walking. A few minutes later, a glint of moonlight at the side of the road attracted her. A metal helm, bashed and spattered with dried blood, sat upside down in a clump of weeds.

Bandits.

As if creeping would make walking barefoot on dirt any quieter, Emma tiptoed to the edge of the road and hid among the trees. *Bandits won't bother me. I don't have any money.* She glanced at the wad of silk as big as a pillow. Marsten paid in gold coins for a small fraction of that amount. A peasant family could live for two months on one of those coins. Bandits would kill for this lump. *It's silly to pay so much for something the spiders have lots of.* Her eyes widened. *It's hard to get. The creepers are deadly.* She shivered again at thinking how close she'd come to the end.

Her resolve cracked and let a few tears out. Between the Banderwigh chasing her, Da missing, and waking up stuck on a web, she wanted to crawl into Mama's lap for the rest of her life and stay there. Assuming, of course, Mama ever woke up. Furious at whatever made her mother sleep, Emma pushed away from her hiding tree and stomped onward. Her mind swam with worry. *Should I stay off the road to avoid bandits? What happened to Da? Don't make noise so the Banderwigh hears me. Why won't Mama wake up? Don't step on thorns, don't drop the spidersilk, watch out for glue traps, and don't stop.*

Her pace had fallen to a slow, careful walk. She absentmindedly plucked threads of web from her hair and dress, shaking her hand until they floated off on the wind. Emerald creeper silk approached the thickness of twine, far tougher than anything a common spider produced. She knew people made rope out of it, tough rope a fraction of the weight of flax. Nan once said wizards used it for special robes. Of course, at the talk of wizards, Emma had had rolled her eyes. She drew the dagger from its sheath, feeling like Princess Isabelle after escaping the castle of the Mad Wizard. She walked along, swinging the knife at branches or vines unfortunate enough to hang close, pretending to be Isabelle fighting a hobgoblin.

"Tamrin Brae, Tamrin Brae," she whisper-sang in a faltering voice, "went to the well one summer's day."

The Banderwigh will hear me.

She sucked in the next line, put the dagger away, and halted in place to listen for anything coming. After a minute of silence, she exhaled and ventured forward. Another deer galloped past, scaring her against a tree. Emma closed her eyes, for the first time in her life disliking the cute forest animal. *Animal!* If she could find a bird, she could ask it to go fetch Nan. *But, what if Nan is still sleeping?* An animal could still lead her east… *Do animals know about east and west?*

Feeling hopeless, she stumbled ahead, staring at the ground. The same tree seemed to go by for the third time before she stopped again, not having a clue where she stood or where she went. A faint chirp carried on the wind. Emma held her breath to listen. It came again: metal, squeaking. She imagined an iron weathervane shifting in the wind, and moved ahead in a turning walk, listening for the direction from which the sound came.

Beyond a thick patch of trees, the forest floor ended at an earthen ridge three times her height. The grating cry of rusted metal had grown louder moving in this direction. She stared up at the three moons, two blue and one green, bright in a sky of cloudless indigo. Emma gathered her hair in front of herself and pressed the spidersilk bundle to her back, sticking it to her dress like a pack. She kicked her feet into the dirt and grabbed at root bundles, climbing to the top and peering over.

Damp earth and pale toadstools bigger than her head filled her nose with an unpleasant musky stink. A short distance from the ridge, the ruin of a building was well on its way to rejoining the earth. Only the hearth and chimney defined it as a former house. A rectangle of stones created the ghost of its missing walls. Some rotting bits of wood remained in the shape of a fence, with a rotting, mushroom-covered plow frame still recognizable at one corner. The scraping turned out to be a fragment of metal gate swinging back and forth on a fencepost. No one had lived here for a long time.

Emma bit her lip and reached past the top of the ridge, grabbing a fistful of grass. With a heavy grunt, she hauled herself up and over, crawling forward until she could catch her breath. A cool breeze picked up, carrying away the sweat that built up from the climb. She peeled the bundle from her back, gasping when it caught on her hair. Stooping over, she set the lump on the grass, stepped on it to hold it down, and pulled her ebon locks free with both hands. She scowled at the iridescent mass of silk stuck to her foot, and hopped. After plucking it from her sole, she threw it to the ground, ready to punt it away for hurting so much, but remembered her bargain with the spider queen and stomped the dirt instead, growling.

The foreboding sight of the destroyed house brought back memories of the awful dream the Banderwigh had forced on her. Branches rustled in a sudden breeze that made the forest seem colder. Emma grabbed the silk and ran, leaping the fallen fence and coming to a halt by the chimney. The hearth space had enough room for her to crawl into and it offered a place to hide at least from three directions.

She curled up against the wall of the old fireplace. Nothing had burned in here since before Mama had been a baby. Only dirt and moss remained inside. Wind howled in the distance, though no air moved. The broken gate hung idle, sparse grass in the space that used to be a home didn't move. For no specific reason, Emma pulled her dagger out and held it at the ready, flat of the blade cold over her knee.

Eyes closed, she heard Da's voice in a faraway memory.

"If you ever find yourself lost in the woods, find a safe place and stay there. Wandering about will only make it harder for us to find you."

She nodded. The snap of a twig opened her eyes. She pressed tight to the stone, barely breathing. *Anyone friendly would be calling my name.* With thoughts of bandits in her head, she stuck the spidersilk to the inside of the chimney, out of sight. Another snap in the distance put both of her hands on the dagger again. Emma looked up, wanting to trade places with the silk and hide in the flue, but it was too small. Not even Tam could fit up there.

Tam.

Despite her anger, tears streaked her cheeks. She wanted to go home, wanted her family. It might only be a boar sniffing around for food. The incantation would let her talk to it. At worst, she could ask it not to hurt her, and at best, it might know how to find town. It had to be harder to eat something that could talk to you, goblins notwithstanding. That thought shed new light on Mama's distaste for meat. Nan thought her silly, but for once Emma was inclined to disagree with her grandmother. Eating animals she could talk to felt wrong. *Can wolves talk to deer?* She scratched at her foot, debating the odd question to take her mind off all the scary sounds creaking and cracking in the night.

Wolves.

Emma scowled at herself for being stupid. She crawled out of her hiding spot and spun around, pointing the dagger in a circle. Nothing there. After a sigh of relief, she took in a great breath, threw her head back, and howled like a lost wolf until her lungs ran out of air. She did it again, adding a pleading tone to a second baying howl that echoed into the woods.

The two long cries left her lightheaded. *Greyfang has to hear me.* She remembered Nan's face, smiling and wrinkled as she learned how to ask the Owl Spirit for the gift of the wildkin whisper. The magic of druids seemed like it only required knowledge of who to ask and what to ask for. Of course, not just anyone could ask of the spirits, but her family had the gift. How much could she figure out on her own?

She sucked in another lungful of ice-cold air, not noticing the drop in temperature as she cut loose with another lamenting howl.

"Ylithir, wolf spirit, carry my plea to the pack!" she shouted.

The dizziness that followed could have been from howling, but she *believed* she had done magic again. Taken by the mood, she dropped to all fours, sitting like a dog, and howled again. As the last traces of her cry echoed to silence, she looked down at her dirt-covered hands and feet, then blushed. *Anyone looking at me now will think I've gone nutters, a wild girl who doesn't live with people.* She frowned. *I don't care. It has to work!*

Her teeth chattered. She stood, rubbing at her arms. "That's strange. It shouldn't be this cold."

Crunch.

Dread fell over her. She didn't have to look to know the Banderwigh had found her. Of course he had, with her making so much noise. The strong cold and sense of evil in the air left her no doubt. She clutched the dagger close to her chest, moving it behind her back as she turned to keep it hidden. Even though she knew what she would see, the shaggy silhouette with piercing yellow eyes made her tremble.

He stood at the gate, mirror-like axe head all but glowing in the moonlight. After a momentary pause, he swung his weapon around and grabbed it in both hands, as he had done before. Emma took a step back. The Banderwigh crushed the old fence under his boots, dead wood cracking and splintering.

"I won't let you hurt anyone else," said Emma, barely hiding the quiver of fear in her voice. "No more like Hannah."

Strong dizziness pervaded her mind. The fallen house became a three-walled diorama with hanging cages. Tam, and two unknown boys screamed and wailed for their mommies. Kimber sat in silence. The burned girl teased Kimber for not having a mother to cry for.

Emma looked away from them. "You are lying."

He growled, moving at her with unexpected speed.

Ready for it, she leapt to the side, leaving the axe embedded in dirt. She pulled her dagger out of hiding and caught the creature unprepared. Her strike sank inches into his thigh; the blade froze over in an instant, becoming painful to touch. Emma refused to let go, and yanked it free, bounding backward.

The Banderwigh unleashed a wail of anguish and stumbled to a knee with a hand on the wound. No blood flowed from his tattered black pants. She gasped at a frosty wisp rising from the tip of the dagger. He growled, surging back to his feet, tearing the giant axe blade from the ground with such force it spattered her with dirt. His next hasty strike flew high, allowing Emma to duck and run around it. She had seen Da fight once. Compared to this creature, he moved swift and with precision. The ponderous axe seemed to drag the Banderwigh around, as if the man had been a simple farmer with little skill and not enough strength to wield such a weapon—before.

"I don't want to hurt you," said Emma. "Please... stop this."

The Banderwigh glowered at her, slouching. Hope sparked within her, but shattered when he reared the axe up over his head. Emma dove left, somersaulting into a run. Behind her, the metal on dirt *thump* of another miss. He roared in rage, filling the air with pure hate. Rapid stomps coming up behind her made her leap away to the right, crashing against the still-standing chimney as he loped by, again swinging his great axe into the ground. She flattened against the stones, unable to breathe.

He loped sideways at her, hauling his weapon up in an erratic rush that betrayed no hint of where it would swing. She shot a one-second glance at the dagger in front of her and, in a moment of blind panic, threw herself forward, plunging the ten-inch blade into the Banderwigh's chest before he could round his axe overhead. White frost raced over the handle, forcing her to release the weapon with a yelp of burning pain. Emma scurried away, rubbing her hands on her dress in a furious attempt to warm her numb fingers.

The Banderwigh screamed in anguish, axe drooping to the ground in one hand. He seemed unable to swing his free arm up to grab the dagger as he staggered forward, falling to one knee. Emma ran to the side, putting some distance between them. The monster collapsed on all fours. Heavy, gurgling rasps came from him, the sound of a wounded beast. The air smelled only of cold, which seemed to freeze her nose with every rapid breath she took. Her mind searched for anything she could use against him.

"I'm not afraid of you! You don't make me sad! You are not scary!"

He rocked back on his heels and roared at the treetops. When his cry faded, the Banderwigh released the axe and clutched the dagger with both hands.

"Go away! Go back to where you came from!" shrieked Emma.

Her confidence didn't last long.

With a wrenching screech of metal on bone, he yanked the dagger from his heart and hurled it to the side. Grunting and rasping, he raked at the ground in search of his weapon. Emma took a step toward the axe, intending to drag it away, but stopped.

Cursed. Don't touch it! Wait, will the curse work on a girl... or only a grown man?

In her moment of indecision, his icy hand sprang out and seized her by the ankle. She screamed as he pulled her to the ground, dragging her close.

His left hand crushed her shoulder into the dirt. Ice crept into her skin, a numbness that spread down her arm and up her neck. He grasped the axe close to the bladed head with his free hand, bringing the gleaming edge hovering over her defenseless neck. She stomped at him, her bare feet able to tolerate touching the frigid creature for only seconds at a time. He ignored her pummeling heels and raised the axe skyward in one hand, animosity burning in its eyes.

She took a breath to scream, but instead howled, kicking at his chest and clawing at the arm holding her down.

Answering howls came from the woods. Blurs of grey, black, and white streaked across the clearing. The Banderwigh started to ram the axe head down, but he vanished in a smear of dark fur. Emma sat up, clutching her frozen shoulder and wailing.

Greyfang had the axe handle in his mouth, rolling in the dirt with the Banderwigh, dragging him around with ease. After three flips, the monster recovered his footing. The alpha wolf hauled him off his feet again, spinning him in a circle. The once-man got his legs to the ground and wrestled with the huge wolf, boots trenching the earth in a battle of inhuman strength. With a baleful growl, the Banderwigh wrenched Greyfang airborne and flung him to the side. He landed, tumbling, and skidded to a halt, dizzy and shaking his head.

The Banderwigh rushed straight for Emma, but didn't get far before Howls at Rain and Runs in Shadow leapt out of nowhere and sank their fangs into his legs, twisting so he fell flat on his chest. Moonsong appeared behind her, nipping at her dress and dragging her away with such force Emma had to hold onto the fabric to keep the mother wolf from tearing her dress off. Stalks the Wind leapt over her, silent, and bowled into the Banderwigh from a blind angle, savaging at his head.

Moonsong stopped dragging her when she reached the fence line, and moved to stand between her and the monster. Emma rolled forward, kneeling next to the black wolf and clinging to her side.

"Thank you," she mumbled into her fur.

Snarls and snaps mixed with grunts and muted thuds. Moonsong twitched, as though she wanted to join the fray, but held her station. Emma got to her feet, pawing at the wolf by her side.

"Moonsong, we have to run away."

The animal didn't react.

Oh no! "Strixian, please give me the gift of the wildkin whisper." She held her arms out, concentrating on her desire. A faint tug of exertion came in time with the flickering white light.

"Moonsong, we need to run. It can't be killed."

The wolf glanced at her, head snapping forward at Howls at Rain yelping in pain. Her pup went skidding away from the fight, driven off by a hard kick to the side. Moonsong snarled.

"Go to him," said Emma, patting her. "It's okay."

The mother wolf looked at her with apologetic eyes and seemed about to do it when Howls at Rain got back up. Greyfang staggered out of the weeds and raced in, taking the axe handle in his mouth again. His weight and strength dragged the Banderwigh to the ground, giving the others free rein to bite anywhere they chose. Wolves yelped, sounds that Emma now understood as cries of pain and gasps of "Cold!"

Howls at Rain swooned over sideways, blood dripping from his mouth. Moonsong bolted to him, preventing him from rejoining the fight. The Banderwigh grabbed Stalks the Wind by the scruff and hurled him ten feet to the side, into a tree. He bounced off and landed on his feet, but staggered.

Runs in Shadow backed away from another grab, snapping at the creature's hand. The Banderwigh twisted his axe side to side, trying to wrench the handle out of the alpha's mouth. Greyfang tried to yell something as he wrestled, but the wooden staff in his clenched teeth made it unintelligible.

The other wolves circled. The Banderwigh glared at Emma, stunned and angered at her unexpected assistance. With a violent shove, he sent Greyfang sprawling to the ground and raised the unburdened axe.

"No!" roared Moonsong. She raced in, a black streak of fur, and sank her fangs into the Banderwigh's side.

Her attack diverted a beheading stroke into a severe gash to Greyfang's chest. The alpha stumbled sideways and careened over. The Banderwigh roared again, reaching for Moonsong's neck. The black wolf evaded his grasp, snarling and snapping her teeth. Emma grabbed one of the healing elixirs out of her pouch and ran to Greyfang, heedless of how close it brought her to the monster or a flying axe blade.

She slid to a halt on her knees, gnawing on the cork. Metal on dirt announced the axe crashing down behind her. Emma's arms shook. She grabbed the little bottle in both hands, emitting a feral snarl while twisting it. The cork popped free at the same time a heavy *thud* came from her left, the Banderwigh's frustrated grunt mixed with a yelp of canine rage, trailed by the sound of snapping underbrush.

Emma pulled Greyfang's head into her lap and poured the elixir into his mouth. She lifted his muzzle and held it shut, rubbing his throat to help him swallow.

"Emma!" shouted a weak sounding Moonsong.

She whirled.

The Banderwigh stood right behind her, axe over his head. The pack rushed at him, but wouldn't get there fast enough to matter.

"No!" screamed Emma, shielding Greyfang with her body. "Why are you so mean! You wanna kill *me*. Leave him alone." She lapsed into sobs. "Please don't hurt the wolves. They were just trying to help me."

Frozen with his axe in the air, the Banderwigh stared at her. Emma kept blocking—as much as her tiny body could—Greyfang's neck, so he couldn't kill the wolf.

As if losing strength, the Banderwigh's arms fell slack. His gleaming axe head fell into the mulch a few inches to her side with a *thud*.

He collapsed to his knees right in front of her. Frost spread out across the ground beneath him and painted a layer of ice crystals on the wolf's fur. White spots appeared at the center of his all-yellow eyes, a trace of a human pupil. Emma stroked Greyfang's mane. The wolf emitted a labored grunt.

Emma held her ground, not moving as the ragged man reached for her and closed both hands around her neck. She shut her eyes, tears streaming down her face.

"I love you, Nan."

Ice spread into her throat. Bone-hard fingers squeezed.

"I love you, Mama an' Da."

Emma shuddered, gurgling for air.

"...ove you T-tam... an' Kim—"

The world seemed to spin away. Snarling neared. The Banderwigh shook from the impact of several wolves against his body. Her air came back, her eyes opened. Coarse, icy hands slipped from her throat to her shoulders. Growling wolves bit into his elbows and legs, struggling to pull him back. The creature's face had changed. His aura of supernatural fear had fallen away, leaving him sallow and drawn, like a broken *man*. His eyes no longer glowed with yellow light, normal, brown... and shedding tears.

28

SAVED

The Banderwigh let out a wheezing cough that puffed ice crystals over her hair, squeezing his fingers into Emma's shoulders, going from holding her down to struggling to hold himself upright. The deathly grey pallor receded from his face. He shuddered, opening his mouth in a silent, mournful cry, stretching sunken cheeks with more wrinkles than they should have had at his age. This man no longer had the air of a powerful monster, rather a wasted and drained shell. The breeze gave up its graveyard chill, allowing a trace of summer night to ease her shivering.

Even the wolves appeared to sense the change and stopped trying to drag him away. Howls at Rain limped sideways, hackles raised in an effort to look more threatening. Stalks the Shadows and Moonsong stood on either side of Emma, watching him. His hands, still clutching her by the shoulders, lost most of their strength as well as their unnatural chill. She reached up and rubbed the front of her throat, still struggling to breathe.

Emma stared at him. Once it no longer hurt to breathe, she extended a tentative hand and touched his cheek, his skin like leather. Widowswood hung in eerie silence. Moonsong nosed at Greyfang who emitted soft growls in response. The other wolves shifted, ready to pounce on him in an instant.

Emma shivered. "Are you…"

"I…" He croaked and coughed, a thin line of saliva falling from his lip. "Do not know."

She glanced at his hands on her shoulders, no longer trying to squeeze the life from her neck. Without the grey in his skin, he seemed close to alive.

"What do you remember?" asked Emma.

He started to teeter over, but she clasped his arms to help keep him steady. "You… So much love for that animal. I saw it…" His eyes grew wider. "A shimmering light in the dark. It made me remember"—he slumped sideways, coughing up a blob Emma refused to look at— "who I used to be."

"Nan said you were cursed."

"My son… Ewan. He went into the forest." Tears flowed along deep wrinkle channels in his face. "We forbade him to go. Ewan didn't listen." He stared off into the trees, eyes wide and wild. "I remember a horrible figure clad in rags of—" He looked down at his tattered clothing and shook with horror. "No! What have I done? What have I become? How many have there been?"

He released her and covered his face, weeping.

Emma fed the second elixir to Greyfang. His injury had grown smaller, but he still didn't attempt to get up.

"I remember a girl."

"Hannah," said Emma. "She came to town a few days ago."

"I killed her," wailed the strange man, breaking into sobs again.

"She's still alive." Emma took his hand in both of hers. "She is nutters, but alive."

His weeping gave way to a belabored sigh. "I killed her spirit. She will not be right again. I stole her childhood." The man shook his head, pulling at his hair. "I can never atone."

"I don't think it was your fault." Emma pointed at the axe. The sight of it made the man jump, startled. "It has a curse that made you bad. A monster had taken your body."

He raked his fingernails over his cheeks, leaving smears of dirt. "I... There were many of us. We had gone out to search, and we found the wretch. I remember believing he had killed Ewan. It killed nine men, but we slew it."

"You took the axe." Emma rubbed his hand.

"Aye. I took it." He gazed into nowhere. "I can still see my hand reaching for it in the leaves. That's the last thing I remember. It... *still* wants me to hold it."

Emma remained quiet for a moment, while stroking Greyfang's fur. Moonsong gave her an urgent look. She focused her intent on the wolf. "I don't have any more elixirs, but I can try the magic."

"What?" The man looked up. "You're making wolf noises." He blinked. "Oh, please tell me I haven't broken you, too." He reached to run a hand over her head, but hesitated.

"No. I'm a druid... or, will be."

He lowered his arms, resting his hands on his legs. "Can you talk to them? Is that why they came?"

"Yes." Emma shifted toward Greyfang. "Uruleth, spirit of life, please grant me the gift of life."

Shimmering green light formed at her chest and spiraled around her arms into the wound. This time, she had already focused on her desire to help him before she spoke, so the glow didn't collect around her hands, instead flowing into the wound. Greyfang's legs twitched as if running in a dream. The injury shrank, closing to an angry scab. Using magic made her feel tired. On top of everything she had gone through that night, she wanted to curl up on the forest floor and sleep right there.

"He's still hurt." She steadied herself and held out her hands again.

Moonsong nipped at her fingers. "No, child. I can smell he will live. You are too weary to focus Uruleth's power. Do not harm yourself."

She rubbed her forehead with the back of her arm and glanced up at the sniffling man. "What happened to Ewan?"

His eyes glazed over. A glassy rattle echoed out of his lungs. "I... After I picked up the axe, something led me to this small, hidden place. I found him in a cage. He didn't recognize me. I took from him, but not for long." He scratched at his head, growling. "My own son screamed whenever he saw me. It broke the haze in my heart. I let him go, but took others." He bent forward, shivering and rocking. "It's been so long, I should be dead by now. My son's grandchildren, if he had any, would be old." He cried. "Dozens I can't remember. Pain. I see a little boy and a girl a bit older." He looked up, locked eyes with her, then glanced away. "You."

"You took me and my brother. But I wasn't sad."

He started to smile, but wound up with a forlorn stare. "Yes, I remember. It hurt. The reverse of sustaining, you pulled strength *from* me."

She fidgeted, not sure what to say.

"I am… glad you saved yourself." He grasped her shoulders again. "You saved me, too."

Crashing and snapping erupted from behind the chimney. The man pulled Emma toward himself as if to hug her. She glanced in the direction of the noise, drawing in air for a scream. Most of the wolves backed away out of sight, except for Greyfang who hadn't gotten up and Moonsong who refused to leave his side. The former banderwigh reached across her back, patting her, about to pull her into an embrace. He wore a strange expression, as though he had experienced great pain for so long, the lack of it brought bliss.

"Your love for that animal broke the spell," he rasped.

"I thought I heard her this way," said a voice so deep it had to be Arnir, one of the watch.

Pine needles and mulch exploded in a flurry of flashing metal and gleaming armor.

Da barreled out into the clearing, running toward her with his left hand outstretched. "Emma!" His eyes narrowed to a vengeful glower as he raised his broadsword, the blade flashing blue in the moonlight. "Unhand my daughter, you fiend!"

"Da!" Emma screamed. "He's—"

In one fluid motion, Da seized the back of Emma's dress, pulling her away, while thrusting his blade at the former banderwigh. steel slid past her face, plunging into his heart. The man bucked and gurgled.

"—not a monster," whispered Emma. She stared on in horror as the once-banderwigh wheezed and fell over backward, sliding off her father's sword.

"Emma!" Da fell on one knee, gathering her tight to his chest with his left arm. "Praise all the gods and their servants! I was so worried. Your mother sent us back out as soon as we returned. She said you'd been taken again."

She continued to stare at the twitching man, blood welling up and out of his mouth. He reached toward her, gurgling.

"Thank…"

His arm fell to the ground. With a gasp, he released his final breath.

"Why did you kill him?!" Emma pounded her fist against his armored chest, making a *thump* on the leather-covered steel. "He wasn't a monster anymore."

Da stood, lifting her off her feet. She squirmed and shrieked, trying to get away. He pointed at the injured wolf, gesturing with his sword at one of his men. "Put it out of its misery."

"No!" Emma's piercing shout stalled them. "If you hurt Greyfang, I will never forgive you!"

"Emma, calm down. The animals are dangerous. I don't know how you survived being kidnapped by that thrice-damned wretch and a pack of wild dogs."

"They're not wild dogs, Da. They're wolves." She sniffled. "They saved me." She stopped pounding her fists into his chest and sagged over his shoulder. "If it wasn't for them, you'd have found me dead. They saved me an' Tam from the goblins too!"

"She's delirious, captain," said Kavan. "Look at her, she's about to faint."

"The wolves did go after the goblins the other day," said Arnir. "Explain that."

Emma stared at him, sniveling. "I broke the spell. He wasn't a monster anymore. Please, Da, don't hurt the wolves."

"Poor girl," said Guard Filner. "She must've 'ad one 'ell of a night. So lucky to be alive."

Emma shivered. "I fell into a nest of creepers, too."

The men exchanged glances.

"That's not funny, Emma," said Da, sounding stern. "I didn't raise a liar."

"Easy, captain, she's..." Kavan twirled his finger around his head. "Needs to sleep."

"Emma, if you got into a creeper nest—" Da couldn't finish; mute, he squeezed her.

"Put me down, Da. I can prove it."

Moonsong growled at an approaching guard.

"Stop them, Da! Please."

He held a hand up in a gesture of delay. Haim lowered his sword, but didn't take his eyes off Moonsong. Da set Emma down on her feet. She ran for the chimney, scurrying into the hearth.

"Emma, that's dangerous. It could fall and crush you." Da chased after her.

She reached up and plucked the wad of silk loose. She backed away, turning to hold up the bundle as big as her whole chest. All the men gasped at the quantity of it. When Da reached her, she handed it up to him.

Whistling in awe, he picked over it. "What's the meaning of this? These hairs..."

"I was stuck in that silk." She shivered, and explained her bargain with the Emerald Queen.

"The girl's gone loopy," said Filner. "Thinks she's talking to spiders now."

Da waved the bundle at him. "And a ten-year-old just strolls into a creeper nest, harvests *this* much silk, then walks away without so much as a numb leg?" He grumbled. "Watch the wolf, but don't harm it if it remains quiet."

"Yes, sir," said the men.

Emma sighed and slumped to the ground. Da put his sword away and took a knee in front of her. He grasped her leg, shaking his head and cringing at all the thistles, nicks, and scrapes along her skin. Emma squeaked each time a thorn or splinter came loose from her; continuing to squirm while he repeated the process for her other leg. Out of the pouch Mama gave him, he took a larger bottle and opened it. The contents smelled like mint candy.

Emma caught the open end with a palm, holding it back. "What's this do?"

"Your mother made it. It will close all the little cuts and keep you from getting sick."

"Give it to Greyfang. He's hurt worse."

"Nonsense, Emma. That's just a wolf. Come on…" He brushed her arm away. She leaned back, but he caught her by the head and fed her some of the liquid sweet. "Oh, don't be difficult, Emma. This is medicine."

She gave up and drank a few mouthfuls of a liquid that tasted cold and minty. In seconds, her legs tingled as if snow fell on her. Her jaw tightened from the oddity of the feeling. All the little wounds closed, even the lingering soreness from the glue trap went away. Da put the bottle away and picked her up. She almost protested at first, disgusted by what he had done to that poor man, but as soon as his arms closed around her, she clung and bawled.

"Da, why did you kill him?"

"There's no such thing as monsters that steal children. It was an evil, twisted wreck of a man. I"—he shivered with anger—"can't imagine what he did to that poor Anders girl. Did he hurt you?"

"Da." Emma sobbed. "He was free. The curse broke. He was free and you killed him. Why?"

For the first time in her life, Emma saw confusion in her father's eyes. He brushed a hand over her hair and glanced over the faces of his men, but they all looked equally at a loss for words.

BROKEN

*M*oonsong edged around, never moving more than two steps from Greyfang. The alpha wolf wheezed, seeming aware of the need to stand, but not attempting to do so. Emma put up a half-hearted attempt to get out of her father's grip. For most of the night, she had been so desperate for him to hold her, but he had killed that poor man for no reason.

He seemed intent on keeping her tight to his chest in a protective embrace. She gave up, and cried on his shoulder, her quiet sniffles the only sound for some minutes.

"Sun'll be up soon," said Kavan, as he returned from pacing the area.

"Aye," called Filner from the area by the gate. "No sign of bandits or anything else."

Da cradled the back of her head, picking a few strands of web away. He gave her a brief look over, as if reconsidering her story about the spiders. Emma squirmed higher so she could peer over his shoulder at Greyfang.

"Your mother was beside herself with worry. We didn't find any other tracks but for that man's boots, Emma. He'd been to the house. We came right back out here to find you."

She scrunched her face in a mixture of glare and sadness. "The curse let him go. He wasn't bad anymore."

Kavan drifted by, squeezing her shoulder. "Poor girl is exhausted."

"Aye," said Da. "Em, I'm sorry our patrol took so long. We went farther out than we intended and we didn't get back until the wee hours. The back door was open and I found tracks. None of the men hesitated to come out here to find you, even after an all-day march."

The men nodded at him, raising hands in salute.

She stared guiltily at the ground. "Thank you, everyone, but you were all gone for three days."

"Poor child," said Kavan. "She's had a fright."

"Good ta find 'er in good 'ealth," said Filner, triggering another murmur of agreement from the men.

"Da, it made itself sound like you an' put everyone sleeping." Emma rambled out a tale of how it led her from the house by impersonating him. At all her yawning and eye rubbing while retelling what happened, the men appeared to think she dreamed it all. "... but one goblin was still alive. It tried to trick me."

"Goblins?" blurted Da, all of a sudden interested. "We cleared a goblin camp that was too close to town."

Emma blearily described what she saw there. Kavan and her father exchanged worried looks.

"I thought you said you'd cleared all the tar snares," said Da.

"Buggers play possum sometimes," grumbled Arnir.

"Obviously, we missed one." Haim shrugged.

"You really were gone for three days," muttered Emma. "Mama wouldn't eat. No one could find you. Not her, not Nan, not the animals."

Kavan raised an eyebrow. "Three days? Impossible, the sun's only just set."

The other men kept quiet.

"Em," said Da, brushing a hand over her head. "You are exhausted."

Emma folded her arms. "You will see. When we get home, everyone will tell you the same. The Banderwigh made you lost so it could get me."

Something in the look she gave him kept his words stalled in his mouth. She set her jaw. He looked at the dead man.

Da trudged over to the body, twisting to keep Emma from seeing it. "This is no monster, at least not in the sense you're thinking of him. Only an evil man." He choked up, hugging the air out of her and kissing her atop the head. "I'm so glad I found you before he could hurt you."

Red eyed, Emma wept. "You didn't have to kill him. He was trying to thank me for setting him free."

"Well, he's free now," said Filner.

Emma glared at him.

"Gonna take this into town," said Da. "See if anyone knows this man. That head's like a mirror. Might be enchanted. Sell for quite a coin in Calebrin. Will split it with the lot of you men."

The guards grinned and raised their arms in salute.

Da stooped. Emma wriggled around to look as the ground came closer. Da's hand opened, reaching toward the handle of the banderwigh axe.

"No!" She shrieked. "Don't touch it!"

Emma thrashed with such ferocity Da had to use both arms to contain her. She beat her fists against his chest, wailing as loud as her voice could get.

"Da! No! Don' touch it! It'll make you into a banderwigh! You'll die!"

"Shh." He stood and moved away from the axe, patting her back and holding her head to his shoulder. "Easy, girl. Shh."

She quieted to sniveling, grabbing around his neck rather than banging on his armor, then whispered, "Please, don't let anyone touch it. You use Mama's potions. You have to believe in a little magic." She sobbed. "Da, don't. It'll turn you into a monster."

Her eyes closed with the comfort of his hand stroking her hair. She hung there, halfway between feeling safe and wracked with guilt over what he had done. Now, she understood how Kimber must have felt. The girl's horrible father had done many awful things, but she still loved him. Emma's contentment evaporated as his neck pulled away from her arms. Guard Kavan, the only man larger than Da, took her into a firm hug.

Emma's eyes widened with horror as Da smiled at her and patted her cheek.

"You need to sleep, Emma. It's time to go home." He shifted his gaze to Kavan. "Hang onto 'er for a moment."

An iron hug held her fast as Da trudged over to the axe. He stooped, reaching for the handle.

"Da! No! It's evil!"

He looked back over his shoulder, shaking his head with disbelief. "Evil…"

As he thrust his arm to grab it, a loud *squawk* made all the guards except Kavan jump. Da, perhaps on edge from Emma's screaming warning, fell back on his rear end. A great raven sailed down from the trees, skimming two feet above the ground, headed right at him. He backpedaled, grabbing for his sword.

The bird glided by in silence, came around in a narrow turn, and landed a foot or two in front of the banderwigh's axe, blocking Da's approach. It flared its wings and squawked at him.

"Nan!" shouted Emma, crying from joy.

"The girl's delusional," muttered Kavan.

The raven spun about, covering itself with its wings. Amid a swirl of ghostly green light and a flurry of loose feathers, the large bird grew into Nan. Kavan's arms fell slack from shock. Da's sword, only halfway out of its sheath, slid back down with a *clack* as he sat there, dumbfounded. Emma slipped to the ground and sprinted on unsteady legs into a hug with Nan. Despite her lack of a cane, the old woman weathered the impact of a frantic child without issue.

"The girl is quite right, Liam. I wouldn't touch that." Nan adjusted her sleeves and folded her arms. "Had you grasped that handle, you would have become another banderwigh and killed all of these men." She thrust a knobbed finger at the corpse. "He, too, was once like you, searching for a taken child."

Da turned his head to glance at the dead man.

"He took the axe and evil got him," said Emma, breaking away from Nan. She retrieved Nan's dagger and put it on her belt before running back to Da's side. "It almost got you."

He looked up at Nan, mouth still open, and wrapped his arms around Emma. The men regarded the old woman warily, shifting around.

Emma shifted, sitting in Da's lap. "Nan..." She pointed at Greyfang. "The Banderwigh almost cut my head off. They saved me."

"He tried to kill you?" Nan gasped. "That is most unusual."

Moonsong raised her head at Nan's approach, mystifying the guardsmen with her lack of hostility. Nan crouched by the injured animal, one hand hovering. She muttered, too low for Emma to hear, and the alpha's entire body glowed with green light for several seconds. Air carrying the scent of a cool spring morning rushed by, the wondrous fragrance gone as fast as it appeared. Greyfang leapt upright and nuzzled with Moonsong, who whined low before bowing her head at Nan. Da went to push Emma behind him when the enormous wolf looked at them and walked over.

Emma grinned. "Do not fear, Da." She touched foreheads with Greyfang, and combed the soft fur of his cheeks with her fingers. "Thank you. I'm *so* sorry he hurt you."

The other wolves emerged from their hiding places, gathering around Nan, who tended to their injuries. Emma leaned into her father, smiling and ready for sleep.

"Let us assume that this weapon is dangerous." Da's voice, so close to her ear, shocked her awake. "What shall we do with it?"

Nan sent the wolves on their way and shook her head. "*You* shall do nothing."

"We can't just leave it here." Kavan gestured at it. "If it's, uhh, evil."

"I do not intend to, my boy." Nan gathered her sleeves up and ambled over to where the cursed weapon lay. "You doubt it is evil? Look at the ground."

The dirt beneath it had turned black, creeping ever outward.

Nan waved her hands about, weaving intricate patterns. "Linganthas, spirit of the wood, hear me. Send forth your power. Destroy this affront against life."

Energy charged the air, though nothing visible occurred for several seconds. The ground at Nan's feet bulged and split. A pair of thorny roots larger than a man's arm surged up and wrapped around the axe. Nan continued gesturing over it as the roots twisted and thickened, engulfing the weapon. The tangle of roots darkened from dirt brown to black, constricting and crushing until a deafening *crack* of breaking wood thundered over the entirety of the forest. Thin beams of white energy leaked out from the seams of the writhing knot, followed by a blast of cold that left a coating of sparkling frost on everything within about fifty feet.

The watch, Da, and Emma all stayed silent as the lump sank into the earth.

Emma walked over to hold her grandmother's hand. "Nan?" She sniffled and pointed at the dead man.

Nan slipped a hand around her back and pulled Emma close. "Do not blame your father for what has happened here. He saw only a creature who threatened his daughter, not the man you set free." She bowed her head. "It is a sad lesson for you, child. But our kind can be monsters too."

FAERIE STORIES

*E*mma held on to Da as the men marched across the forest. The late hour and harrowing chase left her too exhausted to think. Nan, as a raven, sailed over them above the treetops. The old one had no patience to walk all the way back to town. Quiet from what they had seen of magic and curses, the other guards kept their attention to the passing trees, watching for threats.

Surrounded by warmth and safety, Emma set her chin upon her father's shoulder and let sleep take her.

"Em!" shouted Kimber.

Emma startled awake. She yawned and stretched, still in Da arms, then squinted at the sky, blue with morning. The forest was long behind her, and home lay only a short distance away. Mama, tears in her eyes, came running up the road to meet them twenty paces from the porch. She whisked Emma into an embrace that forced most of the air out of her.

"Don't ever do that to me again!" Mama tried to collect herself, but couldn't stop sniffling.

"You beat the bandy-wee?" yelled Tam, as he ran circles around them.

"I'm sorry for going off alone, but you were magic-sleeping and wouldn't wake up." Emma yawned, then smiled at her family. "He won't hurt us now." She gave her father a pointed stare.

Her parents exchanged a glance, Da somewhat apologetic. The remaining guardsmen bowed to him one after the next before heading off down the path to Widowswood proper. Kimber ran over and wrapped her arms around Emma and Mama. She bounced up and down on her toes, crying and giggling.

Nan appeared in the front door. "Beth, poor Em's been up all night. Let her be."

"Only a nap then, or she'll become a creature of the night." Mama smiled, though her eyes still leaked.

Emma drifted in and out of sleep, barely aware of being carried inside, undressed, wiped free of dirt with a damp rag, and re-dressed in a nightgown. Kimber and Tam climbed onto the bed and snuggled close. She put her arms around her siblings and closed her eyes. The rapid murmurs of her parents talking outside may as well have been a lullaby.

"Emma, you should wake." Mama gently nudged her shoulder.

She forced her eyes open and yawned. Tam grinned, winked at Kimber, and they both attacked her sides, tickling. Emma squealed, flailing and kicking at the blanket before succumbing to a fit of laughter.

"It's about mid day," said Mama. "Come to the table. Your father will be here soon."

Still giggling, Emma slipped out of bed and looked around for the dress Nan had made. It didn't lay draped over the shelf where it usually spent the night, nor did it sit folded on the shelf past the foot end of the bed. Joy became dread and her eyes grew wide in preparation to unload a torrent of tears at the thought Da had finally had enough of her disobedience and disposed of it.

"Mama, where is my dress?"

Nan shuffled in from the back bedroom. "Oh, that old thing?" She waved dismissively. "Another week or so and it would've fallen apart... and it was too small for you."

Emma sniffled. "No. Nan... why?" The sense of betrayal made her shrink inward. She covered her eyes and sniveled.

Kimber and Tam exchanged a conspiratorial smile. They hopped off the bed and ran around Emma to either side, taking their places at the table. She sulked down at her toes and trudged to her seat. Mama set plates of sliced cheese, bread, and what remained of last night's stew on the table.

Da, still in his armor, tromped in the front door and sat at the head of the table. He flashed a broad smile, which only deepened Emma's frown. Not only had he killed that poor man, he celebrated the loss of her precious dress.

Emma folded her arms and shot a sour look into her lap.

"You're going to light your nightdress on fire with a face like that," said Nan.

Kimber and Tam erupted with giggles.

Try as she might, she couldn't be angry with them, though it bothered her how everyone seemed so happy her beloved dress was gone. Emma lifted her sullen pout and took a bit of cheese to her mouth.

"There... you need to eat." Mama patted her on the arm. "You're safe here, and I never want you scaring me like that again."

"The monster made you sleepy." Emma swung her feet back and forth. "No one would wake up, and I heard Da calling for help."

"Monster, 'e trick yas." Kimber shook her head. "Was nae Papa."

"He didn't have to die." Emma nibbled on a bit of bread.

Da sighed. "I'm sorry, Em. When I ran out, I saw him reaching for you. I was afraid that man wanted to hurt you."

"It is the way of things, child." Nan took Emma's pale hand in her gnarled fingers and squeezed. "The curse had drained him, and he likely would have passed away soon enough without Liam's help. *If he* had the strength to resist touching the axe again. What is important, is that you broke the magic that had poisoned him. He walks among the spirits now." She smiled.

Emma jabbed the cheese at her plate to pick up crumbs of bread, still horrified at what her father had done. "He would have died anyway?"

Tam and Kimber quieted, though they still fought to keep their giddiness down to mere smiles instead of noise and fidgeting.

"Perhaps days or hours, yes." Nan let go of her arm. "The dark magic fed upon his very essence. Your father spared him an agony."

Da looked at Nan as if to question. Did Nan try to make her feel better or did she speak truth? The look in the old one's eyes suggested sincerity, so Emma let it go.

"All right." She ate a hunk of bread.

"Well now." Nan sat up straight. "You can't run about in your nightdress."

Emma sent a forlorn stare at the empty bit of shelf, then sighed at the dress from the tailor's shop. "Yes, Nan."

Kimber and Tam burst into laughter. Mama put a hand over her mouth to hide a smile.

"What?" Emma looked at them before squinting at Nan. She glanced around at her family all trying not to smile at her. "What's everyone laughing at?"

Nan cackled, and pulled her arm out from under her shawl-covered green robe. She held a bundle of dark blue cloth, which she let unfurl into the shape of a handmade dress. "T'was time to make you a larger one, dear."

Emma squealed and dove out of her chair into her grandmother's arms, crying from joy.

Kimber and Tam piled on to the hug from both sides.

"Easy, now. Your old Nan can't handle so many little bodies in her lap at once."

"Nan!" yelled Emma. "It's beautiful." She wiped her tears. "You can see!" She looked down at the garment in her hands, studying an intricate weave of silver thread binding light blue trim about the neck, the ends of short sleeves, and the knee-length hem. Without a second thought, she peeled off her nightdress and wriggled into the new one. After twisting side to side to admire it, she beamed. "I love it!"

"She'll be wearing that one 'til she marries off," muttered Da.

Mama threw a bit of bread at him.

"Finish your lunch, child." Nan patted her on the head. "You've got a lot of learning ahead of you. I'll need to start the foundations before Beth has you making potions all day long."

Mama stuck her tongue out at Nan.

"Yes, Nan." Emma hopped on her chair and attacked her food. "Will you finish the story tonight?"

"Does the knight kill the dragon?" asked Tam.

"He a' frozed!" yelled Kimber. "Pincess Izbell nee'ta give 'im ae magic potion."

Tam furrowed his brow. "When's he gonna fight?"

Emma laughed a spray of bread crumbs onto her plate.

"Perhaps tonight, perhaps tomorrow." Nan winked at him. "There's always a story to be told if you know where to listen."

"Nan, do the wolves like stories too?" asked Emma.

Her grandmother grinned. "Of course. Where do you think I heard them from?"

Emma laughed, but a second later, her eyes went wide. How many of the creatures from her other stories could be real if banderwighs existed? She bit her lip, unable to think of the forest the same way again. If Nan's stories had been true all along, could faeries be real too?

Kimber smiled, her emerald green eyes sparkling. Tam grinned and kept pestering Nan about Sir Steelsong the knight, and what sort of dragon he'd wind up fighting.

And as for Emma, she felt happier in that moment than she had in a long time. Kimber looked far different from the apple-selling beggar; she'd come to life, wanted, and happy. The glint in Tam's eye said he itched to get back into trouble. If that didn't show he'd returned to his old self, nothing would.

A shiver ran down her back when she remembered her deal with the spider queen. She'd have to return for silk soon, which meant being around spiders again. But for now, she could put thoughts of giant fuzzy green critters—and banderwighs—out of her head.

She was home.

fin

The adventures continue in book 2 - Emma and the Silk Thieves!

Once again safe at home, Emma clings to the comfort of family and tries to put the fright of the Banderwigh behind her—but deeds, even good ones, often have consequences.

With a new reality of spirits and magic open to her, Emma feels a strong connection to Widowswood. She means to make good on her promise to the Spider Queen, bringing a monthly supply of silk in trade so humans cease their trespass upon the forest.

A guild of thieves infiltrates the quiet town, lured by the incredible value of enchanted spidersilk flowing so freely from the forest. At first, they don't realize the source is a ten-year-old girl, but once they learn, they'll do anything to control her.

Stuck between protecting her family and protecting her forest, Emma draws courage from her grandmother's stories and makes a choice—that could cost her life.

ACKNOWLEDGMENTS

Thank you for reading Emma and the Banderwigh!

Additional thanks to Courtney Lynn Rose for the suggestion of taking the idea that became this story and running with it.

To Orion Rodriguez, thank you for your amazing editing. This story is much better off for you having worked with me on it.

ABOUT THE AUTHOR

Originally from South Amboy NJ, Matthew has been creating science fiction and fantasy worlds for most of his reasoning life. Since 1996, he has developed the "Divergent Fates" world, in which *Division Zero*, *Virtual Immortality*, *The Awakened Series*, *The Harmony Paradox*, *and the Daughter of Mars series* take place. Along with being an editor at Curiosity Quills press, he has worked in IT and technical support.

Matthew is an avid gamer, a recovered WoW addict, Gamemaster for two custom RPG systems, and a fan of anime, British humour, and intellectual science fiction that questions the nature of reality, life, and what happens after it.

He is also fond of cats.

Visit me online at:
Facebook: https://www.facebook.com/MatthewSCoxAuthor
Pinterest: https://www.pinterest.com/matthewcox10420/
Goodreads: https://www.goodreads.com/author/show/7712730.Matthew_S_Cox
Email: mcox2112@gmail.com

OTHER BOOKS BY MATTHEW S. COX

Divergent Fates Universe Novels

Division Zero series

- Division Zero
- Lex De Mortuis
- Thrall
- Guardian
- Harbinger
- The Shadow Fixer
- Neuroshock

The Awakened series

- Prophet of the Badlands
- Archon's Queen
- Grey Ronin
- Daughter of Ash
- Zero Rogue
- Angel Descended

Daughter of Mars series

- The Hand of Raziel
- Araphel
- Ghost Black

Virtual Immortality series

- Virtual Immortality
- The Harmony Paradox

Prophet of the Badlands Series

- Prophet's Journey
- Prophet's Mercy

Divergent Fates Anthology

(Fiction Novels - Adult)

The Roadhouse Chronicles Series

- One More Run
- The Redeemed
- Dead Man's Number

Faded Skies series

- Heir Ascendant
- Ascendant Unrest
- Ascendant Revolution

Temporal Armistice Series

- Nascent Shadow
- The Shadow Collector
- The Gate to Oblivion
- The Queen of Discord
- The Burning Alchemist

Vampire Innocent series

- A Nighttime of Forever
- A Beginner's Guide to Fangs
- The Artist of Ruin

- The Last Family Road Trip
- The Phantom Oracle
- How Not to Summon Demons
- Ordinary Problems of a College Vampire
- A Vampire's Guide to Surviving Holidays
- An Introduction to Paranormal Diplomacy
- A Vampire's Guide to Adulting
- How to Stop a Vampire War in Six Easy Steps
- Ancient Vampire Death Cults and Other Annoyances
- Hunting Vampires for Fun and Profit
- A String of Seriously Unlucky Events
- The Summer of Completely Usual Strangeness
- Demonic Crisis Management for the Modern Vampire

Standalones

- Wayfarer: AV494
- Axillon99
- Chiaroscuro: The Mouse and the Candle
- The Spirits of Six Minstrel Run
- Sophie's Light
- The Far Side of Promise anthology
- Operation: Chimera (with Tony Healey)
- The Dysfunctional Conspiracy (with Christopher Veltmann)
- Of Myth and Shadow
- The Girl Who Found the Sun

Winter Solstice series (with J.R. Rain)

- Convergence
- Containment
- Catalyst
- Catacombs

Alexis Silver series (with J.R. Rain)

- Silver Light
- Deep Silver
- Silver Quarrel
- Silver Crucible
- Silver Heart

Samantha Moon Origins series (with J.R. Rain)

- New Moon Rising
- Moon Mourning
- Haunted Moon

Vampire For Hire series (with J.R. Rain)

- Moon Master
- Dead Moon
- Lost Moon
- Vampire Destiny
- Infinite Moon
- Vampire Empress
- Moon Elder
- Wicked Moon
- Moon Blade

Maddy Wimsey series (with J.R. Rain)

- The Devil's Eye
- The Drifting Gloom
- Dark Mercy
- Primal Wrath

Samantha Moon Case Files series (with J.R. Rain)

- Blood Moon

Immortal Operative (with J.R. Rain)

- Broken Ice
- Broken Wing

Four Elements series (with J.R. Rain)

- The Elementalist
- The Black Rose
- The Wakefield Curse

Witches series (with J.R. Rain)

- The Witch and the Hangman

Zeb Clemens series (with J.R. Rain)

- The Beast of Devil's Creek
- Wanted: Undead or Alive

Young Adult Novels

The Eldritch Heart Series

- The Eldritch Heart
- The Cursed Crown
- The Sapphire Soul

Evergreen Series

- Evergreen
- The World That Remains

- The Lucky Ones
- Nuclear Summer
- The Nuclear Frontier
- The World We Make
- The Threat Unseen

Progenitor Series

- Out of Sight
- Out of Mind

Diary of a Teenage Fey

(Short story series)

- Elder Horror
- The Hag of Barrow Falls
- Babysitter's Nightmare
- Lharakki
- Bauble for a Soul
- Simulacrum
- Amorphous
- Manticore

Standalones

- Caller 107
- The Summer the World Ended
- Nine Candles of Deepest Black
- The Forest Beyond the Earth

Middle Grade Novels

The Adventures of Ubergirl series

- My Dad is a Mad Scientist
- Aliens Ate My Homework
- The End of all Halloweens
- Dr. Infinity and the Soul Smasher

Tales of Widowswood series

- Emma and the Banderwigh
- Emma and the Silk Thieves
- Emma and the Silverbell Faeries
- Emma and the Elixir of Madness
- Emma and the Weeping Spirit

Standalones

- Citadel: The Concordant Sequence
- The Cursed Codex
- The Menagerie of Jenkins Bailey